Paul Hendy is 37 years old with a showbiz age of 28. Although he never made it as high as the C-list, you may have seen him hosting such shows as *Don't Try This at Home* and *Wheel of Fortune*, which had been running successfully for 20 years until Paul did one series and they cancelled it. He lives in London with his partner Emily and Ernie the cat. This is his first novel.

T0316375

DIARY OF A
C-LIST CELEB

Paul Hendy

BANTAM BOOKS
LONDON · TORONTO · SYDNEY · AUCKLAND · JOHANNESBURG

DIARY OF A C-LIST CELEB
A BANTAM BOOK : 0 553 81625 X

First publication in Great Britain

PRINTING HISTORY
Bantam edition published 2004

1 3 5 7 9 10 8 6 4 2

Set in 11½/13½pt Garamond by
Kestrel Data, Exeter, Devon.

Bantam Books are published by Transworld Publishers,
61–63 Uxbridge Road, London W5 5SA,
a division of The Random House Group Ltd,
in Australia by Random House Australia (Pty) Ltd,
20 Alfred Street, Milsons Point, Sydney, NSW 2061, Australia,
in New Zealand by Random House New Zealand Ltd,
18 Poland Road, Glenfield, Auckland 10, New Zealand
and in South Africa by Random House (Pty) Ltd,
Endulini, 5a Jubilee Road, Parktown 2193, South Africa.

The Random House Group Limited supports The Forest Stewardship
Council® (FSC®), the leading international forest-certification organisation.
Our books carrying the FSC label are printed on FSC®-certified paper.
FSC is the only forest-certification scheme supported by the leading
environmental organisations, including Greenpeace. Our
paper procurement policy can be found at
www.randomhouse.co.uk/environment

MIX
Paper | Supporting
responsible forestry
FSC® C018179

Printed and bound in Great Britain by Clays Ltd, St Ives plc

DEDICATION

For Emily, who stopped me becoming Simon Peters.

And for C-list celebrities everywhere . . . you
know who you are.

Men have a solicitude about fame; and the greater share they have of it, the more afraid they are of losing it.

Samuel Johnson (1773)

Fame, I'm gonna live forever, I'm gonna learn how to fly . . . high!

The Kids from Fame (1980)

DIARY OF A
C-LIST CELEB

1 JAN

If my career were a horse, they would have shot it by now.

Yes, I know New Year's Day is traditionally a time for looking forward, being positive and having an open mind about the future, but at the moment I can't. This is mainly because:

a) I've got the mother of all hangovers from last night's party.

b) I'm in panto.

c) The panto is in Grimsby.

'Oh no it's not.'

'Oh yes it bloody well is!'

It's not that I hate panto and it's not that I hate Grimsby. I just feel, at this stage in my career, I should be somewhere else, somewhere different, somewhere . . . BETTER THAN THIS.

Now, you might think I'm being hard on myself, after all I have had my own prime-time game show on network television in the last year. I use the term 'prime-time' as an abbreviation for the new TV-exec-speak, 'prime-time-*day-time*' (thanks to Dale, the two-thirty in the afternoon slot is now a very popular one). My show, *Simon Says – 'The game show where you do as I say, not as I do!'* did very well in the ratings and on two occasions we actually beat the BBC's

11

re-runs of *Murder She Wrote*. The problem is that the big cheeses over at ITV Network Centre are undecided as to whether the series should 'go again'.

Quote: 'We're not sure if Simon Peters is big enough to fill Dale's slot.'

That's what they said. I kid you not.

So, at the moment I'm in TV limbo-land, not cancelled but not re-commissioned either. Which is why I'm in pantomime . . .

'This is your five minute call, Mr Peters.'

. . . In Grimsby . . .

'You have five minutes until the custard-pie routine.'

Oh bugger.

2 JAN

I have to admit I was in a bit of a bad mood yesterday, but that's what happens when you mix together a hangover, career disillusionment and 200 screaming kids throwing half-sucked Opal Fruits at you. I refuse to call them Starbursts in the same way that Marathons will never be Snickers and Jif will never be Cif. God, it's so depressing, I'm starting to sound just like my Dad.

Did I mention I was in pantomime?

I'm fourth on the bill (I should be second). I'm appearing with Mimi Lawson (yes, *the* Mimi Lawson), Ricardo Mancini (what a twonk) and Vince Envy (don't laugh). We're performing at a brand-new theatre. If you look up the word 'theatre' in the dictionary, it says, **'theatre** *n. a place where people go to be entertained.'*

Not in Grimsby they don't.

Apparently, when it was opened late last year, they held a competition in the local paper to name this new theatre in the middle of Grimsby. Guess what the winning name was? You're ahead of me on this one, aren't you? Yes, it was The Grimsby Theatre. What a stroke of genius. It does exactly what it says on the can. It's a theatre in Grimsby; let's call it The Grimsby Theatre. So simple it's beautiful. Unlike the place itself, which is a dump.

I'm playing the part of Simple Simon (the producer's idea of a joke) in *Snow White and the Seven Drunken Dwarfs*. It's not actually called that; it's just that the dwarfs who are playing the dwarfs always seem to be drunk. They pick fights with each other, chat up the dancers and wave their willies in the air, often all at the same time. I think I should point out their willies are normal size, and a normal-sized willy on a little man's body can be a very impressive sight. Not that I've been looking, of course, one of the dancers told me.

The dancer's name is Jason.

Disney copyright prevents the producers from using the dwarfs' names from the film – Sleepy, Bashful, Doc etc., – so in our show they're called Sniffy, Dozy, Prof, Blusher, Grumbly, Snoozy and Smiler. Off stage we call them Flasher, Farter, Shitter, Shagger, Pisser, Groper and Smiler (he really does just smile all the time). Two of them, Pisser and Shitter, appeared in the movie *The Sleeping Princess*, and another two, Farter and Shagger, played small furry things in *Starfighter IV*, which you have to admit is pretty impressive. Occasionally they perform in a club act, which is a mickey-take of The Chippendales. They do a strip routine and call themselves The Chipolatas. After tonight's panto they're doing a show in a local nightclub and have asked me if I want to go along and watch them. I'm not sure that I do.

I think I'll let Jason go in my place.

6 JAN

We've only got one show today, and as I have some spare time on my hands, I thought I'd give you an idea of who's who in the show.

Here are the biographies as taken from the programme:

MIMI LAWSON as Snow White

Mimi stole the nation's heart at the age of five when she won the televised talent show Tomorrow's Stars Today *(ATV). She had her own TV show,* Here's Mimi!, *by the time she was six and was playing Annie on Broadway by the time she was seven. The following year she starred in her first Hollywood movie, the now cult classic* Mimi and Mo *('Two gangsters terrorize America . . . and they're only eight!'). Mimi's hit song 'I'm Daddy's Little Girl' (RCA) knocked The Bay City Rollers off the number one spot and stayed there for a record eighteen consecutive weeks. At the age of sixteen, Mimi was asked to star in the West End production of* Flares *playing the part of Sugar alongside Vince Envy. Soon after that she decided to retire from life in the public eye to spend more time with her dear mother. Now, at the age of thirty, MIMI'S BACK! She recently appeared in* The Bill *(Thames), playing the part of an ex-child star who has fallen on hard times, and her new album 'Daddy's Big Girl' (Telstar) is currently on sale in the foyer. Mimi is delighted to be making her theatrical comeback in Grimsby.*

I feel I should have warned you that biographies in theatrical programmes are often great works of fiction. Here is a rough translation of what it all means:

Mimi Lawson is barking mad.

She went from child star to has-been as soon as she hit

puberty. She had a TV show at six, a Hollywood film at eight and a Class-A drug addiction by the time she was fifteen. Her descent into drug abuse and alcoholism has been well documented, as have her three failed marriages, including one to a fake sheikh (the tabloids had a field day with that one).

All of this is strangely absent from her biography, as is her ill-advised attempt in 1986 to host the late-night Channel 4 youth show *Bad!* (it was).

My favourite line in the biog is, *'Now, at the age of thirty . . .'*

THIRTY? That would have made her a foetus when she won that talent competition. Now that's what I call a child prodigy.

Her mother, by all accounts, was a bit of a tyrant. If she and Joan Crawford were the only two mothers left in the world and Mothercare decided to hold a 'Best Mum in the World' competition, Joan would win it hands down. Mrs Lawson managed young Mimi's career from the age of five to fifteen. They fell out when Mimi started working on *Flares* and haven't spoken since. In a candid moment she told me she misses her mother and hopes one day they'll be reunited. Having lost my mother at the age of thirteen, and because I haven't spoken to my dad for three years, I can empathise with her in this respect.

Mimi's supposed to be 'clean' now, and if she weren't the showbiz-super-bitch-from-hell I'd almost feel sorry for her.

And now ladies and gentlemen, fanfare please . . . it's the one you've all been waiting for. I give you the biography, as it appears in the programme, of Mr Ricardo Mancini (bear in mind he wrote all this himself):

RICARDO MANCINI as Prince Ricardo

How does one describe Ricardo Mancini? An actor? A singer? A dancer? A comedian? A magician? (that one goes without saying). The truth is Ricardo is all of these things and so much more. He is an all-round entertainer, but even that description doesn't really do him justice. His brooding good looks and sparkling personality have won him legions of female fans. He started his career working as a magician and first came to prominence when he won the live televised grand final of Your Big Moment *(YTV). Hailed as Britain's Answer to David Copperfield, he went on to host his own one-hour special* Mancini's Magic! *(Granada) and one series of* The Magic of Ricardo Mancini *(BBC). Despite all this early success, Ricardo always wanted to be, in his own words, 'more than just another good looking magician'. His first love has always been acting and he recently made a guest appearance in* The Bill *(Thames), playing the role of Nino, a sexy magician with an attitude problem. Ricardo is delighted to be reviving the role of Prince Ricardo in this, his fifth consecutive pantomime for Johnny Goldberg Productions.*

I HATE HIM, I HATE HIM, I HATE HIM, but then again Ricardo Mancini's one of those people you can't help but hate.

Ricardo likes to pretend he's from Sicily, but he was actually born in Halifax and his real name's Richard Manky. After winning *Your Big Moment* on Yorkshire TV, Manky was given his own network show on ITV, but totally blew it due to his serious attitude problem. The BBC snapped him up and signed him to an exclusive three-year golden-handcuffs deal. Halfway through filming the first series he head-butted the Head of Light Entertainment and, with that, the Beeb refused to use him again. Because of his massive ego and a reputed drug problem, his career took a nosedive and his life seemed to spiral out of control. He quickly became tabloid fodder, always in the gossip columns for dating some pretty pop star, soap actress, or in one case a lap dancer from Stringfellow's. Nowadays, he's convinced he's a bigger star than he is and he hates it when people don't recognize him (which is often). Mimi Lawson might be the super-bitch-from-hell, but at least she once had genuine talent. Ricardo Mancini is a thirty-five-year-old nobody who could have been a big star but threw his chance away. He's hardly worked over the last three years, apart from the odd summer season in Weymouth and, of course, panto. The fact that he's done five consecutive pantomimes for Johnny Goldberg explains why he's second on the bill and not me.

You will stop me if I start to sound bitter, won't you?

VINCE ENVY as Oddjob

Vince first shot to fame in the early 1960s with his band, Vince Envy and the Jealous Guys. He had a string of hit records, including 'Just a Rebel (With a Heart Of Gold)', 'Tears of Pain (In the Rain)', and his all-time-classic number-one double-A side 'Cream Sweater, Blue Jeans'/ 'Jessica'. He was also a resident singer on TV's favourite pop show Go Go Go! *(ATV). Throughout the Seventies Vince was instantly recognizable as The Man with the Tan in the famous Golden aftershave commercials. The 1980s saw Vince move into musical theatre, and he was the first British star to play the role of Mr Love in* Flares *opposite Mimi Lawson. He also appeared as Benny in* Oh Romeo, *Slick in* Swingbeat *and created the role of Carter in* King Tut: The Rock 'n' Roll Mummy. *More recently Vince appeared in* The Bill *(Thames), playing the role of Jed, an aging rock 'n' roll star with a drink problem. This is his fifteenth consecutive pantomime for Johnny Goldberg Productions and Vince is happy to be reviving the role of Oddjob in* Snow White.

Vince is from the old school of showbiz and is always playing in charity golf days for The Variety Club of Great Britain. I like him and I spend a lot of time in his company. He's very fatherly towards me and keeps offering me little nuggets of advice.

'Talent isn't enough these days,' he often tells me. 'You can't just be famous, you have to be *infamous*.'

Vince really has done it all. One thing this biography doesn't mention is that, in the mid-Sixties, he spent a couple of years working as a lounge singer in Las Vegas. He tells some great anecdotes: late-night drinking sessions with Frank Sinatra and Sammy Davis Jr, how he once got into a bar fight with Dean Martin over a showgirl and how the mob put a contract out on him in a case of mistaken identity.

Vince keeps telling me how he's really popular in Albania and that his 1963 double-A side 'Cream Sweater, Blue Jeans'/'Jessica' has been re-released there and has been number one all over the Christmas period.

The trouble is, when he's had a few he does go on a bit and he tells all these stories with a real sense of sourness. I sometimes feel a little bit sorry for him. In a way he's everything I hope I never become. He's been married four times, has no children and has a bit of a drink problem. He seems dissatisfied and generally unhappy with his lot, and despite all the things he's done in his career, he's always moaning about showbusiness as if it owes him something. When he sings his solo 'Cream Sweater, Blue Jeans' – how they jemmied that into the plot of *Snow White*, I will never know – he knows the good days have gone and that it won't get any better than this.

*　　*　　*

Just in case you're interested, here's my biography:

SIMON PETERS as Simple Simon

Yorkshire-born Simon started his career working as a bluecoat at the famous Ketley's Holiday Park in Bridlington. During his time there he hosted the Glamorous Granny and Knobbly Knees competitions — 'Very often the same person would win both,' he jokes. Simon worked hard to develop his own comedy act, which he toured around the working men's clubs of Yorkshire and the north east. In 1993, he came third in one of the regional heats for the TV talent show, Your Big Moment *(YTV). Simon's burning ambition was to be a TV presenter and his big break came in 1995 when he was chosen from 400 hopefuls to host the popular Saturday morning children's show* A.M. Mayhem *(Nickelodeon). He went on to present many other kids' TV shows, including* The Gungemeister *(Disney Channel),* Kidzonly *(Nick Jr),* The Road Crew *(CBBC) and* MadFerrit! *(two series for Children's ITV). 1999 saw Simon move away from children's television and into daytime TV with his hit game show* Simon Says, *'The show where you do as he says, not as he does!' (Carlton). Simon is delighted to be appearing in* Snow White *at The Grimsby Theatre.*

Well, that's my career. Talked up in some places, made up in others. What can I say? I was a bluecoat (where I lost my virginity), I was a comedian, (where I died a death at every club I played at) and now I'm a game-show host (desperate for a shot at the big time). I am 29 years old and I'm going to be thirty in December. I don't mind admitting that I'm dreading it.

Now you probably noticed in my biography that I came

19

third in one of the regional heats of the TV talent show *Your Big Moment*. The more discerning reader might have observed from Ricardo 'Manky' Mancini's biography that he came first in that very heat and then went on to win the grand final. I feel I should point out that my hatred and bitterness towards him has nothing to do with this fact.

Besides, it was all rigged anyway.

A man who worked with a friend of my uncle knew someone who went to school with the sister of one of the people who built the set for the show and he said the reason Mancini won the heat was because the producers needed a magician to 'balance up the final'. They already had five pop singers, so the inclusion of a magician made it more of a variety show. Mancini pretends he doesn't remember me, but he's always got a smug look on his face that suggests he does. Come to think of it, he's always got a smug look on his face full stop.

You're probably wondering who came second in my heat. It was a parrot. A singing parrot to be precise. He was actually very talented and last month I saw him in an episode of *The Bill*.

8 JAN

One of the dancers, Pippa, smiled at me from the stage today while I was waiting in the wings. At least I *think* it was me. Manky Mancini was standing behind me, leering at all the dancers as he always does; surely she wouldn't be smiling at him? The thing about Pippa's smile was that it wasn't just a 'villager's smile'. The dancers spend the entire show as villagers who do nothing but stand around all day and then occasionally burst into a dance number. Whatever they do, they do it with these slightly scary smiles on their faces. I think they must learn how to do it at a very early age, as soon as they start going to dance lessons.

'Nice toes, naughty toes, nice toes, naughty toes. Very good girls, now for the next three hours we're going to sit here and practise grinning inanely.'

Dancers have more training than any other profession I can think of. Most of them start to learn to dance at the age of three or four. They go to dance lessons twice a week and learn every style of dance known to man: modern, tap, jazz, ballet, freestyle, ballroom, contemporary and national (where they have to learn the national dance of Lithuania or something). They perform in amateur shows, take exams and enter competitions all over the country. They do all this right up to the age of sixteen, when they go off to full-time dance college for *three solid years* of modern, tap, jazz, ballet etc. At the end of all this, after a 15-year apprenticeship, they come out into the glamorous world of showbiz and get a job in pantomime.

In Grimsby.

As villagers who smile a lot.

But the smile Pippa aimed at me wasn't a 'dancer's smile'. She smiled with her eyes and that's something they don't teach them at dance college.

12 JAN

I think I'm in love.

This afternoon I was in the theatre car park and I saw Pippa get out of her car (a cobalt-blue Mazda MX5 1.8 injection with alloy wheels and tan leather trim). She looked absolutely stunning, with her long blond hair, big blue eyes and Coke-bottle figure. Some women spend small fortunes on nips and tucks, silicone and collagen; God gave it to Pippa for nothing. This is the sort of girl I desperately want to go out with. She was wearing a pair of faded blue Levi's, a long white leather coat and Prada sunglasses. She was soft focus, backlit and walking in slow motion. If this were the Seventies then she would be the girl from the Harmony Hairspray adverts.

I caught up with her just outside the stage door.

'Nice car,' I said.

'What?' she snapped.

For a moment I wasn't sure that she recognized me as being from the same show as her.

'Nice car,' I repeated, my confidence fading fast.

'Oh right . . . thanks,' she said, suddenly realizing who I was.

She opened the stage door.

'I think Mazda have got the rear differential just right this time.'

What on earth was I was talking about? Pippa just ignored me.

'So, how long have you had it?'

'My boyfriend bought it for me.'

My heart stopped. She was absolutely, 100 per cent, without doubt, the sort of girl who would have a boyfriend who would buy her a sports car.

'Or rather my ex-boyfriend.'

My heart started again.

'We split up just before I came to do panto, but he let me keep the car.'

He let her keep the car! She was absolutely, 100 per cent, without doubt, the sort of girl who would have a boyfriend who would buy her a sports car and then, when they split up, would let her keep it.

I couldn't think of anything to say to her. My mouth was dry and I knew the nervous rash on my neck would be starting to show. I felt completely out of my depth, in at the deep end without my water wings and unable to touch the bottom. Drowning not waving. Floundering in a sea of my own insecurities.

By now we were inside the stage door and she was asking Gordon, the stage doorkeeper, for her dressing-room key. I didn't want to let this moment pass and I knew that, if I did, the next time I spoke to her I would find it even more difficult. I spluttered and stammered something about it being great that the MX5s have passenger air bags fitted as standard. She flashed me a smile, but this time it was a dancer's smile. I could tell I was losing her.

What was I doing even beginning to think that a girl like her would be attracted to a guy like me?

But then, as he's done so many times in the past, *The Other Me* took over, Mr Confidence, Mr Personality, Mr Showbiz, the man I become when I'm 'on'. So much more entertaining than the real me, so much more interesting.

'*Of course she'll be attracted to you,*' he whispered in my head. '*You've had your own game show on prime-time daytime television.*'

The radio at the stage door was playing a song by the boy band *4Real!* The DJ was saying that their third consecutive single had gone straight into the US charts at Number One, the first British act to do that since *The Beatles*.

'*4Real!* are officially massive,' said the DJ, somehow managing to emphasize all the wrong words in all the wrong places, as only DJs on local radio stations can. 'The American chicks just can't get enough of Bad Boy Troy, as I think the papers are calling the cheeky lead singer Troy Coral.'

The Other Me seized the opportunity and launched into his favourite amusing anecdote, telling Pippa his story of how *4Real!* made their first ever TV appearance on *MadFerrit!* the kids show he used to present, and that he was the first person *ever* to interview them on live television. A fact that is confirmed in their official auto-biography *4Bidden!*

'It's funny to think that they've gone on to be worldwide super stars,' said *The Other Me*. 'When I first interviewed them, they were a bunch of acne-ridden wannabes.'

'Really?' she said, with a distant look in her eye.

'Troy was a bag of nerves.'

'Was he?'

'Yes, at the time he was excited to meet me, someone off the telly.'

'It was Troy who bought me the car.'

She is absolutely, 100 per cent, without doubt, the sort of girl who would have gone out with Troy Coral.

The Other Me quickly did a runner out of the stage door, and all I could hear was my normal self saying, 'So what's the torque ratio on the MX5 like these days?' But it was too late. By then she was in her dressing room.

16 JAN

Charley O'Neil is my best friend and she's driving up from London to see the show tonight. We met about six years ago when I was hosting *A.M. Mayhem* for Nickelodeon. It was my first presenting job. She was working as a junior researcher on the show and we just hit it off. Charley is one of the funniest people I've ever met and seems to be able to get on with absolutely everyone. She has an unruly mass of red curly hair and eyes the colour of emeralds. She's always so full of energy and when you meet her, you think, Why can't I be more like that? and, Wouldn't the world be a better place if everyone was like Charley?

She reminds me of my mum.

Charley is also really good at her job and is now working

as a senior researcher on the popular BBC daytime show *Coffee Morning with Mike and Sue*. It's great because she gives me all the gossip about them; he's an egomaniac of dubious sexuality and she's a man-eating alcoholic. Oh, and in case you're wondering, it's true, they really do hate each other.

I never thought I'd have a best friend who's a girl. Wasn't it Billy Crystal who said that men and women can never be friends, because the sex part always gets in the way?

Well, with Charley and me it never has. OK, it nearly did once when we were drunk, but we both agreed never to mention it and have been best friends ever since.

I'm pleased she's coming to see the show. I surmise from this that:

a) She must be a really good friend to drive all the way from London to Grimsby to watch a pantomime.

Or

b) (the more likely reason) She can't believe Mimi Lawson's still alive and is driving all this way to see it for herself.

Whatever the reason, I know it's another night on the beer. Whey hey.

It's four in the morning and as usual I'm suffering from insomnia. I arrived back from the club at two thirty and I've had a few to drink, so if there are any spelling mistakes, I apologize now.

The night started well enough. Charley *said* she enjoyed the show, but friends always say that, don't they. I've never once had a friend come backstage and say, 'God, that was crap.'

We went for a drink in the pub behind the theatre, where the cast and crew seem to de-camp at the end of each show. After a couple of beers, Pippa and another of the

25

dancers Sharone (I'm pretty sure her name is just Sharon, but she insists on it being pronounced Shar-*own*) said they were off to a local nightclub. I quite liked the idea of a bit of a boogie, and because I fancy the pants off Pippa I said that I'd go too. I persuaded Charley to come with us, although at first I don't think she really wanted to.

Word quickly spread.

Vince Envy was a little bit tipsy by this point, but said he wanted to come along, as did a handful of dwarfs. Before I knew it there were seventeen members of the cast and crew wanting to go to The Club. That's what it's called, The Club. I'm really starting to appreciate Grimsby's simplistic way of naming things.

For some reason, if you work in showbusiness, it's your God-given right not to have to pay to get into nightclubs. All you have to do is blag it. Pippa claimed she was the queen of blags and called up the club to arrange the guest list. Sharone booked the taxis – from The Grimsby Taxi Company, no doubt – and when they arrived we all piled in and set off.

Picture the scene, one game-show host, one aging pop star, three stage crew, five dwarfs and six glamorous dancers in heavy make-up (Jason's was the heaviest). Oh, and Manky Mancini tagged along too.

The rest of the evening is a bit of a blur. You know when you've been drunk and keep having flashbacks and thinking, I didn't do that, did I? Well, the whole night is a flashback.

If this were a movie, cue the montage sequence:

. . . arguments at the door over the guest list . . .
   . . . not sure whether to let Jason in, in his black leather catsuit . . .
   . . . tequila slammers all around . . .
    . . . Charley, Farter and me dancing to 'YMCA' . . .

... more tequila slammers ...

... me jiving with Pippa (yesss!) ...

... Charley jiving with Shagger ...

... Jason jiving with Gordon the Stage Doorkeeper(!) ...

... me buying a round of drinks for everyone (£78.55. Ouch.) ...

... a large tattooed skinhead smiling at me in the toilets ...

... telling Manky Mancini that I should be second on the bill and not him ...

... Jason podium dancing ...

... Vince on the mike trying to sing ...

... Manky chatting up Pippa ...

... Shagger kissing Sharone ...

... Sharone kissing Gordon the Stage Doorkeeper ...

... Gordon the Stage Doorkeeper trying to kiss Shagger

... Shagger and Shitter fighting with Gordon the Stage Door-keeper ...

... Shagger and Shitter fighting with a six-foot bouncer ...

... Vince telling everyone he's Number One in Albania ...

... Mimi Lawson sitting alone at the bar ...

... Vince telling me I'm like a son to him ...

... Mimi Lawson smiling at me ...

... Jason leaving with the large tattooed skinhead ...

... Vince and Mimi arguing ...

... telling Pippa I think she's lovely ...

... Pippa telling me she thinks I'm drunk ...

... outside club ...

... police sirens ...

... goodnight, Pippa ...

... no kiss ...

... turning my back ...

... persuading the police to let Shagger go ...

... Manky Mancini jumping in a taxi with Mimi ...

... Mimi blowing me a kiss! ...

> > > > > > *. . . no more taxis . . .*
> > > > > *. . . walking back to the hotel with Charley . . .*
> > > > > > *. . . seeing panto poster . . .*
> > > *. . . drawing a moustache and glasses on Ricardo Mancini . . .*
> > > > > *. . . back at the hotel . . .*
> > > > *. . . mini bar . . .*
> > > *. . . telling Charley Pippa is Mrs Right . . .*
> > *. . . Charley telling me that Pippa is Mrs Right Now . . .*
> > > *. . . telling Charley this is different and Pippa is The One . . .*
> > > > *. . . Charley telling me I wouldn't know The One . . .*
> > > > > *. . . if 'The One' was standing in front of me . . .*
> > > > > *. . . peck on the cheek from Charley . . .*
> > > > > *. . . Charley going back to her room . . .*
> > > > *. . . sleep . . .*
> > > > > **. . . Why did Mimi Lawson blow me a kiss? . . .**
> > > > *Sleep.*

17 JAN

I woke up looking like Homer Simpson when he has dribble coming out the side of his mouth.

There was a note from Charley at reception:

Peters, you old tart!

Sorry I missed you. I've had to go back to London to sort out a problem on Mike and Sue *(she's probably back on the drink again).*

Re: Pippa scenario. On second thoughts, I think she's perfect:

> *a) She's a dancer.*
> *b) She's got blond hair.*
> *c) She's got big tits.*

What more could a man ask for?
I loved the show; you really were great.

See you when you get back to London.
Call me.
Charley xxx
P.S. Or maybe Mimi Lawson is The One????
(. . . Ahem!)

I went in to the theatre and everyone was a little bit sheepish with each other. I avoided Mimi, Sharone avoided Shagger and everyone avoided Gordon the Stage Doorkeeper.

Jason arrived, still wearing his black leather catsuit and proclaiming he was in love with Colin, the large tattooed skinhead who was coming to watch the show this afternoon, 'So could we make it wonderful *dahlings,* just for him?'

I didn't get a chance to speak to Pippa, but she did flash me a smile again. I wasn't close enough to see if it was a dancer's smile or a real one. I know Charley was being sarcastic about her being perfect, but I think maybe she is.

She really has got everything I look for in a girl.

19 JAN

Shitter told me that Sharone told Shagger that Pippa has got a little bit of a thing for Manky Mancini. I can't believe it, surely she's not the type of girl who just goes for someone because they're good-looking and drive a nice car.

I hate it when people are that shallow.

20 JAN

Mimi has been acting very strangely; if she wasn't *the* Mimi Lawson, well-known showbiz-super-bitch-from-hell, then

I'd say she was almost flirting with me. It really wasn't a pretty sight.

23 JAN

There's nothing I'd love more than for my dad to come to see this show, sit in the audience and think, That's my boy. But the show finishes in a week's time and I know that's not going to happen.

I haven't spoken to my dad for over three years. We fell out over a stupid little comment that was made, and we're both too stubborn to be the first one to get in touch. My dad is retired now. He worked as a stand-up comedian for forty-two years and prides himself on the fact that he performed in every working men's club in Yorkshire and was never 'paid off' once.

He *was* a very good comic. He would wear a black velvet suit, a black velvet bow tie and a pink ruffled shirt. He'd hold the microphone in one hand, while leaning on the mike stand with the other. He had total command of his audience, and when I was a kid he was my hero. I was in awe of him. I would sit at the side of the stage with a bottle of Vimto and a packet of crisps and just laugh and laugh until I couldn't laugh any more, even though I'd heard him tell the jokes a thousand times before and even though I didn't understand half of them. To me, he was a star. To me, he was the funniest man in the world.

He appeared on one episode of *The Comedians* in 1974, but that was the pinnacle of his career. Although he wouldn't admit it, the fact that he'd never 'made it' ate away at him and left him feeling resentful of other people's success. I remember when I was about ten years old, the whole family used to sit down to watch *The Tommy Cooper Show*. My older brother David and I used to sit on the rug in front of the fire and my mother, who was already quite ill by this point, would lie on the sofa. The three of us thought Tommy was hilarious, but I have a vivid memory of turning around and seeing my father sitting there, gripping the arms of his chair and scowling at the television, bitter at the fact that it wasn't him making the nation laugh. My father never laughed at other comedians. In fact, he never really laughed much at all. The only time he seemed to come alive was for the forty-five minutes he was in the spotlight doing his act.

I went to see him perform about five years ago and was surprised to see that he was still wearing the same black velvet suit, black velvet bow tie and pink ruffled shirt. His act, like his stage clothes, had started to look dated and worn around the edges: lots of mother-in-law gags and jokes about the Irish. They were the same jokes I remembered as a child, but somehow they didn't seem funny any more.

My father never gave up showbusiness, showbusiness gave him up. The phone stopped ringing and my dad stopped working. When he retired it wasn't just the spotlight on the stage that went out. He became rude, bad-tempered and irritable, and whenever I saw him, all he wanted to do was argue. It was one of these petty arguments that led to us falling out and we haven't spoken since.

All I've ever wanted is for my dad to tell me I'm funny. I want to make him laugh, and when he's laughing I want him to feel proud and for him to think my mum would have been proud too.

Charley keeps telling me that I should swallow my pride and get in touch with him and I know one day I probably will.

Just not today.

24 JAN

My agent is the legendary Max Golinski.

Some people in the business call him a gangster, but I'd never call him that in case he kneecapped me. He's a small man in his early fifties, and I'm sure in a previous life he was a cold-hearted killer. Just a minute, what am I talking about? He's an agent, in *this* life he's a cold-hearted killer. I can honestly say he scares me. I would never leave the agency for fear of waking up with a horse's head in my bed. When he speaks, Max spits his words out like bullets from a machine-gun and his speech is peppered with Yiddish expressions, half of which I'm sure he doesn't understand, the other half he just makes up. I'm not entirely convinced he's even Jewish. I think he just pretends to be because he thinks it's good for business. Having said all that, he is one of the top agents in the country; his negotiating skills are legendary and every producer in the television industry fears him. I'm very lucky to be on his books. I know this because he keeps telling me I am.

Max hates panto with a passion and I think he only drove to Grimsby because I told him there were a couple of good-looking dancers in the cast. He turned up to watch the show with his assistant, Scary Babs, who, like Max, has managed to achieve near mythical status in showbusiness circles. She's in her mid-fifties, has peroxide-blond hair and always has a cigarette hanging out of the corner of her mouth. She's fiercely loyal to Max – he calls her his Rottweiler – but she has a memory like a sieve. I've been with the agency five years and she still can't remember my name.

It was a shame that they saw this afternoon's show. It was the old-age pensioners' matinee and, with the sound of snoring and the smell of wee, it was quite possibly the worst show we've ever done. Vince Envy was drunk, and instead of his 'Cream Sweater, Blue Jeans' song, he launched into an Irish sea shanty about some old tart from Dublin. The language was colourful to say the least, but what was most disconcerting was that all the pensioners enjoyed it and joined in the chorus. Vince kept taking his wig off and his teeth out and telling the audience he was Number One in Albania. He went down a storm and was the only member of the cast the audience seemed to like.

The rest of us died a death.

Everything that could go wrong did go wrong. Part of the scenery collapsed in the forest scene, two of the dwarfs had a fight during 'Whistle While You Work' and it took me twenty five minutes to get four pensioners on stage for the singalong at the end. I told the usherettes not to choose people with Zimmer frames, but they wouldn't listen.

Probably the worst moment came when I sang 'When You Wish Upon A Star' to Mimi as Snow White. Just after the line 'Your dreams come true,' there's a pause in the music, and during that pause one of the OAPs in the audience broke wind. They actually farted on the off beat and it filled the gap perfectly. I know comedians who would give their right arm to have timing as good as that. It was even in the right key. Now, this wasn't just a tiny trump or a petite poop, oh no, this was the loudest raspberry you've ever heard, a rip-roaring, cheek-blowing, paint-stripping, good old-fashioned fart. It was the sort of fart you can only really produce under heavy medication. That was bad enough, but the next line of the song is *'Like a bolt out of the blue.'*

Cue hysterical laughter from the band.

Backstage, Mimi was very complimentary and kept telling me how she thought I'd handled the situation very well.

Agents are supposed to be encouraging and full of praise. Max said he thought the show was shit. That's all he said, 'Shit'. High praise indeed from the master of under-statement.

I asked Scary Babs what she thought.

'Don't ask me, dearie,' she said. 'I was in the bar.'

They didn't hang around after the show, Max had arranged to take Mimi out for dinner – I think he must be trying to sign her onto his books – I kept hinting that I was hungry but Max just told me to 'get a McDonalds'. On his way out I also noticed him giving Pippa his card and telling her to give him a call when she was next in London.

25 JAN

Today I was shopping in Boots for some eyelash tint. I looked up and who should be standing there but Mimi Lawson. She did the whole *fancy-seeing-you-here* routine, and asked if I wanted to go for a coffee in the theatre bar. I reluctantly agreed and ended up sitting in there for over an hour. In that time I had one orange juice and a Jaffa Cake. She had four Mars Bars, eight cups of coffee and fifteen cigarettes. She was hyper, wide-eyed and wore a constant manic smile, a sort of 'dancer's smile' gone wrong; it was almost as if, after years of being forced to smile like that, she'd forgotten how not to. She told me I was a good listener.

GOOD LISTENER?

I couldn't get a word in. I only managed to mention my show, *Simon Says*, once. The rest of the time it was 'me me me' (maybe that's why they called her Mimi). I heard about her mother, her three marriages and how she'd been having an on-off relationship with a guy for years but it just wasn't working out. I asked how her dinner with Max had gone, but she obviously didn't want to talk about it. Instead she announced she was thinking of turning to God. It was at that point that I made my excuses and left. On my way out of the bar I bumped into Pippa and Manky Mancini, who were on their way in. Pippa looked beautiful, although I couldn't help noticing that she was wearing the same clothes as yesterday. Manky took off his sunglasses and nodded casually in Mimi's direction, but she shot him a filthy look. He turned back to me and gave me a smug, knowing wink. I grabbed him in a headlock and punched him very hard, several times in the face.

Of course I didn't do that at all, I just smiled at Pippa and said, 'It's not what you think.'

She smiled back and said, 'Neither is this.'

26 JAN

I'm not looking forward to tomorrow at all. Tomorrow's always the worst day of the year.

27 JAN

My mum used to love comedy and my one abiding memory is of her howling with laughter at the comedians who used to appear on television in the late Seventies and early Eighties.

She was an amazing woman and the complete antithesis of my father. He was funny on stage, but off stage it was my mother who was the life and soul of the party. She was a ball of energy, always so outgoing and gregarious. She never had a bad word for anybody and was full of enthusiasm for everything she did.

My mum met my dad in 1961 in a variety show at The

Regent Theatre in Rotherham. She was one of the dancers and my dad was a bottom-of-the-bill comedian performing alongside acts such as Elroy the Armless Wonder and Bob Beamon and his Comedy Pigeons.

They fell in love and were married in 1964.

My mum's burning ambition was to be a comedienne herself, but it wasn't really the done thing and I don't think my father liked the idea of her being funnier and possibly more successful than he was. She gave up showbiz to have my brother in 1966 and I came toddling along seven years later.

When we were growing up, my brother showed no interest in showbusiness at all (he now works as an accountant in Doncaster). Of course, my mother never minded this, but I know she was really pleased when I started to perform at an early age. Without being a pushy stage mother, she was always really encouraging to me in everything I did.

'You can do it, son,' she used to whisper in her soft voice.

My mum died of cancer on 27 January 1986. She was forty-three years old. She left a great big hole in the middle of my life and no matter what I do I just can't seem to fill it.

I wonder if I'd have made her laugh?

28 JAN

This morning I spoke to Charley, who always manages to cheer me up. She told me she's having a complete nightmare with Mike and Sue. Yesterday Sue punched Mike before they went on air and gave him a black eye, which the make-up artist had to keep covering up every time they went to a VT. The director was screaming 'no close-ups' and kept telling the cameramen to pull back. This resulted in Mike and Sue being unable to read the autocue and they started to argue live on air. Apparently it was a classic piece of television and Charley's going to send me a tape of it.

She asked me how the panto was going and I told her tomorrow is the night of the company meal.

'Tomorrow night's the night, then?' said Charley.

Company meals are legendary in panto circles as the last chance to get off with someone from the cast.

'Yes,' I said. 'Tomorrow's the night I get off with Pippa.'

'It wasn't Pippa I was talking about,' she said.

29 JAN

We've just finished the evening show and everybody's getting ready for the meal.

I pride myself on being a sharp dresser and always put a lot of time and effort into my appearance. I showered using the hotel's lavender and primrose shower gel and washed my hair with Asda's own-brand anti-dandruff shampoo (I suffer with the odd flake here and there.) After towelling myself dry, I dabbed a splash of Blue Stratos aftershave behind my ears and styled my hair using Falcon hairspray for men. A lot of producers have suggested that I have my hair cut and restyled because it looks too Eighties, but to be honest I quite like it long at the back with a demi-wave perm.

I glanced in the mirror and thought I looked a little pale, so I covered my face in Mr Bronzer's Self-Tanning Lotion (you have to be careful how you apply it, though; if it's not evenly spread it can look a little blotchy). Finally, before getting dressed, I sprinkled Dr Cornbuster's Foot Powder between my toes. This is purely as a preventative measure, you understand, although I admit I don't have the best-looking feet in showbusiness.

I like to think that I'm well known for my fashion sense, and for some time now I've been leading a one-man crusade to bring bright and colourful clothing back to the fore. The good thing about being a television presenter is you can buy all the clothes you wear on screen for 25 per cent of the cost. So, courtesy of *Simon Says*, I'm wearing my best pink and electric-blue Hawaiian shirt, with surfer motif, and my pleated two-tone burgundy trousers from Top Man.

I have just caught sight of my reflection in the mirror and, although I say it myself, I look pretty damn cool.

Tonight is the night I'm going to teach Manky Mancini a lesson in style. It's also the night that I make a play for Pippa.

30 JAN

This morning I woke up next to Edwina Currie.

It scared the life out of me and I screamed out loud, but luckily my wail of horror, shock and disbelief didn't wake her. My head was spinning from all the wine I'd consumed the night before. I knew I was drunk, but how did I end up in bed with Edwina Currie? I closed my eyes and prayed I was dreaming, but when I opened them again she was still there. I'd never noticed it before, but lying there asleep, with last night's make-up smeared across her face and big globules of mascara forming in the corners of her eyes, the former government minister did bear an uncanny resemblance to Mimi Lawson; she had the hair and everything. I was so transfixed, it was a good ten seconds before it suddenly hit me:

'OH MY GOD, I SLEPT WITH MIMI LAWSON!'

I screamed again and this time she ran her hand across my chest, murmured something incomprehensible and fell back into a deep sleep. She started snoring and I thought I was going to be sick.

I lay there for about ten minutes, trying to piece together what had happened . . .

At the restaurant there was the usual kerfuffle over who should sit next to whom. Everyone was hovering, not wanting to get stuck sitting next to Gordon the Stage Doorkeeper. There were five different tables and I was desperate to sit next to Pippa, but Manky Mancini beat me to the last available chair on the dancer's table. I was running out of options. There were two chairs free on the band's table, but to sit in one of those would mean a night of drinking games, farting competitions and quoting lines from obscure Monty Python sketches. There was another chair on the wardrobe department's table. I would have sat on that, but all the women who work in wardrobe smell. The only other available chair was at the table occupied by Smiler, Pisser, Shagger, Farter, Jason the Gay Dancer, his boyfriend Colin the Tattooed Skinhead and, of course, Mimi Lawson. I thought this was my best option and took up my place between Shagger and Pisser.

The evening was really good fun and the wine flowed freely. Someone kept playing footsie with me under the table, but at the time I couldn't tell whether it was Mimi Lawson or Colin the Tattooed Skinhead. For a short while I thought it was Farter, but then I realized his legs weren't long enough.

I kept looking over at Pippa's table, trying to catch her eye, but she seemed to be deep in conversation with Manky and his hands were all over her. He kept trying to be flash by buying champagne for all the girls and sending crates of lager over to the crew's table. At one point he sent over a pint of lager for me; I smashed the glass, leapt across two tables and stabbed the jagged edge right through his heart.

Of course, I didn't do that at all, I just smiled and said, 'Cheers.' Pippa eventually came over and asked me what was the matter with my face. I immediately went to the toilet and looked in the mirror. My Mr Bronzer's Self-Tanning Lotion had reacted with my Blue Stratos aftershave, and under the restaurant's ultra-violet lighting had made my face look all streaky. I tried washing it off, but it only made it worse. I spent the rest of the evening looking like a bloody zebra.

Vince was really drunk and staggering all over the place. He kept coming up to me and putting his arm around me.

'My record's Number One in Albania,' he slurred. 'Has been for weeks.'

'I know, Vince,' I said, trying not to sound too condescending. 'You've already told me.'

Suddenly his mood changed and he became very angry.

'I've got no-one, Sshimon, I've been married four times and never had any children. I'm shixty-eight years old and I've got no-one. I thought there was someone special in my life, but there's not.'

He was shouting by this point.

'She's let me down again,' he bellowed.

'You've always got me, Vince,' I said in a jokey, we're-all-drunk-together type way.

'I appreshhate that,' he said, suddenly calming down. 'I bloody love you, lad. You're my beshht friend, you are.'

He sounded as if he meant it.

'You're my best friend too, Vince.'

I didn't mean it at all.

'Can I offer you shome advice, Shimon?'

'Of course you can, Vince.'

'Have shhhillren.'

He was really starting to mumble now.

'What's that, Vince?'

'Have shhhillren. Showbishness won't look after you in your old age and the public don't really love you at all. They shay they do but they don't. You can have a Number One record in Albania but no-one cares.'

He started prodding me with his finger to emphasize each word.

'Your. Career. Counts. For. Nothing. The only thing that matters is shhhillren.' He was obviously finding it difficult to fight back the tears. 'Have children. Everything else is just shallow and meaningless.'

'You're right, Vince,' I said before excusing myself and going to the toilet to check my fake tan.

When I returned everybody was arguing over the bill.

'. . . Why don't we just split it between everyone?'

'. . . Well, I never had the popadoms, so I'm not paying for those.'

'. . . The dancers didn't have anything to eat so I don't think we should pay as much as everyone else . . .'

Next came the line that you hear at every meal for twenty-five people or more.

'Who hasn't paid? One person hasn't paid!'

Never be the person who collects the money after a large company meal. It's a thankless task and people just think you're being bossy. After forty-five minutes of arguing, everybody claimed to have paid but we were still short by thirty-one pounds and seventeen pence. Having already paid for himself and all the dancers, Manky Mancini threw in another thirty quid and said, 'I'll pay that and I'm sure Peters will add the one pound and seventeen pence.'

I picked up the money and in one quick violent movement rammed it into Manky's self-satisfying gob.

I know you expect me to say that I didn't do that, but actually I did. I picked up the money and tried shoving it into his mouth, only to be pulled back by Shagger and Pisser.

'Calm down, lads, we've all had a drink,' said Farter, clinging onto my leg.

Even Mimi chipped in with the old classic, 'Leave it, Simon, he's not worth it.'

We returned to our respective tables and decided to have one more round of drinks. It was at some point during the next ten minutes that Mimi managed to manoeuvre herself into the seat next to mine. She

41

started telling me how she'd fancied me since the first day of rehearsals and how I was different from all of the other men. Before I knew it she was sitting on my knee and talking dirty in my ear. Maybe it's selective recall, but it all goes a little hazy after that. I remember the restaurant owners putting some music on and Mimi doing a strange sort of lap-dance for me. I know someone took photographs and I have an image of Manky Mancini pointing over at me and Pippa bursting out laughing. Vince wasn't laughing; he was just staring at us with a distant look on his face.

After we'd finished the drinks, the rest of the cast decided to move on to The Club in Grimsby town centre. Mimi grabbed my hand and said she didn't really want to go clubbing.

'What would you like to do instead then?' I asked in what could have been misconstrued as a slightly flirtatious manner.

'I want to take you back to my hotel and cover you in whipped cream.'

Now, of course, if I'd known that in the morning she'd turn into Edwina Currie, I would have found the whole idea objectionable, but at that moment in time, after four bottles of Liebfraumilch, three gin and tonics, two pints of lager, a brandy and a cigar, I have to say I found the whole idea rather appealing. So, we went back to her Travel Lodge and, true to her word, she covered me in whipped cream.

Unfortunately the rest is a little bit of a blank. All I remember is at one point I think she started to moo . . .

I must have drifted off again, because when I woke Mimi was making a cup of tea using the complimentary teabags and long-life milk that Travel Lodge so kindly provides. I pretended to be asleep but, squinting through one eye, I could see that she looked old and haggard, like Maggie May. The morning sun was in her face and it really did show her age.

She put a cup of tea on the bedside cabinet and disappeared into the bathroom. This was an embarrassing situation to be in. How best to play it? As far as I could see it I had three options:

The *'wasn't that a great night, let's do it again sometime'* approach where both parties are completely cool about what happened. They share a cigarette, discuss how much they enjoyed the sex and talk openly about the fantasies in which they would like to indulge in the future.

Or:

The *'let's pretend it never happened'* approach where both parties talk about the weather, the state of the economy and the one-way system around Bury St Edmunds. Anything to avoid mentioning the fact that just four hours previously they'd been rutting like wildebeests.

Or:

The *'typical male'* approach, where one party (Mimi) takes a shower, the other party (me) runs from the room as fast as he can without saying a word.

I think you can guess which one I plumped for.

I went straight to the theatre, locked my dressing-room door, waited for the show to start and only came out for the scenes I was in.

I spent the rest of the day smelling of sour cream.

Somehow I successfully managed to avoid Mimi. At the end of the two shows I knew she was waiting for me outside the stage door, so I left through my dressing-room window (I use the term 'dressing room' very loosely, 'dressing cupboard' would be more appropriate). My dressing room is actually on the second floor and I had to shimmy down a drainpipe to make my escape. Excessive, I know, but I just couldn't face her.

I went straight to the pub and drank six pints of lager in quick succession, but it did nothing to take away the images in my head of last night's proceedings. I was aware of people gossiping. Some wag put Mimi's old hit 'I'm

Daddy's Little Girl' on the jukebox and everyone started singing along and changing the words to 'I'm Mimi's Little Boy'. Somebody started to howl. Were they howling because it was such a bloody awful song or had somebody heard something last night? When I thought I heard someone moo I decided I was getting paranoid and caught a taxi back to the hotel. As the taxi drove past the theatre, Mimi was still waiting outside the stage door. She looked as though she'd been crying.

I did the decent thing and hid on the back seat.

31 JAN

Pippa and I were driving along in her open-top sports car. We were laughing and her long blond hair was flowing in the wind. The car span out of control and as it twisted and turned in mid air we began to kiss. There was no avoiding the crash. At the point of impact Pippa's breasts became great big air bags that exploded in my face and enveloped my whole body until I started to suffocate.

Petrol was leaking from the tank.

In amongst the twisted wreckage Pippa was sitting astride me, making love to me slowly and rhythmically. She smiled and with one hand flicked open a Zippo lighter. The petrol ignited, engulfing us in a ball of flames.

A vision of hell.

Pippa had now become a hideous, shrivelled old crone; half Mimi Lawson and half Edwina Currie. She was writhing around on top of me, riding me faster and faster. She was screaming, barking, oinking, mooing and at the point of climax she tossed her head back, let out a piercing screech and turned into Ricardo Mancini.

I woke up drenched in sweat.

*   *   *

Today was the last day of the pantomime. When I arrived at the theatre, there was a note for me saying, '*Don't ignore me, Simon.*'

It was written in a childish scrawl. An image of Glenn Close in *Fatal Attraction* flashed through my mind. I felt relieved that I didn't own a rabbit.

I decided that the decent thing would be to let her down gently by giving her some of 'The Old Peters Charm'.

'Mimi, you're a beautiful and talented woman and I will never forget our evening together. I feel we shared something special and unique and no-one can take that away from us. It's unfortunate, nay heartbreaking, that at this point in our lives, destiny decrees that we cannot be together. I will always have the memory, you will always have my heart and we will always have Grimsby.'

Of course that's not what I actually did. I figured, Home tomorrow, no more panto, no more Mimi Lawson. If I could avoid her for another ten hours then I might just get away with it.

During the last show of a pantomime, it's traditional to play last-night gags. Sometimes they're hilarious, sometimes they're embarrassing and sometimes they're just plain crap. The best one tonight was played on Manky Mancini. He was in the middle of his solo 'I Command Thee!' (taken from *Moses. The Musical!*) when Pisser, Shitter and Shagger ran on behind him with two buckets of water each. Shitter stood on Shagger's shoulders and Pisser passed him the water. Manky was so busy posing to the audience that he didn't have a clue what was going on. Just as he got to the line, 'let the wind blow, let the rain fall' Shitter did just that: six big buckets of water all over Manky's head. I was watching from the wings (stage left, knowing that Mimi's next entrance was from stage right) and it really was a glorious moment. Manky was furious. The band gave

Shitter, Shagger and Pisser a standing ovation and I think I'd have enjoyed it even more except for the fact that every time I looked at Manky, I thought of last night's dream and it made me feel ill.

At the end of the show everyone was hugging, swapping numbers and promising to keep in touch. They won't, of course, it's just the done thing.

Mimi was nowhere to be seen, so I slipped away to my dressing cupboard, collected my belongings and went out the stage door to start loading up my car. I have to admit my car is a bit of an old wreck. I call it Ringo because it's an old Beetle and the timing's out. A previous owner had painted it in the colours of Noddy's car and I haven't quite got round to changing it. The main body is yellow, the wheel arches are blue and the roof is red. I like to think it has character. Unfortunately, every time I go on a journey of over twenty miles, it inevitably breaks down and I have to get the AA out. I think I'm their least favourite member. They actually call me up, ask me where I'm going and say they'll have someone standing by.

I was just putting my make-up suitcase in the car, when there was a tap on my shoulder.

Mimi, I thought.

This was the moment I'd been dreading. I thought about making a run for it. I could jump into the driver's seat, slam the door and speed away with the wheels screeching, like in a Hollywood movie.

But I didn't, I decided to face the music. In the cold night air I could feel little beads of perspiration forming on my upper lip. I took a deep breath and turned around.

Pippa stood there, looking more attractive than I'd ever seen her look before.

'Expecting someone else?' she said with a big beautiful smile on her face.

'No,' I said, trying desperately not to drool. 'Not at all.'

'Nice car.'

I couldn't tell whether she was being sarcastic or not.

'Thanks.'

'What's the torque ratio on the rear differential?'

We both laughed. There was a pause, but this time it wasn't an embarrassed one.

'So what's going on between you and Manky Mancini, then?' I asked.

'Nothing,' she said. 'What's going on between you and Mimi Lawson?'

'Nothing.'

'I think you fancy her.'

'No I don't, I think she's a silly cow.'

'Well apparently she moos like one.'

'Pardon?'

'Nothing.'

We looked at each other for what seemed an eternity.

'Nice working with you,' I said.

'Nice working with you, too.'

She smiled.

'Have you got a pen and paper?' she asked.

'Er . . . no, why?'

'Because I want to give you my number.'

She then did a really cool thing: she licked her finger and then used it to write her phone number in the dirt on the bonnet of my car.

'You'd better hope it doesn't rain tonight.'

She pecked me on the cheek, turned around and went back into the theatre. I swear to God I would have married her there and then. I finished loading my car and was just putting in the last bag when Pippa tapped me on the shoulder again. She'd obviously been to get a piece of paper, or maybe she was coming back for more than a peck. I turned around quickly and, just like my dream, Pippa had turned into Mimi.

'Expecting someone else?' she said with a great big grimace.

The look on her face should be a textbook case study for drama students. It was one of pain, anguish and intensity, with just a hint of underlying turmoil. Her hair was matted, her eyes were dark and hollow and her make-up was smeared all over her face.

'You look nice,' I said.

'Why – have – you – been – ignoring – me,' she hissed through clenched teeth. She was obviously finding it difficult to hide her feelings towards me, so I decided to turn on The Old Peters Charm.

'Mimi, you're a beautiful and talented woman and I will never forget our evening together—'

'DON'T GIVE ME THAT SHIT!' she screamed with pure venom. 'You just don't understand what's been going on, do you? You don't understand at all. I've heard it all before, Simon. You men are all the same; you just want to see what it's like to spend a night of passion with Mimi Lawson.'

'No, it wasn't that at all. I was hideously drunk . . .'

With hindsight that wasn't very tactful, but luckily she wasn't listening.

'*The* Mimi Lawson, the little girl next door who never grew up.' The anger was subsiding now and she started to sob. 'All my life I've been used and then rejected. There've only ever been two men in my life who've told me they loved me, and one of them has just let me down.'

I knew I was drunk, but I certainly couldn't remember telling her I loved her.

'Who was the other one?'

'My daddy,' she said, her eyes filling with tears.

Oh my God, I thought. *She's not going to sing, is she?*

'I'm still Daddy's little girl.'

She is. She's going to sing.

And right there on the pavement, she sang all six verses of 'I'm Daddy's Little Girl.' When she finished there was an uncomfortable silence for what must have been a minute.

Then we hugged each other, swapped numbers and promised to keep in touch.

1 FEB

LONDON

Thank God that's all over. I am never doing panto again. Yes, I'm back in London, back to the bright lights, back to the hustle, the bustle, the glitz, the glamour, the celebrities, the champagne, the canapés, the paparazzi, the parties, the premieres, the anxiety over not being invited, the worry, the nervousness, the loneliness, the desperation, the uncertainty, the insecurity, the unemployment. I'm really going to miss panto, I hope they book me again for next year.

2 FEB

8.30 a.m.

Oh bugger. It rained in the night and I forgot to copy Pippa's number from the bonnet of my car.

I've been home for just twenty four hours and the post-panto blues have already set in. When you do a show like a pantomime, you're with the same group of people ten hours a day, six days a week for eight whole weeks and, love them or hate them, you become a family. When the show finishes and everyone goes home, it's a shock to the system and you can't help but feel a little sad.

I've been in this situation before and the trick is to stay motivated.

3 FEB

Bored.

4 FEB

Bored.

7 FEB

Really bored.

9 FEB

The one thing that's keeping me sane is the thought that any day now Max, my agent, is going to call me and tell me that the executives at ITV Network Centre have recommissioned my game show *Simon Says*. I've got a really good feeling about it. It's as if it's meant to be.

10 FEB

Bored.

12 FEB

Bored. Bored. Bored.

14 FEB

I have only received two valentine's cards. The first one was from a local estate agent saying:

> *Dear Homeowner,*
> *We would love to sell your flat for you.*
> *You know it would be nice.*
> *So don't be shy and give us a call.*
> *We'll get you the right price.*
> *Happy Valentine's Day from Merton & Merton Estate Agents XXX*
> *(We have a list of people on our books who are waiting to buy a flat like yours. If you are thinking of selling in the near future please don't hesitate to contact us on the above number.)*

That one obviously doesn't count. Besides, my flat's rented and isn't mine to sell. Even though it's rented, I've managed to make it my own by covering the walls in framed signed photographs of all the famous people I've ever worked with. Charley says it's a bit naff and keeps trying to persuade me to at least take down the signed photograph of me. I disagree, I think it's important to leave a couple of clues to whose place it is, just in case Loyd Grossman and the *Through the Keyhole* team ever decide to pop round. For the same reason, I bought the entire works of the French philosopher Jean-Paul Sartre just so Loyd would say that whoever lived in this house was obviously a person of great intellect.

The second valentine's card was a real mystery. It was large and padded with a painted picture of a vase of roses on the front. It was either from someone with no taste whatsoever or from someone with a real sense of humour.

Inside there was just a large question mark written in lipstick.

Maybe it was from Pippa?

I can't believe that having had a prime-time daytime game show on network television I only received one genuine valentine's card. Maybe all the other cards went to the TV Company and they haven't bothered to pass them on yet. I'll call Max tomorrow and ask him to find out.

15 FEB

Maybe I won't call Max about the missing cards; it might sound a little conceited.

16 FEB

What if there weren't any other cards?

18 FEB

I have to stay positive. I have to keep telling myself that the exciting thing about a career in showbusiness is that you never know what's round the corner. What drives you on is the hope and the optimism that the next job is the Big One. There's nothing quite like the anticipation and exhilaration you feel when the phone rings, and you pick it up and it's your agent on the other end of the line with some unbelievable news.

19 FEB

'*Simon Says* has been cancelled.'

Max gave it to me straight. I thought he could have maybe dressed it up a little, eased it into the conversation, broken the news in a more gentle manner, but no, he told it as it was.

'*Simon Says* has been cancelled.'

'But surely if—'

'No ifs, Simon, no ifs. There's an old Yiddish expression, "*Az di bobe volt gehat beytsim volt zi geven mayn zeyde.*"'

'What does that mean?'

'If my grandmother had testicles she would be my grandfather. Try not to get too depressed about it.'

Try not to get depressed about it?

I wouldn't have thought of being depressed if he hadn't said that.

20 FEB

My life is a black hole, my career an abyss.

21 FEB

I think I'm coming down with something.

24 FEB

I have just spent the last three days doing absolutely nothing. Somehow seventy-two hours of my life have just disappeared, and I can't think of one single thing of interest that happened.

26 FEB

This morning I spent three hours just looking at myself in the bathroom mirror. All I could see staring back at me was the face of an unemployed game-show host. What's worse, it was the face of an unemployed game-show host with really bad nasal hair. I am alarmed at the rate at which it grows. I recently read an article that said if you didn't cut your nasal hair it would grow to be two foot long. The thought of this made me feel ill. I should do something about it, but what's the point? I am truly past caring.

27 FEB

The phone rang and, hoping it was Max with news of some work, I snatched up the receiver.

It was Mimi Lawson.

For a moment I was stunned and couldn't think what to say, then I put on my best Indian accent, told her she had the wrong number and hung up. She called again and left a message on my answer machine. I think she was trying to sound sexy, breathy and husky, but instead it sounded like she had asthma. I think I'll screen my calls from now on.

Why hasn't Max called me? If he's not going to call me then I'm going to have to call him. It's not as if I'm scared of him or anything.

1 MARCH

There are lots of little jobs that need doing around the flat. The cold-water tap in the kitchen sink has been dripping since I returned from Grimsby, but I can't seem to get round to fixing it.

Vince Envy left a message. What is it with Vince? Doesn't he realize the panto's over now and it's time to move on. He doesn't seem to be able to grasp the notion that when you work on a show, you say you'll keep in touch but you never actually mean it.

He sounded like he was calling from a bar. He was slurring his words and having a conversation with himself, as if he didn't know he was speaking to an answer machine. I always had a soft spot for Vince, but he has to realize that I'm a very busy showbusiness personality. I made a mental note to call him back, knowing full well that I never will.

I'm going to start writing a 'Things To Do' list, and top of that list is to call my agent.

I'll do it tomorrow.

2 MARCH

I spent the whole day watching television.

Well not exactly the *whole* day – I didn't get up until one thirty in the afternoon, but when I did I just lay on the settee, flipping from channel to channel. This would probably be acceptable if I was improving my mind by watching Discovery or The History Channel but I wasn't, I was watching the home shopping channels, and the trouble is, there are so many of them. It's as if I'm caught in their evil spell. Once I start watching I can't stop. The crappier the channel, the more enjoyment I get from watching it.

5 MARCH

I spent four hours watching *Going-Gone TV*, the auction channel where viewers call in to bid for various items. The trouble is, of course, all the items are rubbish.

Today they were selling a breadmaker, a flashing torch, a man's signet ring, a pack of four 'rebound' pillows, a selection of towels, an 'Improve Your Memory' cassette, a rechargeable oscillating toothbrush and a multi-dish marinader.

The constant dripping from the tap is like Chinese water torture. I'm going to get up first thing tomorrow morning and fix it.

6 MARCH

I woke up at two thirty in the afternoon. The reason I got up so late is because I didn't get to bed until about four in the morning, and the reason for that is that I was watching *Late Night Going-Gone TV*.

I think I'm addicted.

8 MARCH

I feel sorry for the presenters. They have to talk about an object with real relish and enthusiasm, even though it's quite plainly crap. They're not allowed to use even a hint of irony or sarcasm.

Today's presenter was Tony Dobson, who used to be the showbiz reporter on *Coffee Morning with Mike and Sue* (how the mighty have fallen). He has a really deep fake tan and teeth that are simply too white. He has a really over-enthusiastic presenting style; he sells everything as if it's the best product in the world and he can't quite believe how you, the viewer, are managing to live your life without it.

The show is completely live and the presenters have to keep talking until someone calls up to make a bid. There was a great moment today when nobody called for thirty-six minutes. That might not sound like a long time, but when Tony Dobson only had a Sherlock Holmes Beanie Bear to talk about, he did struggle slightly. I could imagine a producer screaming at him in his earpiece to 'Fill . . . fill . . . fill'. He did OK for about eighteen minutes, but then began to flounder. He was stammering and had a look of panic in his eyes. He was sweating profusely. By twenty-four minutes, desperation had really set in. He started pretending to be Dr Watson to the Beanie Bear's Sherlock Holmes, creating little crime scenarios and doing the voices for both characters. I swear, by thirty minutes he was almost crying. I nearly called in just to put him out of his misery.

Going-Gone TV is the presenter's graveyard. Please God, don't let me ever have to work there.

10 MARCH

I seem to have a real problem motivating myself. I've been home from panto for well over a month and I still haven't called my agent, trimmed my nasal hair or done anything about the dripping tap in the kitchen. I feel so unfit; I really ought to get some exercise.

On *Going-Gone*, they were selling a stain remover, a kitchen knife, a foot spa, a portable karaoke machine, a unisex bicycle, an electric pepper mill, a Beanie Bear dressed as Evil Knievel and a diamanté brooch in the shape of a unicorn.

11 MARCH

A hand-delivered note was pushed through my letterbox:

Please call me.
I'm desperate to speak to you!
M.

An image of a naked Edwina Currie danced across my mind. I've really got to do something about this situation before it escalates.

I'll call her.

Tomorrow.

Maybe.

12 MARCH

Just when you think things can't get any worse, Ricardo Mancini has a four-page spread in *OK!* magazine: RICARDO MANCINI SHOWS OFF HIS NEW LONDON APARTMENT. He has absolutely no shame. The photographs are sad with a capital 'S'. One of them, '*Ricardo relaxes in his bedroom*' shows Manky lying on a leopard-skin rug pretending to read a copy of *The Undiscovered Self* by C.G. Jung. He is wearing glasses (obviously going for the intellectual look), a leather jacket with tassels on it, tight blue denim jeans and cowboy boots (I'm sure he's just trying to copy me). He's not wearing a shirt underneath the jacket and you can tell he's put some make-up on his pecs to create the illusion of definition.

In another photograph, '*Ricardo is late for an important business meeting*', he's wearing a suit with the sleeves rolled up, striking a real male model pose; the one where they appear as if they're checking the time on their watch and simultaneously looking slightly off camera, as if something really interesting is happening behind the photographer's head. He also has one eyebrow raised in a quizzical manner and he's pouting in a way that would have put Marilyn Monroe to shame.

The article talks about how the former 'Italian stallion' has now mended his ways and finally found a 'nice girl' to settle down with.

I turned the page and couldn't believe what I saw. It was Manky lying on a white leather sofa, wearing a white Aran jumper, white cotton slacks, white socks and white patent-leather slip-on shoes (which made me feel quite jealous because I've always wanted a pair of those). That was bad enough, but lying next to him was Pippa. She looked gorgeous in a slightly transparent white silk dress which the article reliably informed us was by Chanel. Their arms were entwined and the headline screamed *RICARDO'S NEW LOVE*.

'*I was looking for love in the wrong places,*' he is quoted as saying. Well, I suppose he's right: drug dens and lap-dancing clubs aren't the ideal place to meet your soulmate. '*but then I met Pippa while we were both appearing in a musical in the West End.*'

Musical in the West End?

Panto in the Arse End, more like!

I couldn't stop staring at the photograph and thinking how terrible it is that celebrities allow magazines like *OK!* into their homes and end up selling their love and trading their personal affairs.

I phoned Charley to ask her if she'd seen it and to tell her how naff I thought it was, but she said she thought the one of Manky and Pippa was quite nice. She seemed almost pleased that they were together.

'But they're prostituting their private lives,' I shouted.

She said she'd heard from someone on *Coffee Morning* that he'd been paid five grand for it.

FIVE GRAND?

I wonder if *OK!* would do an 'at home' with me?

I must call Max.

Why am I putting off calling him?

13 MARCH

I flick open the magazine and there is a picture of Edwina Currie and me standing outside Number 10, Downing St. Edwina is looking into my eyes adoringly.

SIMON PETERS FINDS TRUE LOVE!
The popular game-show host speaks exclusively for the first time of his love for Edwina Currie.

Edwina wears a blue twinset with pearls, Simon, a puce Hawaiian shirt and matching slacks.

'We fell in love, the moment we saw each other,' said Edwina.

Asked if they could hear the sound of wedding bells, Simon winked cheekily, squeezed Edwina's hand and said, 'Watch this space.'

I must stop eating cheese before I go to bed.

16 MARCH

Vince Envy left another message. He sounded really drunk and the only part I understood was when he started singing an obscure Irish song about 'The Son I Never Had.'

I deleted the message. I know the decent thing would be to return his call and offer him some friendship, but deep down I don't really want to (it's not even that deep down; on the surface I don't want to call him back). I feel as though Vince Envy is a warning to me. I could end up like him if I don't sort myself out.

Why can't I snap out of this boredom and lethargy? At least I haven't started drinking yet. Television seems to be my only vice. Why am I so obsessed by it?

18 MARCH

That bloody tap was dripping all through the night. At one point I had to turn up the telly so I couldn't hear it.

19 MARCH

. . . a vibrating travel clock, a tool box, a carpet cleaner, a French manicure set, a left-handed can-opener, thirty-two different paint brushes, a globe made of lapis lazuli, a collection of Elvis Presley CDs, a six-piece luggage set, a moisturizer that reduces cellulite, a Swing-Easy golf club, a pair of scissors that will never go blunt and a Beanie Bear dressed as a cowboy . . .

Obviously I'm watching the channel with a detached sense of irony, but some people do actually call up and bid for these things.

What sort of lives do these sad individuals lead?

20 MARCH

Today I bid for a *Motivate Yourself* video.

Chad Steele, the American self-help guru, was Tony Dobson's guest. He was selling books, videos and audio cassettes. My video cost £12.99 plus £4.50 p&p, and it will be delivered within three working days.

22 MARCH

'*The Plumber's Mate*,' an amazing invention that can fix a dripping tap in the blink of an eye.' Tony Dobson's words, not mine. It looked like a spanner and a couple of washers to me, but Tony assured me that 'over the next few years it could save you thousands of pounds in plumbers' bills'.

It cost £29.99, plus £6.50 p&p.

I ordered two.

24 MARCH

'*The Ab-solution*, the ultimate in abdominal training.'

It might look like a long thin metal bar, but apparently not. According to Tony, who was wearing Lycra today and really shouldn't have been, The Ab-solution hardens your abs, strengthens your lower back and tightens up your obliques.

I don't know what your obliques are, but Tony, the man in Lycra, said that this would tighten them. I couldn't stop myself from calling up. It cost me £160.99 plus £19.50 p&p.

Mimi Lawson left another message. She said she was in London next week and did I want to meet up for a drink as there was something she wanted to talk about? I chose to ignore it. Her voice sounded shaky and emotional, as if she'd been crying about something. I should never have given her my number. I should have been straight with her from the start and told her there was no future for us. Why can't I be strong? Why can't I tell people what I really feel?

25 MARCH

'*Be Strong!* and *Tell People What You Really Feel!*, two videos that will change your life for ever.'

I exist in a strange TV twilight zone where *Going-Gone TV* is broadcasting only to me. I'd been watching it for twenty-four hours solid when Chad Steele, the American self-help guru, turned to the camera and said, 'Simon Peters, you really need these videos.'

Suddenly it's me on the screen. I'm presenting *Going-Gone TV*. My face is orange and my teeth are fluorescent white. I'm talking in an American accent and trying to sell a gadget that plaits nasal hair. The next item I have to auction is Mimi Lawson. She's dressed in a pantomime cow costume. She's mooing. Nobody calls in for two hours. We fill by singing 'I'm Daddy's Little Girl' twenty-three times.

I woke up and Tony Dobson was selling a pair of garden shears for people with arthritis.

I turned off the television and went to bed.

26 MARCH

I think I must be getting paranoid because this morning I thought I saw Mimi sitting on the wall opposite my flat, but when I looked again she was gone.

28 MARCH

I called Charley at 7.30 a.m. She was about to go into a production meeting for *Coffee Morning*, but listened for half an hour as I poured my heart out.

I told her how missing my mum and not speaking to my dad for three years has left me feeling like an orphan. I told her all about my night of hell with Edwina Currie and how one-night stands just leave me feeling empty. I told her how upset I was at only receiving two valentine's cards and how I can't face up to the fact that I'm going to be thirty in December. I told her about my concerns over my nasal hair, how my career is going nowhere, how I'm scared of my agent, in love with Pippa, jealous of Ricardo Mancini, avoiding Mimi Lawson and feeling guilty about not wanting to speak to Vince Envy. I also told her I was addicted to crap television.

'Simon,' she said sympathetically, 'it's a shame about your mother, but that happened seventeen years ago and you can't keep using that as an excuse every time you feel a bit down. If you want to speak to your dad, just pick up the phone and call him. It's as simple as that. As for all the other stuff, it's just *life*. You've got to put it all into perspective and, to be honest, you don't know what real problems are. There's a bloke on *Coffee Morning* today who rowed across the Atlantic, even though he's only got one arm.'

'Did he row single-handed?'

'That's a crap joke, Simon.'

'Sorry.'

'Now only having one arm in life is a problem.'

'Yes, but Charley, I've got a problem,' I said. 'I feel I'm destined always to be a B-list celebrity.'

'Simon, darling, you're not a B-list celebrity.'

'Thanks, Charley.'

'You're C-List, everyone knows that.'

I can always rely on Charley to make me feel better.

2 APRIL

'*Motivate Yourself!*' '*The Plumber's Mate*' and '*The Absolution*' all arrived in the post. I watched the video, fixed the tap and did 25 'Ab-solution' stomach crunches.

4 APRIL

I decided to call Max and really lay it on the line to him. If he couldn't get me some work then I'd have to find an agent who could. I would put my foot down and demand a meeting with him.

Scary Babs answered the phone and when she finally stopped coughing and wheezing I told her I wanted to speak to Max. She put me on hold and ten minutes later I was finally connected.

'Max,' I said.

'Peter,' he said.

'Simon,' I said.

'Whatever,' he said. 'Where have you been, you great big *shlump*?' I didn't have a clue what a *shlump* was, but I knew it wasn't a term of endearment.

'I've . . . been . . . erm . . . doing some writing.'

'No you haven't, you lazy *alter kaker*, you've been watching television for the last two months.'

God, he scares me. Max seems to have an uncanny knack of knowing exactly what I'm doing at all times.

'No . . . not at all,' I lied. 'I've been . . . erm . . . developing some game-show formats.'

'Will you stop with the shit already. Come into the office on the twenty-third. We'll have a meeting.'

And with that he hung up.

I'm glad I sorted that out.

7 APRIL

This is the new me.

Today I spent forty-five glorious minutes using my *Remington Chrome-Plated Nasal Hair Trimmer*, which was delivered this morning. I also did 50 '*Ab-solution*' stomach crunches.

11 APRIL

Painted my bedroom ceiling using the *Extendable Roller Brush©* and did 100 stomach crunches.

14 APRIL

Washed Ringo using my *Power-Jet* hose, grouted the bathroom tiles using *Supa-Grout*, cleaned the windows using *Wonder-Brite* and made the flat more energy efficient by installing *Cosy-Therm!* loft insulation. I nearly called Mimi to tell her it was best if we didn't see each other again, but I didn't feel quite that motivated.

150 stomach crunches.

16 APRIL

I think I've overdone it on the *Ab-solution* and I'm suffering from severe stomach pains. I dismantled it and put it in the loft.

I'll get it out again when I'm feeling better.

18 APRIL

Improve Your Memory audio cassette arrived in the post.

I don't remember ordering that.

20 APRIL

Things have definitely taken a turn for the better. This has to be the pinnacle of my career so far. I've called everyone I know: my agent, Charley, old school friends, people who I've only ever met once and some people who I've never met at all but whose numbers, for some reason, are in my phone book. I almost called my father, but at the last moment chickened out. But I called everyone else. The reason?

I am in *Heat* magazine.

A couple of weeks before I started rehearsing for panto, Charley invited me to a charity ball at the Grosvenor Hotel in Park Lane, which she'd been invited to through *Coffee Morning*. It was wall-to-wall celebrity. I really was the only one I'd never heard of. They took a big group photograph of all the guests and they've printed it in *Heat* this week. Unfortunately, in the caption underneath the photograph, they have me listed as one of The Chuckle Brothers. Admittedly it is very difficult to tell that it's me. I'm right at the back, it's very poorly lit and Richard Madeley's hand is completely obscuring my face (he just had to wave, didn't he?)

But one of The Chuckle Brothers. Pur-lease!

When I called Charley, she didn't seem overly impressed.

'But my ears are in *Heat* magazine!' I protested.

'They look like the ears of a Chuckle Brother to me,' she said.

I don't care. I, Simon Peters, am in *Heat* magazine.

Yesssss!

23 APRIL

Meeting with Max.

I made a real effort to look like someone who he would want to have on his books. I wore my favourite bright yellow Hawaiian shirt (courtesy of the *Simon Says* wardrobe budget), mustard-yellow trousers (Burtons) and a pair of off-yellow converse baseball boots (BHS). I looked in the mirror and thought I looked pretty damn sexy, a tad too much yellow perhaps, but hey, this is showbiz.

It's strange but I can't look in the mirror these days without pretending to be a game-show host. I ask my reflection general knowledge questions and then increase the tension with a '*You can bank the money if you want to,*' and, '*Remember, if you pass, five seconds of time will be deducted.*' At one point I became a bizarre cross between Richard Whiteley in *Countdown* and Robert De Niro in *Taxi Driver*. '*Is that your final answer? Is that your final answer? Well I don't see anybody else answering.*'

I really must stop doing this as I think I might look a bit stupid.

I drove to Max's office, or at least I attempted to. Ringo broke down on the Westway and I had to abandon him. I should have waited for the AA to come, but I knew Max would kill me if I was late. I walked along the road, trying to hail a cab. It started to rain and I began to panic. My walk turned into a jog and I stuck my thumb out, hoping to hitch a lift. At one point a car swerved to avoid hitting me and I tripped up the kerb, ripped my trousers, cut my knee and landed face first in a deep puddle. The rain was getting heavier and, as I picked myself up and began to run, a lorry pulled up alongside me.

'You're that bloke off *Simon Says*,' shouted the driver from his cab.

He told me this as if he was telling me something I didn't know.

'That's right,' I said, still running along.

'The show where you do as I say not as I do,' he said, quoting my catchphrase. This guy was obviously a fan.

'That's right.'

The rain was now beating down. I was short of breath, drenched to the skin and my knee had started to bleed.

'I've got a good one for you,' he shouted.

'What's that?' I said, hoping he'd offer me a lift.

'Simon says buy an umbrella!'

He pipped his horn and drove off, laughing hysterically. I swear he even drove through a large puddle just to splash me.

I began to sprint.

I arrived at Max's office with two minutes to spare. I was sweating and breathing heavily and my clothes were dirty, bloodied and soaking wet. The office is very plush with cream carpets, cream leather couches and framed photographs of all the artistes Max represents on the walls. Where one's photograph is situated is indicative of one's success. Mine's in the basement outside the gents' toilet.

I went to the reception desk to let Scary Babs know I'd arrived. She removed the cigarette from her lips and gave me a disapproving look.

'You look like a bloody wet banana,' she said in her inimitable scouse accent. She burst out laughing and the laughing inevitably led to one of her coughing fits. Once she'd recovered, she said that Max was in a meeting, which was going on for longer than expected. She told me I could sit and wait so I headed for one of the cream leather couches.

'Not there!' she shrieked and pointed towards a wooden seat in the corner. 'There.'

Exhausted, I sat down and closed my eyes. When I opened them again I noticed that Scary Babs was looking at me and frowning. Or at least she would have been frowning if the botox hadn't prevented her from doing so.

'Your face is all streaky,' she said.

Damn that Mr Bronzer's Self-Tanning Lotion.

Max kept me waiting for an hour and a half. I was absolutely fuming and I spent the entire ninety minutes plotting word for word how I was going to tell him exactly what I thought about him and his agency. I would tell him that I haven't had a job or an audition since I came back from panto, how I don't feel he hustles for me, how he never treats me with any respect and how he seems to forget that he works for me and not the other way around. How dare he keep me waiting for an hour and a half?

'Peter, get your arse in here.'

It was Max, summoning me from his inner office. I pushed open the thick heavy door and went inside.

'Peter.'

'It's Simon,' I hissed through clenched teeth.

'Whatever . . .'

This is the moment I tell Max Golinski that he's nothing but a sadistic bully.

'*Coffee Morning with Mike and Sue* have been on the phone . . .'

This is the moment I tell him to take his agency and stick it up his arse.

'. . . they want you to be their regular showbiz reporter.'

That was the moment I leant over the desk and kissed him.

25 APRIL

I start on *Coffee Morning* in two weeks' time. It's a three-month non-exclusive contract, working two days a week at £450 a day. My job is to go on location and interview lots of showbiz personalities. I also have to present occasional live inserts into the programme.

This is a big break for me. I will be appearing on a popular daytime show on network television, twice a week for at least the next three months. Who knows what it will lead to?

2.07 a.m.
I've just realized that for Tony Dobson it led to *Going-Gone TV*.

3.02 a.m.
I wonder if my dad will watch it?

26 APRIL

Mimi Lawson was definitely outside my flat this morning. She sat on the wall for two hours looking up at my window.

She's starting to scare me now.

27 APRIL

I've certainly climbed up one rung of the showbiz ladder. Max called and asked me if I could pop into the office to sign the contract for *Coffee Morning* as they needed it urgently. He didn't get Scary Babs to call me, he called me himself.

I didn't want to risk Ringo, so instead decided to go on the Tube. On the way, I stopped at a newsagent's to buy a couple of Cohiba cigars in readiness for a celebration. I was sure it was the sort of thing Max would like.

I hate the Underground at the best of times, and today it was absolutely packed. I don't think people realize what a pain it is for a famous person to travel on public transport. It's not the staring, the nudging, the pointing and the giggling that upsets me; it's when none of these things happen that I get really paranoid. Some people just carry on reading their books or looking out of the window as if they've never seen me before in their life. Don't people watch television these days?

I was recognized once on the journey, though. A man with greasy hair and bad teeth poked me in the ribs.

'You're that bloke off telly, aren't you?' he boomed in a very loud voice.

A few people looked up from their newspapers.

'That's right,' I said putting on my best 'I'm just a normal guy going about my everyday business' face.

More people started to stare. I was pleased I'd made an effort with my clothes (bright red Hawaiian shirt with flame motif and lime-green trousers). The man with the bad teeth shoved a ripped cigarette packet into my hand.

'Here,' he bellowed. 'Sign this for me, would you, mate?'

'Sure,' I said modestly.

I took the packet and casually started scribbling my name.

'I love your show,' he shouted. 'What's it called again?'

By now everyone was looking and starting to whisper. I noticed a very attractive girl with long blond hair sitting at the far end of the carriage. She'd been studying the Tube map, but was now starting to take an interest in me.

'*Simon Says*,' I said, trying to look nonchalant, as if this sort of thing happened all the time.

The man looked surprised.

'Eh?'

'*Simon Says*,' I repeated, this time loud enough for the blonde girl to hear.

The man stared at me blankly.

'*Simon Says*, the show where you do what I say and not what I do!'

I was really playing to the audience now and flashing my best showbiz smile to the whole carriage. I gave a cheeky little wink to the blonde girl.

'Sorry, mate,' said the man, snatching back the cigarette packet, which I hadn't even finished signing. 'I thought you were one of The Chuckle Brothers.'

There was a silence.

Everyone returned to their newspapers and the attractive blonde girl went back to studying the Tube map. I even heard somebody tut.

I am never travelling on public transport again.

When I arrived at the office Scary Babs was quite nice to me, which proves I'm on the way up. She let me sit on the leather couch, offered to make me a cup of tea and told me conspiratorially that Max was in with a new client. As an artiste you hate it when your agent takes on a new client; you feel he's being unfaithful to you.

Agencies seem to have a three-tier system of artistes on their books. At the top are the 'The Big Earners', the stars who can command massive fees and are in the enviable position of being able to pick and choose their work. In the middle you have 'The Workers', the artistes who've been around for some time, they're always going to work but haven't quite made it big yet. Finally, at the bottom, you have 'The New Talent', all the youngsters coming through who will one day be one of the 'The Workers' and, if they're lucky, one of 'The Big Earners'.

I seem to have been 'New Talent' for the last five years now. Maybe *Coffee Morning* will change all that.

I didn't mind having to wait for Max. I knew I had something important to do to fill the time. All I had to do was wait for the right moment. After about twenty minutes, Scary Babs asked me if I would look after the reception desk while she nipped to the shops to buy some cigarettes.

'I'm down to sixty a day,' she said.

I waited until she'd gone and knew this was my opportunity. I made my way to the gents' toilets in the basement and, using the screwdriver I'd bought from *Going-Gone TV* (Screw4U, £9.99 plus £3.50 p&p) I took down the photograph of me. I felt like I was on a secret mission. Quickly and quietly, I went back upstairs to the main office. I made sure the coast was clear and removed the photograph of Mickey Spillers, the TV chef from *Too Many Cooks* (what his photograph was doing opposite the main entrance, I have no idea), and put my photograph in his place; I was just tightening the last screw when Scary Babs walked back through the door. She'd caught me red-handed and I knew there was no escaping her wrath. She was short of breath from her trip to the shops and for a moment she just stared at me.

'Don't worry, dearie,' she wheezed. 'All the artistes do that. It's like bloody musical chairs with those photographs.'

She started to cough. It was the sort of hacking cough you only get from a lifetime of nicotine abuse. Just as she was starting to bring up phlegm, I heard Max opening the door to his office and showing his new client the way out.

'Ah, Peter, I believe you know this young lady . . .'

I turned from tending to Scary Babs.

'Phillipa Snape,' Max was saying. 'We're going to have to do something about that surname though . . .'

I couldn't believe it was her.

'. . . go double-barrelled maybe, that's all the rage at the moment . . .'

She was more beautiful than I remembered.

'. . . or lose it altogether; it's always good if you can just be known by one name . . .'

Max made the action with his hands that indicated her name in lights.

'Pippa!'

My heart skipped a beat.

She was tanned as if she'd just come back from a holiday, and she'd had her hair dyed black and chopped into a short funky bob. It had a really severe fringe, as if someone had put a pudding bowl on her head and cut around it. On anyone else, the hairstyle would have looked ridiculous; on Pippa it looked perfect. We stood there, looking at each other for what seemed an age.

'How's the car?'

Is that the only conversation I've got?

'I sold it,' she said. 'I wasn't happy with the remission on the ignition transmission.'

I smiled to let her know I knew she was joking, but didn't laugh, just in case she wasn't.

'I like your hair.'

'Thanks,' she said. 'They put a pudding bowl on my head and cut around it.'

This time I burst out laughing. 'That's a good one.'

She didn't even smile. 'It's true.'

There was a silence that bordered on the uncomfortable.

'I was going to call you but the rain washed your bonnet off the phone number of my car.'

'All the words are there folks, they're just not in the right order.'

That was Max trying to be funny.

'So, what are you doing here?' I asked, this time carefully enunciating each word.

'Max asked me to pop in to see him. I quite fancy having a go at being a TV presenter.'

For a split second I despised her. You can't just *quite fancy having a go at being a TV presenter*. That's what I hate about the way people perceive this job. Every actor/actress/dancer/singer/model/wannabe thinks they can just *have a go at being a TV presenter*. Don't they understand? TV presenting is the art of communication, a skill and craft that people have to hone through years of hard work and experience. It's a career choice and a life's calling, not just something you *fancy having a go at*.

Who am I kidding? The real reason I despised her in that moment was because I was jealous of her. I knew she'd be famous in no time at all. I knew it would be easy for her. I knew that under Max's guidance she would go from being 'New Talent' to a 'Big Earner' without ever having to be a 'Worker'. Within six months she would be on the front cover of *Loaded* magazine and hosting *Top of the Pops*. Pippa had A-list written all over her. I knew it, Max knew it and I think even Pippa knew it.

'Max told me you've just got a gig on *Coffee Morning*,' she said. 'Congratulations.'

She smiled that smile and all my hatred and jealousy disappeared in a flash.

'He also said you might be able to give me some tips on how to be a presenter.'

The Other Me stepped in.

'Yeah sure, I can tell you what you need to put on your showreel, which producers are good to see, what to do at auditions, that type of thing. Why don't we meet up for a coffee?'

'Coffee would be great,' she said.

She wrote her number down on a piece of paper and handed it to me.

'I would have written it on the bonnet of your car,' she said, 'but it looks like it's going to rain again.'

Everyone laughed. Even Scary Babs, which wasn't a pretty sight as it set off one of her coughing fits again.

'So, are you still going out with Manky Mancini then?' enquired *The Other Me*.

'Yes,' she said, but it was difficult to tell whether she was happy about the fact or not. 'But call me anyway.'

She pecked me on the cheek and with that she was gone.

The Other Me danced his way back into the office, grabbed Scary Babs's hand and kissed it.

'She's way out of your league, dearie.'

Scary Babs was back to her old self and desperately trying to burst my bubble.

'She might be out of my league, Babs, but there's always the chance of a good run in the FA Cup.'

The Other Me licked his index finger and mimed the sign of a number one.

'One-nil to Peters.'

Boy, I was on form. I waltzed into the inner office, signed the *Coffee Morning* contracts, gave one cigar to Max and lit the other one for myself.

'It doesn't get much better than this, Maximondo,' said *The Other Me*, blowing a perfect smoke ring.

'Yes it does, Peters, it gets a lot better than this. Now get your feet off my desk, stop smoking in my office and never ever call me Maximondo again.'

I heard the sound of breaking glass. It was *The Other Me* jumping out of the window.

'Now, listen to me very carefully,' said Max, lighting his own cigar. 'Whatever you do, don't mess up the *Coffee Morning* gig. I've been working on getting you this for months.'

'Don't worry, Max, I won't let you down.'

And I meant it. I finished the cigar outside and treated myself to a cab home.

3.46 a.m.

Things are going really well at the moment, but I hate it when I haven't got anything to worry about.

4.03 a.m.

The incident on the Tube this morning really upset me, and that bloody lorry driver who splashed me the other day.

4.19 a.m.

What does it take to be popular with the public?

29 APRIL

I have a theory that celebrities are like football teams. At the top of the premiership and qualifying for Europe, you have Dale Winton. Now you might be surprised that I put Dale in the premier league.

'What about your pop singers and your movie stars?' you may well ask. 'What about your Noels and your Bruces?' (That's Gallagher and Willis, by the way, not Edmonds and Forsyth.)

Well, they're in some sort of Celebrity Super League, a league I don't even dream about and one I know I'll never play in.

'Know your limitations,' as my old careers teacher Mr Maxwell used to say, ambition being something that was frowned upon at my school. I feel I do know my limitations. I'd be happy as one of those Nationwide League Division One-type celebrities, alongside your Carol Smillies and your Jeremy Beadles. But at the moment I'm not even that. No, at the moment, in footballing terms, I'm sitting on the subs bench at Accrington Stanley, squeezed between Vanessa Feltz and that scouse bloke who won the first series of *Big Brother*.

Maybe *Coffee Morning* will change all that.

I really do feel indebted to Max for getting me the work. I know it's his job, but I think he pulled out all the stops and did some tough negotiating to make the producers believe I was the guy for the gig.

The man is a god amongst agents and I can't think why I ever doubted him in the first place.

30 APRIL

I called Charley this afternoon and told her the good news about *Coffee Morning* and that we'd soon be working together. She said she already knew but was too busy to talk because of problems with Mike and Sue. They'd had an argument and were refusing to speak to each other. Apparently Mike had counted all the words in the script and was upset to find out that Sue had forty-three more than him.

'There's a party on May the sixth,' said Charley. 'One of the producers is leaving – there's always someone leaving this show. Anyway, there's a party to celebrate. It'll be a good chance for you to meet everyone.'

In the background I could hear someone shouting and cursing and using some of the most obscene language I've ever heard.

'Who's that?'

'It's Sue,' she said. 'Got to go, see you next Friday.'

2 MAY

LWT CORDIALLY INVITES YOU AND A GUEST TO A RECORDING OF A CELEBRITY AUDIENCE WITH BILLY FOX

To be honest, I can't stand Billy Fox. He's about 80 years old, he sings off key and his jokes have more corn than a bowl of Kellogg's. He's one of those old-style entertainers who TV bosses keep giving game shows to just because he was funny in the 1963 Royal Variety Performance. The sort of person who should retire and give some young blood (i.e., me) a chance.

None of that mattered when the invitation dropped through my letterbox, though. All of a sudden, I loved Billy Fox. I've never been referred to as a celebrity before (apart from when I've said it about myself), but now here it was in writing, 'celebrity'. This meant so much to me. I called Charley to tell her the good news.

'Charley,' I said. 'I've been invited to *A Celebrity Audience With Billy Fox.*'

'But you hate Billy Fox.'

I couldn't see her but I knew she was smirking.

'No, I don't, I just think he's a bit old for prime-time television, that's all.'

'*He should retire and give some young blood, i.e., me, a chance,*' said Charley.

I have to admit her impression of me was pretty good.

'Anyway,' I said. 'I'm going to be in the audience with all the other celebrities.'

'But you always say the celebrities in those programmes are a bunch of no-hopers who'd turn up to the opening of an envelope.'

'You know what this means, don't you?' I said, ignoring her.

'You're officially a no-hoper?'

'Somebody at LWT had to write down a list of celebrities and they thought of me. I AM A CELEBRITY.'

'Simon—'

'I hope they put me next to Carol Vorderman.'

'Simon—'

'I wonder if I'll have to ask a question?'

'SIMON!'

'What?'

'It's a gag.'

'Pardon?'

'It's a gag,' she said and burst out laughing.

She'd made the invite on her computer at work and decided to send it to me as her way of welcoming me to the *Coffee Morning* team. I can see the funny side now, but at the time I was a little upset.

I wouldn't have gone anyway, I hate Billy Fox.

3 MAY

5.40 a.m.
A Celebrity Audience with Simon Peters.

I'm standing in the middle of the stage holding a microphone and leaning on the stand. I'm wearing a black velvet suit, black velvet bow tie and pink ruffled shirt. Three cameras are pointing at me, but I don't have a clue what I'm supposed to do. There's no autocue and nothing's been rehearsed. I can't sing, I can't dance, I can't tell a joke. I can't even think of one amusing anecdote.

The audience is made up of obscure celebrities from the 1970s and they start to heckle me. Instead of asking the pre-arranged questions about my career, they start to ask me really difficult general knowledge questions. Little Jimmy Krankie asks me to explain the Pythagoras theorem, while Sid Little shouts out a question about thirteenth-century Italian literature.

'Who directed the classic 1926 film *Metropolis*?' demands Bernie Clifton.

'What's the chemical symbol for hydrogen?' yells the lead singer of Showaddywaddy.

'Which of Röntgen's discoveries was described as the greatest landmark in the history of diagnosis?' screams the woman who used to be Olive in *On the Buses*.

The celebrities start to invade the stage. Mike Yarwood and former Leicester City centre forward Frank Worthington lead the charge and everyone else soon piles in. John Noakes, Peter Purves and Geoffrey from Rainbow man the cameras while Donny Osmond, Suzi Quatro and Peters & Lee fight over the microphone. Magnus Magnusson wrestles me to the ground while Vince Envy picks up a baby and starts singing 'The Son I Never Had.'

It's at this point that my dad starts to strangle me.

'In Racine's tragedies, in spite of certain recurrent, rhetorical and poetic devices, the characters and their moods are clearly differentiated,' said my dad. 'How far and in what ways is it possible to argue that this is achieved?'

It was the shock of this that made me wake up.

I didn't think my dad knew who Racine was.

4 MAY

I finally built up enough courage to call Pippa, but unfortunately her answer machine was on. She hadn't bothered with a personalized message so I heard a pre-recorded voice with an American accent.

'*Your call cannot be taken at the moment. Please speak after the tone.*'

I tried to leave a message sounding all sexy, but halfway through, one of the peanuts I was eating became lodged at the back of my throat. I started choking, coughing and fighting for breath. Instead of doing the sensible thing and just putting the phone down, I carried on speaking, and by the end of the message my voice was like one of those computers that teach children how to spell.

'I'm actually turning purple now,' I strained, sounding like Bobby Davro doing a bad impression of Stephen Hawkins. 'I'll have to call you back.'

5 MAY

Mimi Lawson is definitely stalking me.

I've always dreamt of having a stalker (it's a real status symbol), but to be stalked by someone who is more famous than oneself is just weird.

Simon,
I need your help.
M.

Once again the note had been hand delivered and looked as if a child had written it. It made the hairs on the back of my neck stand up. I looked out of the window but she was nowhere to be seen.

12.02 a.m.
If I started going out with Mimi, maybe I'd be able to get some publicity out of it.

6.03 a.m.
No, the thought is too hideous even to contemplate.

6 MAY

Bit drunk and really tired, so I can't write too much.

I've just returned from my night out with Charley and a few members of the *Coffee Morning* production team. It's a good job Mike and Sue weren't there, as everyone quite plainly hates them as much as they hate each other. The team loves to bitch about them to anyone who'll listen. I listened for hours and it was brilliant.

Here are just some of the bits I remember:

Sue is always late, wears no knickers, doesn't shave her armpits, has terrible flatulence, awful halitosis and hairy toes. She's into toyboys, suffers from a mild form of Tourette's Syndrome and is having a passionate affair with the acting deputy head of finance at the BBC, Martin Davies.

Mike, on the other hand, really fancies himself, wears a toupee, chats up all the young male researchers, goes to gay clubs and collects bestial pornography. He loves dressing up in women's clothing, has been arrested for exposing himself on Brighton Beach, was the secret lover of José (the Latin pop sensation) and without Sue's knowledge is also having a passionate affair with the acting deputy head of finance at the BBC, Martin Davies.

I think I'm really going to enjoy working on this show.

At one point during the evening, someone mentioned that Mike was totally self-obsessed.

'All presenters are self-obsessed,' said Charley.

'Yeah, but not me,' I protested.

'Especially you.'

The conversation moved on, but I kept trying to get it back to the subject of me not being self-obsessed.

At the end of the night we piled into a kebab shop.

'It's brilliant that you're going to be working on the show,' said Charley, giving me a great big hug. 'I think you're going to be great.'

'I'm really looking forward to it,' I said, through a mouthful of doner. 'Max did a great job getting it for me.'

'Pardon?'

'Max did a great job getting the gig for me,' I repeated, this time wiping a big blob of chilli sauce from my chin. 'Apparently he worked on it for me for months.'

The strange look in her eye was gone as soon as it came.

'What a great agent,' she said, kissing me on the cheek before saying good night. 'See you at work.'

'Yeah, see you at work.'

I caught a cab home and it's now 2.30 in the morning.

I'm in such a good mood I might give Pippa a quick call.

7 MAY

6 a.m.

I woke up.

I was on the settee and I still had the receiver pressed to my ear.

I remember calling Pippa last night and I remember the answer machine kicking in. There was a beep and I began to speak. I told Pippa's machine how I thought she'd make a great presenter and, with her personality and her looks, she'd go a long way in this business. Obviously, I'd had a few to drink, and that's when I started to ramble. I think I said something about her being gorgeous and how she'd be better off without Manky Mancini.

That's where my memory stops. The rest is a blank.

Knowing my luck she's got a digital answering machine that can record for hours.

Please God, don't let me have snored.

9 MAY

Tomorrow I start work on *Coffee Morning*. I'm excited about it, but at the same time more than a little nervous. They've thrown me in at the deep end and I have to present a live on-location insert from the set of ITV1's new daytime soap *Trafalgar Way*.

Presenting live television is a completely different discipline to pre-recorded TV. When you're filming pre-records, there's a safety net at the back of your mind; you always know if it all goes wrong, you can just do it again. With live television there's no second chance. When you say something to the camera, within a beat the nation hears it, and that's a very scary thought.

I have presented live TV before, but that was on kids' telly and it was different. If something went wrong when I was hosting *A.M. Mayhem*, it didn't matter. It was all part of the fun and it was only a bunch of snotty-nosed school kids watching anyway. If any adults *were* watching they'd only tuned in to see the low-cut tops and miniskirts of my co-presenter Jo Heeling.

Coffee Morning is different. *Coffee Morning* is a BIG SHOW. It's an institution watched by the world and its dog, and if the world and its dog ever miss it, they can read about it in the tabloids the next day. I called Charley to tell her my fears.

'Don't worry,' she said. 'You'd be able to do this job with your eyes closed.'

'Yeah, but then I wouldn't be able to read the auto-cue.'

'With wit like that, you'll be fine. The one thing you've got to remember is that Mike and Sue are the bosses. Everyone thinks the producers are in charge, but they're not. Mike and Sue rule. Mike loves it when it's called *The Mike and Sue Show*, instead of *Coffee Morning*. Sue loves it if you do a little bit of flirting.'

'With her or with Mike?'

'With her,' she said. 'Although on second thoughts, Mike might enjoy it too. Oh, and Simon?'

'Yes?'

'When you're on location, you don't get an autocue.'

I spent the rest of the day on the toilet.

10 MAY

'Coming to you on location in thirty seconds . . .'
The voice in my ear sounded like a late-night radio DJ about to play a request especially for me. It was calm and soothing, like warm melted chocolate being poured all over my thoughts. Whoever she was, she'd done this a thousand times before and her reassuring tones made me feel much less nervous.

My earpiece was slightly uncomfortable and didn't fit my ear properly. You can get personalized earpieces made, which fit exactly, but you have go to a place in the West End where they make hearing aids. I've never quite got around to it. Today I was wearing a standard-issue earpiece, which the soundman had given me. I don't like using other people's earpieces because you never know who's worn them before you. I once appeared on a kid's show where they had different guest presenters each week. I was in my dressing room and the soundman came in.

'We had a good show last week,' he told me cheerily. 'It was all about the environment. You remember Scruffy, that

86

environmental protester who spent three months up a tree. He was the guest presenter, he used that very same earpiece.'

I know it might be psychosomatic, but I swear my ear itched for a month.

I heard a click and then a hiss as they switched my talkback to 'open'. I was now hearing everything from the gallery as well as the studio output. I could hear the director, who obviously wasn't quite as calm and collected as The Chocolate Voice. He sounded nervy as he barked instructions to the vision mixer and cameramen.

'Hold it on two . . . hold it . . . and coming to three . . .'

In the background I could just pick out Mike and Sue talking. I heard Sue's often imitated posh Edinburgh accent, followed by Mike's smooth, some might say smarmy tones. He was introducing me on location.

'The new soap opera, *Trafalgar Way*, has been the surprise hit of the year . . .'

The Chocolate Voice cut in, louder than Mike's, more in command, **'Coming to you on location in twenty seconds . . .'** The director was shouting now and I could hear him clicking his fingers, *'give me the two shot . . . give me the two shot . . .'* Mike was continuing to speak '. . . brought to you by the same team that made – **fifteen seconds to location** – it's the tale of everyday city folk – *close up on Sue* – the trials and tribulations – *close up on Sue* – and starring the very popular actress – *NOT THAT CLOSE* . . . **ten seconds to location . . .'**

Now it was Sue speaking.

'. . . **ten** – we've sent along one of our – **nine** – reporters to find out more – **eight** – new face to the *Coffee Morning* team – **seven** – of you might already recognize him – **six** – viewers used to watch his amusing daytime game show – **five seconds to location** – do what he says and not what

87

he does – **four** – think he looks a bit like one of The – **three** – Chuckle Brothers, – *they're laughing . . . give me the wide shot . . . give me the wide . . .* **two** – let's go over to Simon – **and cue Simon.'**

For a second I was lost, hypnotized by the voices in my head.

The red light flashed on top of the camera and I knew I was supposed to do something.

'And cue Simon.'

The Chocolate Voice was still calm, but firmer this time, more insistent.

I opened my mouth to speak but nothing came out.

That's when it hit me.

Four million people watch this show.

A wave of fear swept through my body. I could feel the beads of perspiration on my top lip and I knew my nervous rash would be starting to show on my neck. I was aware that I was just standing there staring. I tried to blink, but I couldn't even do that.

A thousand thoughts raced through my head in slow motion: Did Sue just say I looked like one of The Chuckle Brothers? Four million people. I wonder if The Chuckle Brothers are watching this? I wonder if Pippa's watching? I wonder if John Goff who I used to walk to primary school with is watching? Four million people. Whatever happened to John? I heard he got married, had three children and became a gasman. Did I turn off the gas? I left the flat in a bit of a hurry, trying to avoid Mimi Lawson. She wasn't there this morning, though. She only seems to be there every other day. Strange. Four million people. What's this cameraman's name again? What's that signal he's giving me? I wonder if my dad's watching this? I bet he thinks I look really stupid. I bet four million people think I look really stupid.

'**Cue Simon.**' Calm.

Max will kill me for this.

'**Cue Simon.**' Still calm.

I'll probably never work again.

'**SPEAK YOU FUCKER!**' Not so calm.

Suddenly there was a new voice in my ear. A voice I hadn't heard since I was thirteen.

'You can do it, son,' she whispered.

That's when *The Other Me* stepped in.

The Other Me knew instinctively that if he started speaking straight away it would look as if he'd frozen and because of that he'd never be given another chance. The only thing to do was to bluff his way out of it by pretending it was a technical fault. He put his finger to his ear, looked slightly off camera and shook his head.

In my earpiece, I was aware of the panic in the gallery.

'*His talkback has gone down, he can't hear us.*'

Stay calm, I thought. Force them to go back to the studio.

'*Let's come back to the studio . . .*'

'**stand by studio . . .**' *camera two give me a wide, camera one give me a single, camera three give me a two shot . . .*'

In the background I could hear Mike asking if his hair was OK and I could just pick out Sue swearing at the head of sound for not having sorted out the talkback.

I might just get away with this, I thought.

The director was apoplectic: '*Is that VT ready? Camera one, I said a two shot, not a fucking wide!*'

'**And cue Mike.**'

'Well, we seem to have some gremlins in the works today.'

'And on Simon's first day as well,' said Sue sympathetically. 'A real baptism of fire.'

They both laughed.

'They're laughing. Give me the two shot, the nation loves to see them laugh.'

'Just to explain to the viewers, Simon is wearing an earpiece so that he can take direction from the director . . . it's a small piece of plastic that just slips inside one's ear, much like a hearing aid.'

'I think our viewers know what an earpiece is, Michael.'

'Oh God, they're going to start arguing again.'

'Well, some of them might not actually, Susan.'

'Let's try the live link again.'

'I think it's important that the viewers are aware of the technicalities involved in the making of a – **Mike, throw to Simon** – television programme . . . and . . . talking of which – **coming back to you on location in five seconds** – fingers crossed, I do believe we can now cross back over to Simon Peters who is on the set of the new soap *Trafalgar Way*. Simon? – **Cue Simon . . . Please God, cue Simon.'**

The Other Me smiled and left it just long enough for four million people to know that it wasn't his fault. He put his finger to his ear one more time.

'Thank you, Mike. Yes I can hear you now.'

In my ear I heard the director cheering and the Chocolate Voice breathing a huge sigh of relief.

Suddenly, I felt totally in command.

'I think somebody forgot to put fifty pence in the meter,' said *The Other Me*.

There was a nervous laugh from the gallery.

'Yes I'm here on the set of *Trafalgar Way*, the first ever daytime soap opera to give *EastEnders* and *Coronation Street* a run for their money in the ratings war. They're calling it "The Soap with a Dope", referring, of course, to Norman Brigstock, the character that really seems to have captured the nation's heart. He's played by that great character actor David Nicholas, and David joins me now . . .'

With that I was away. The words flowed beautifully and the time seemed to fly by. It was supposed to be a five-minute item, but while I was in the middle of presenting a piece to camera about the wardrobe department, the Chocolate Voice whispered in my ear that I would have to cut the item down to three and a half minutes because of the hiatus with the talkback. I simultaneously heard the information, understood it and carried on speaking without even faltering. *The Other Me* even managed to get in a gag about the dress sense of one of the characters.

'Tracy Brigstock is to fashion what Russell Grant is to hang-gliding.'

Lesley Charles, the actress who plays the part of Tracy Brigstock, really giggled at that one, and by this point I was getting big laughs from the gallery. I was definitely on a roll. I'd just finished a quick tour of the props cupboard when the Chocolate Voice informed me I had thirty seconds to fill until I had to throw back to the studio.

'Well, that's it from the set of *Trafalgar Way*. Don't forget, you can catch the show every weekday at one thirty in the afternoon with a repeat at five thirty-five. Before I hand back to the studio, I'd just like to say what a great pleasure it is to be appearing on *The Mike and Sue Show* . . .'

The Chocolate Voice started counting down from ten to zero.

'I've been a big fan for years and it's a real honour for me to be working alongside two such great icons of the broadcasting world. This is Simon Peters on the set of *Trafalgar Way*, saying back to you, Sue. Oh, and by the way, Sue, love that dress.'

The Other Me said 'love that dress' at exactly the same time as the Chocolate Voice reached zero.

It was perfect.

I heard Sue give a very girly giggle.

'Well thank you very much, Simon,' she said. 'He was very good, wasn't he? Hopefully we'll be seeing a lot more of Simon Peters in the weeks to come. Coming up, swimwear for fat ladies.'

The Chocolate Voice cut in.

'Thank you, location, and you're clear . . . Simon, you were brilliant.'

I stood there in a state of shock. The cameraman put his camera down and shook my hand.

'Well done, mate, you did really well there.'

The soundman started to remove my microphone and earpiece.

'Sorry about the talkback,' he said. 'These things are always going wrong. I thought you handled it really well, though.'

A guy with thinning hair and horn-rimmed glasses came up and patted me on the back.

'We didn't meet before,' he said. 'I do the satellite up-link. I thought you handled that really professionally.'

I didn't have a clue what the satellite up-link was, but I shook his hand anyway.

I switched on my mobile phone and it rang immediately. I let it ring long enough for people around me to realize that the personalized ring tone was the theme tune to *Simon Says*.

Nobody seemed to recognize it.

I looked at the caller ID and it flashed the word CHARLEY. I pressed the green button.

'I just wanted to say well done,' she said quietly. She was calling from the studio.

'Yeah, it went OK,' I said modestly. 'It would have been better if the sound guys had sorted out the talkback though.'

'Absolutely.'

'Bloody soundmen.'

'Typical.'

'Useless.'

'I couldn't agree more.'

Trust Charley to be the only one to suss me.

'I could see it in your eyes,' she whispered. 'But don't worry about it, no-one else noticed. Everyone's saying how great you were.'

'What about Mike and Sue?'

'They loved you – "*I must say it's a really great pleasure for me to be appearing on The Mike and Sue Show!*"'

Once again her impression of me was spot on.

'"*Oh, and by the way, Sue, love that dress.*" You bloody creep, Peters. You want to watch that Sue; she likes her toy-boys.'

'I think I've got enough problems with Mimi Lawson.'

A small beep in my ear informed me that I had a call waiting. I looked to see who it was. Part of me desperately wanted it to say DAD, but it didn't. It flashed the word AGENT, which is the next best thing. I told Charley I'd speak to her later and pressed the green button.

'Simon?'

In five years, Max had never called me Simon. He usually called me 'Peter' or 'Peter you *schmuck*', or if he was in a really bad mood 'Peter, you *farshtinkener*!' But never Simon.

'Yes, Max?'

There was a silence at the other end of the phone as if Max was choosing his words carefully. Either that or he was finding it really difficult to pay me a compliment.

'You did well,' he said and hung up.

Those three words meant so much to me. I swallowed hard and had to fight back a tear. Charley could have spent the whole day telling me how wonderful I was, how I was the best thing on television and how it was only a matter of time before I had my own prime-time show on Saturday night television, but it was those three little words from Max that made my life complete. It's not as if what Charley said didn't mean anything to me, because it did. It's just that I *expected* Charley to say that. I never expected to hear Max Golinski say, 'You did well'.

I came home and spent the entire afternoon watching my bit of the show over and over again. The great thing about 'live' television is that you get a real adrenalin rush from it. You experience a genuine, natural euphoria that lasts for hours and you feel a sense of elation that you hope will never end. I've heard it's possible to become addicted to appearing live. Presenters become obsessed about getting their next fix. It has to be live, anything else is just a weaker drug that doesn't give that same buzz. Studio pre-records are just the methadone to live TV's heroin. You get junkies who are desperate for their next hit. They'll appear on anything as long as it's live.

I guess that's why some people end up on QVC.

13 MAY

I had to nip to the supermarket to get a loaf of bread. Before I go out these days, I always peep through the curtains to check the coast is clear and that Mimi's nowhere to be seen. I couldn't see her anywhere, so I left the flat and crossed the road to where Ringo was parked. I was just putting the keys in the lock when I caught sight of Mimi at the far end of the road.

Suddenly, it was as if I was in a movie, a thriller where the hero is being pursued by a ruthless female psychopath.

STALKER!

FADE FROM BLACK:

EXTERIOR – A LONDON STREET – EARLY EVENING

AN ESTABLISHING WIDE SHOT

The street is tree-lined and there are cars parked on either side of the road. The camera tracks in as SIMON comes out of his flat and walks casually to his BRIGHT RED FERRARI. He is twenty-four years old, handsome and rugged (a young ROBERT REDFORD). He is just putting his keys into the lock when he hears A NOISE. He turns. It is obvious from his reaction that he doesn't like what he sees.

> SIMON:
> Shit.

We see what he is looking at. It's A NUTTER at the other end of the road. She's in her early forties and looks as though she hasn't slept for a month.

CUT TO: A CLOSE-UP on THE NUTTER. She shouts.

> NUTTER:
> SIMON!

She starts to run towards SIMON.

CUT TO: CLOSE-UP on SIMON. He looks gorgeous, but there's a look of fear in his piercing blue eyes.

SIMON:
Shit!

He has to act quickly. There's a sense of urgency in his movements.

CLOSE-UP on SIMON fumbling with the car keys.

A WIDE SHOT on THE NUTTER running down the street.

SIMON opening the car door and getting in. He is starting to perspire (but in a cool way).

CLOSE-UP on THE NUTTER. As she runs, she has a manic look of determination on her face.

A BIG CLOSE-UP of the keys going into the ignition. SIMON tries to start the car.

Nothing.

We see THE NUTTER even closer. Relentless in her quest, like the T-1000 in *Terminator 2*.

SIMON tries to start the car again. Nothing.

THE NUTTER, closer still.

On SIMON now. He knows the situation is fraught

with danger, but he still manages to look sexy. He speaks through gritted teeth.

SIMON:
Come on . . . come on.

He is panicking. He glances in the rear-view mirror where we see THE NUTTER larger than life. She is nearly upon the car. He tries the engine once more, but again it fails.

SILENCE.

All we can hear is SIMON breathing heavily.

He looks in the rear-view mirror. She's not there.

He checks the wing mirror. Nobody.

He looks over his shoulder, through the back window.

THE NUTTER has completely disappeared.

He checks the rear-view mirror again, but this time we see SIMON'S reflection. We notice his strikingly attractive chiselled features and we see the realization slowly dawn on him. She has gone and he is safe. The experience has left him drenched in sweat and totally exhausted. He closes his eyes, rolls down the window and breathes a huge sigh of relief.

He opens his eyes.

Suddenly THE NUTTER reaches in through the open window. She's screaming.

We see a Hitchcockian-style 'track in, zoom out' on SIMON'S face.

> SIMON:
> Noooo!

In desperation, he tries to start the car one last time. The engine bursts into life with a throaty roar. SIMON engages first gear, slams his foot on the accelerator and lets the clutch out sharply, causing the wheels to spin.

> NUTTER:
> Simon, we have to speak.

The upper part of THE NUTTER'S body is inside the car. Her legs are outside and she has to start running to keep up as the car starts to accelerate. She puts her arms around SIMON'S neck and is desperately trying to hold on.

> SIMON:
> LET GO OF ME, YOU LOONY!

> NUTTER:
> BUT I HAVE TO TELL YOU SOMETHING . . .

SIMON sees his chance. He throws the car into a sharp left-hand bend.

CUT TO: SIMON'S POINT OF VIEW.

The speed of the turn causes THE NUTTER to release him. She disappears from inside the car and has to carry on running in a straight line. SIMON glances over his shoulder just in time to see THE NUTTER sprawled in a rhododendron bush. As the car pulls away she picks herself up and is shouting something. He can't quite make out what it is, but it sounds like:

NUTTER:
I'll be expecting you, maybe!

INTERIOR – CAR

SIMON:
(*to himself in a cod American accent*):
You can expect me all you want, honey, but you ain't never gonna get me.

SIMON smirks, flips open the glove box, takes out a CD and pops it into the machine. He prides himself on his impeccable taste in music and this particular album is his all-time favourite: STATUS QUO'S GREATEST HITS.

He searches for track four and then gently pushes the play button. The Quo start to sing 'Rockin' All Over The World'. SIMON adjusts the mirror and checks his reflection one last time. He gives a roguish grin and a cheeky wink. He's a hero, conquering malevolence and iniquity and bravely fighting the forces of evil.

He runs his fingers through his hair, drops the car down into second and speeds off into the London night.

MUSIC SWELLS.

FADE TO BLACK.

THE END

I bought the loaf of bread from the supermarket, but I was too scared to go straight back to the flat in case Mimi was still lurking outside. I decided to go for a drive to clear my head. I drove for two hours. I only actually travelled three miles, but that's London traffic for you. When I finally returned, Mimi was gone. I went to bed but couldn't sleep.

2.32 a.m.
Why won't she leave me alone?

2.56 a.m.
Can't she see that, not only am I not interested in a relationship with her, I'm actually petrified of her.

17 MAY

'Showbusiness is like a bath, sometimes it's hot and sometimes it's cold.'
It was Max.
He'd called me first thing this morning and I knew he had something good to tell me, otherwise it would have been Scary Babs on the phone. Before he released the information though, he had to give me his usual pseudo showbiz psychobabble.
'When the bath's hot,' he continued, 'the phone doesn't stop ringing, everything goes your way and nothing can go wrong. When the bath is cold, you can't get arrested.'

He was starting to mix his metaphors, but I stuck with him.

'Hot and cold, like the waters of the Zambezi.'

He was really losing me now.

'Do you know what you are, Simon?'

'No, Max.'

'You're tepid.'

'Thanks, Max.'

And there's me thinking he was going to give me some good news.

'Or at least you were tepid. Now you're veering towards the lukewarm.'

'Actually, Max, I think you'll find tepid *is* lukewarm. Technically they're the same thing.'

'Don't get pedantic with me, *groyse macher*, I'm trying to give you some good news.'

'Sorry, Max.'

'Now let's be honest, over the last five years you haven't been hot or cold. You've been somewhere in the middle. As I say, lukewarm.'

I didn't like to point out that he'd actually said tepid.

'You've never been freezing cold, but you haven't exactly set the world of television on fire, have you?'

'No, Max.'

I was now growing tired of the hot and cold analogy and was silently praying Max would hurry up and tell me the reason he'd called.

'Well, things are starting to heat up for you, *my boy*.'

My pulse quickened. In five years Max had never called me '*my boy*'. I'd only just got used to him calling me Simon but '*my boy*' was a real term of affection. I'd only ever heard him say that to one other person, and that was Mick McGovall, the builder turned TV presenter who hosts the popular DIY show *McGovall the Shovel*.

He's earned Max an absolute fortune.

'The Beeb have been on the phone and they want you for a pilot.'

For a moment I felt a slight stab of disappointment. My immediate thought was, Not another pilot. A pilot is when a production company tries out a show to see if it works, before the all-powerful commissioning editors decide to give the go-ahead for a series. The trouble is, they make lots of pilots and some of them never see the light of day. Especially the ones I make.

Take a Chance, *Pick a Card*, *Mind-Benders!*, *Time-Wasters!*, *Fact-Finders*, *The Home Straight*, *Higgledy-Piggledy*, *Roadhogs*, *Seconds Away*, *Deception*, *Perception*, *Travesty!*, *Dichotomy!*, *Suckers!*, *The Wannabes*, *The Could-Have-Beens*, *Hook, Line and Sinker* and *Evolution: The Story of Man* . . . All great shows that I did the pilots for, but for some inexplicable reason they were never actually commissioned. All with the exception of *Evolution: The Story of Man*. The trouble with that was, when they came to make the series they actually got Professor Robert Winston to present it. He was OK, but at least on the pilot I tried to inject a little humour into what was otherwise quite a dull subject. Winston just never did that.

'Forget about all of those other pilots you did.' How did Max know I was thinking that? 'They were all for independent companies, this is for the Beeb.'

My feelings of disenchantment were quickly lifted. Max was being enthusiastic about this, and when Max was enthusiastic about something, you couldn't help but be swept along.

'What's more, it's prime time.'

'Prime-time Daytime?' I asked hesitantly.

'Prime-time *Prime time*,' said Max, like a poker player finally revealing his trump card.

This was the phone call I'd been waiting for all my life.

'It's a game show called *The Swizz Quiz.*'

Max was on a roll now, relishing each new piece of information he fed me. My head started to spin and I had to sit down.

'The producers saw you on *Mike and Sue* and think you're perfect for it.'

My heart was pounding and I felt as if I couldn't breathe.

'If the pilot's successful the series will go out Saturday nights at seven o'clock on BBC1.'

That's when I started to hyperventilate.

'This could be the big time, my son. This could make you a star.'

Suddenly I was in a different place. It was as if Max was speaking to me in slow motion. His voice floated through my mind and I was able to swim between the words and understand exactly what each one meant – *'BIG TIME', 'A STAR'* and, best of all, *'MY SON'*. I don't think Max has ever called anyone *'MY SON'*, not even McGovall the Shovel.

'Are you still there, Simon? . . . Simon?'

I snapped out of it and something inside me wanted to maintain an air of professionalism.

'Is it a good format?' I asked, my voice sounding distant and detached, as if I took this sort of call all of the time.

'That's not important, you *alter kaker*,' said Max.

I know *alter kaker* means 'old shit'. What happened to *Simon. My boy. My son?*

'The important thing is, if they like the pilot, the series will go out on Saturday nights.'

Sometimes you couldn't argue with Max's logic. His philosophy has always been, it doesn't matter if it's crap as long as it's got a good time slot.

'Oh, and Simon?'

'Yes, Max?'

'Don't mess this up, I've been negotiating it for months.'

'But I thought you said they saw me on *Coffee Morning with Mike and*—'

'Never mind that now,' said Max. 'The date for the pilot is June twelfth.' He hung up. Max has an unusual habit of never saying goodbye at the end of telephone conversations, so you're just left there holding the receiver, wondering if you've upset him. Apparently he does it to everybody.

18 MAY

I called Charley and told her that I was going to be hosting a prime-time Saturday night game show for BBC1. She screamed with delight but then I told her it was just a pilot.

'Not another one.'

She started to laugh.

'You have to do pilots,' I said. 'It's part of the business.'

'Yes, but you've been on more pilots than a British Airways stewardess.'

'Yes, very funny, Charley.'

'You've done so many pilots, I'm going to start calling you Pontius.' She was really on a roll now. 'Not one of your pilots has ever been broadcast, let alone commissioned into a series. What's this one called?'

'*The Swizz Quiz.*'

'Maybe they should call it *The Gas Boiler Show*.'

'Why's that?'

'Because the pilot will never go out.'

She burst into a fit of giggles and I couldn't get any more sense out of her, so I told her I'd see her tomorrow at the *Coffee Morning* studio. As I put the phone down, I could hear her shrieking with hysterical laughter and making some glib remark about pilot whales.

She can be a little cutting sometimes, although I know she only does it so I don't get my hopes up. *The Swizz Quiz* is different from all the others, though; I just know it is. I've got a feeling deep down that this is the show. This is *The One*.

19 MAY

Things just seem to get better and better. Today, I was offered two great jobs . . . Oh, and I saved a man's life.

Usually I'm on location for *Coffee Morning*, but today I had to be in the studio to present an item on bizarre world-record attempts.

I've always loved television studios. Even now, after five years of working in this industry, I still get the same buzz when I'm in one. I love the big heavy studio doors and the red flashing 'on air' sign above them. I love the large lights that hang from the ceiling and the long poles the 'sparks' use to adjust them. I love the cameras and the cables and the unnatural colours. I love the illusion of a television studio, how nothing's as it seems. I love how the set always looks much bigger when you see it on the telly and how the stars are much smaller when you see them in real life.

There are always far more people working in a television studio than you'd expect and I still have no idea what half of them do. What I do know is that the wardrobe department always fusses, the make-up department always gossips and the sound department always moans.

It was good to finally meet all the people who usually talk to me in my earpiece. I'd imagined the Chocolate Voice to be a sexy diva of Caribbean descent, big brown eyes, long slender legs and soft, honey-toned skin. She was actually a white forty-five-year-old mother of three from Bromley in Kent, but she seemed very friendly and said how well she thought I was doing, so obviously I liked her immediately. I'd expected the director to be a highly strung chainsmoker, tall, thin and wiry, with a balding head and no dress sense. When I met him he was exactly that.

During rehearsals, Mike and Sue came over to say hello. Mike was a little aloof, but Sue was very complimentary, and if she wasn't twenty years my senior, I would say she was almost flirting with me. What is it with older women and me?

The item was simple enough. I had to do a five-minute piece about three different record attempts and then segue into the latest *4Real!* video. Before the show started we had a rehearsal on camera, so everyone knew what they had to do and where they had to stand. The three record attempts were a man trying to flip 150 beer mats and catch them in one fluid movement, another man trying to eat twenty meat and potato pies in under two minutes and a woman who claimed to have the longest toenails in the world, my job being to measure them. Never let it be said that I don't do quality television.

Once we were live on air, my item seemed to be going very well. The man caught all the beer mats and the woman did indeed have the longest toenails in the world (a combined length of 2m 21cm, fact fans).

Then Archie Rimmer stepped forward.

I started the clock and he began his meat-pie challenge. He was on his third pie when he suddenly started to choke. He was an elderly gentleman from Yorkshire and he struck me as a little bit of a character, so I thought he was pretending and playing to the cameras.

'He's so confident, he's even got time for a little joke,' I said.

Then his lips turned blue and his face became an unusual shade of scarlet.

Panic swept through the studio. I noticed the look of fear on the floor manager's face and the worry in the make-up lady's eyes. In my earpiece I could hear the Chocolate Voice screaming with terror and the director shouting, '*Please God, don't let him die on air, but if he does, camera three give me a close-up of it.*'

Suddenly, like a hero riding to the rescue on a white stallion, *The Other Me* stepped in to save the day. Surrounded by chaos, he was the quiet in the eye of the storm. My mother had taught me first aid as a boy and I knew all about the 'Heimlich Manoeuvre'. In one swift movement I was behind the man, who by now was fighting for his life. The whole studio fell silent and everyone stood there with their mouths wide open. Archie Rimmer glanced over his shoulder at me. He was purple now and his eyes pleaded for help. I was running out of time. I put my arms around the choking man's chest and clenched my two hands together, giving the effect of one large fist. I knew what was required of me and gave a short, sharp violent jab into Archie's sternum.

It had no effect.

I had to stay calm; I knew I'd only get another two attempts at this. I punched him again, but still Archie continued to choke.

The Other Me could hear the Chocolate Voice's nervous breathing in his ear and the director whispering, '*Closer on three. Closer on three.*'

At the back of my mind I was aware this would be making great television and I could imagine millions of viewers sitting on the edge of their seats, praying for me to save Archie.

I had one last chance.

Summoning all my strength, I gave one final, mighty blow to Archie's breastbone. He seemed to explode, and a half-chewed piece of gristle shot out of his mouth like a bullet from a gun, hitting camera three right in the middle of the lens. Camera three had the red light on, and from the collective 'Yeeuuuccch!' in the studio, I could only imagine the picture that had just been broadcast to the nation.

There was a moment's silence when no-one in the studio seemed quite sure what to do. *The Other Me* seized his moment and took control again.

'Well, we certainly *hammed* that up,' I quipped. 'When they said *Archiechokes* on *Mike and Sue* today I thought they were talking about a cookery item.'

The Other Me quickly turned to camera one, forcing them to cut to the close-up of me.

'That's one for Denis Norden,' I said. 'Now I don't know about breaking the record for eating meat and potato pies, but I think we've just set a new world record for projectile vomiting. We'll get this man a glass of water, while you check out the latest video from *4Real!* which ironically could be Archie's theme tune: it's called "All Choked Up".'

I glanced over to the monitor; my image disappeared and was replaced by Troy Coral, the lead singer of *4Real!* wearing a cowboy hat and standing on the bonnet of an American Buick. The Chocolate Voice informed everyone that we were on VT and the studio erupted into a spontaneous round of applause. Members of the crew were shaking my hand and slapping me on the back. Sue came over to me. She leant in close and that's when I realized that the production team hadn't been joking about the halitosis. For a moment it looked like she was heading for my lips, but I managed to turn my head just in time and she ended up giving me a great big wet sloppy kiss on the cheek. Even Mike gave me a nod of approval, as if to say *Yes, that's how I'd have handled it* (saving Archie's life, that is, not avoiding Sue's kiss).

With all the celebrations, I'd completely forgotten about Archie Rimmer. He was lying on the floor, surrounded by St John Ambulance men, who didn't really look as if they knew what they were doing. Archie looked up and when he saw me, he grabbed hold of my hand and shook it vigorously.

'You saved my life.'

'It was nothing,' I said, as if I saved lives every day of the week.

'I'll never forget what you did for me today.'

Archie squeezed my hand and looked deep into my eyes, then he started to cry.

I felt a bit of a lump in my throat and had to swallow hard to stop myself sobbing in front of the crew. The Chocolate Voice came back over talkback and informed everyone there were thirty seconds until we were back on air. I'd finished my job for the day, so I shook Archie's hand one last time and made my way to the Green Room (the room where the guests can sit, relax and have cold coffee and stale croissant before and after their appearance on the show). It wasn't a green room at all, but a pastel shade of pink. It was empty, so I poured myself a mineral water and took a swig of it. I noticed that my hand was trembling and I was sweating heavily.

I'd saved a man's life.

More impressive than that was the fact that I'd saved a man's life on national television.

I heard a noise behind me and spun round to see Charley standing there.

'My hero,' she said, clutching her chest and lifting one

heel in the air in the style of a 1940s screen heroine. I knew she was joking, but I could tell by her eyes that she was impressed by what I'd done.

'I didn't know that you knew Heimlich.'

'Oh yes, I went to school with him,' I said in my best Eric Morecambe voice. We both laughed.

'You've certainly impressed the powers-that-be,' said Charley.

I knew that she had something to tell me, but I shrugged as if to say, I just saved a man's life, I don't care what the powers-that-be think. I was a hero now and had to remain cool. I took a long hard slug of water, raised one eyebrow and looked off into the middle distance.

'Really?' I said, trying to appear nonchalant. I managed to make my voice sound like gravel and it even had a slight American drawl. I couldn't help thinking that I probably looked like Bruce Willis in *Die Hard*.

'My God,' said Charley. 'You looked just like Bruce Willis then.'

'Did I really?'

'No, not Bruce Willis,' she said. 'Who am I thinking of?'

'Clint Eastwood?' I suggested, narrowing my eyes in a typical hard-man stare.

'No, not him.'

'Mel Gibson?' I offered, instinctively sucking in my cheekbones.

'No . . . not Mel Gibson.'

'Who, then?'

'One of The Chuckle Brothers,' she said. 'Barry, I think it is. Now stop pouting your lips, raising your eyebrows and doing that stupid squinty thing with your eyes.'

'Yes, Charley,' I said, trying desperately not to pout or squint.

'Now, do you want the good news, the really good

news or the unbelievably good news?' she asked with a big smile on her face. I could tell that she was dying to tell me.

'I'll have the good news, please, Charley.'

'I've been promoted. I'm now a producer.'

'That's brilliant,' I said. 'Congratulations.'

I couldn't help feeling slightly disappointed that the good news didn't concern me.

'What's the really good news,' I asked quickly.

'The really good news is we want you to cover a film premiere on June fifth.'

'What's so special about that?'

'Well, Mr Blasé, *Coffee Morning* have the exclusive rights to the premiere. You're going to be the only reporter allowed into the party with a film crew, but if you're not interested, we could always get Jenny James the weather girl to do it, we're very happy with her at the moment . . .'

'What's the film?'

'. . . she seems to get an awful lot of press. The tabloids love her and there was an article about her in *The Sunday Times*. The execs have been saying that maybe Jenny could start covering some of the showbiz stories, the ones you're not interested in. Oh, by the way, it's *The Young and The Brave*.'

I couldn't believe it. *The Young and The Brave* is set to be the biggest film of the year. A Second World War epic that's already been tipped to sweep the board at the Oscars. Some of the critics are already calling it 'the film of the century'. Every famous young film star in Hollywood is in it and it's been reported that most of them are coming over to Britain for the world premiere. To have access to the party is incredible, but to be the only reporter allowed in with a film crew is unbelievable. This was a job I had to do.

'Charley, I love films,' I said. 'I know loads of movie trivia. Go on, test me.'

Charlie just stared at me blankly.

'I know that Nicolas Cage is Francis Ford Coppola's nephew, and I know that Michael Caine's real name is Michael Micklewhite.'

Still Charley said nothing, but I think she was impressed by my knowledge of the film world.

'Please, Charley, please. I really want to do this. I love reporting, I love films and I love parties. I'm the man to do a report on a film party.'

There was just a hint of desperation creeping into my voice but I felt I had to prove to Charley how perfect I was for this job. Another piece of movie trivia popped into my mind.

'I know that in *Citizen Kane*, Rosebud was a bicycle that he owned as a kid. Jenny James wouldn't know that. Jenny James is a bloody weather girl who doesn't know what a bloody cumulus is.'

'It's a sledge.'

'No, it's not, it's a wispy cloud.'

'No, Rosebud was a sledge.'

'What?'

'In *Citizen Kane. Rosebud* was a sledge, not a bicycle. And by the way, it's fluffy, not wispy.'

'What, the sledge?'

'No, the cloud. Cirrus is wispy, cumulus is fluffy and I was only joking about Jenny James. You're the one who's going to cover the premiere.'

I gave her a great big hug and kissed her briefly on the lips. When I released her she raised her eyebrows at me.

'Sorry,' I said.

'I can't wait to see what happens when you hear the

really good news,' she said. 'We also want you to fly to New York to interview the boy band *4Real!*'

I opened my mouth to speak, but Charley beat me to it.

'Yes, I know. You were the first person to interview them on live TV – "*They were really pleased to meet me, because I was off the telly*".'

Her impression was good, but I don't think my voice is quite that squeaky.

'You fly out on June ninth and fly back on the eleventh.'

'Wow!' I said. 'I'm shooting the pilot for *The Swizz Quiz* on the twelfth, I hope I won't be too jet-lagged.'

'Welcome to the world of a successful TV presenter.'

I gave her another hug and this time I heard her sigh.

'Maurice,' she whispered in my ear.

This was an embarrassing situation. I was cuddling my best friend and she was calling me by the wrong name.

'Maurice?' I said, not wanting to appear rude.

'Maurice Micklewhite,' she said. 'It's Michael Caine's real name. You called him Michael Micklewhite.'

We stood there, looking at each other for what was probably a moment too long. Then Archie Rimmer walked in and started pestering me again.

'You saved my life,' he said and started to hug me, regardless of the fact that I was still hugging Charley.

He started to sob.

'One day, I'm going to pay you back for this, lad,' said Archie.

'Don't worry about it,' I said.

What's he going to do? Leave me a meat and potato pie in his will?

20 MAY

I'm on page three of *The Sun*.

There's an article about me saving Archie Rimmer's life. It's right next to the picture of 'Shelley (18) from Stoke on Trent'.

TV HORROR FOR MIKE AND CHEW
AND THAT'S NO CHOKE!

The King and Queen of daytime television, Mike and Sue, watched on in horror yesterday as one of their guests nearly choked to death, live on air. Archie Rimmer (72) had a piece of bacon lodged in his throat when attempting to break the world record for eating fifty bacon sandwiches in under one minute. Unknown TV presenter Peter Simmons (35) was on hand to administer first aid. 'I could have died,' said Archie (pictured below). A safety executive for the BBC said, 'This was just an unfortunate incident . . . all the usual safety precautions had been taken.'

I can forgive them for getting my name wrong and I can just about forgive them for saying I'm 35 but *'unknown TV presenter'* was the one that really hurt. Surely the headline should have been *SUPER SIMON SAVES SUE'S SHOW*.

Maybe I shouldn't worry about it too much. Everything else seems to be going so well for me at the moment. I've just read my diary back from February and March and realized what a sad git I must have been. All I did was watch television and get depressed.

My mother once said to me that *'if you won't be worrying about a thing in a year's time, then it's not worth worrying about now'*.

That's going to be my philosophy from now on.

The next month is going to be very busy for me and I really think I ought to be more professional about my job and start trying to get fit. The irony is that now I'm becoming more successful I haven't got that much time to do it. I would go to the gymnasium but I've never really bought into the whole gym culture thing. I always feel pale, puny and slightly intimidated, as if the people in the gym know I don't really belong.

What other ways are there of keeping fit? Jogging is definitely out and I've never been that keen on the idea of swimming (I know the chlorine and disinfectants are supposed to kill all the germs, but the idea of splashing about in the general public's body fluids makes me feel a little squeamish.)

What I really need is to be able to get fit with the minimum amount of effort.

21 MAY

I'm no longer addicted to *Going-Gone TV*, but I tune in every now and again just for the amusement factor. I watched the show for a couple of hours and was just about to turn over when Tony Dobson, who looked more orange than ever, started telling me about *The Pulse Toner*, which is a battery-operated belt that sends out small electrical pulses and causes your muscles to contract; apparently it has the same effect as doing 100 sit-ups. With its pads and conductive gel, it looked like an instrument of torture.

I've never liked Tony Dobson as a presenter, but he certainly knows how to say the right thing.

'It's a genuine get-fit-quick solution. A workout without any work!'

Then Tony said the magic words. 'You can wear this while you're watching television.'

It cost £74.99 plus £12.50 p&p and will be here within three working days.

22 MAY

So this is what the life of a celebrity is like? Today I received an invite to a charity ball at the Marriott Hotel in Grosvenor Square on 1 June, in aid of something called LAB. The accompanying letter says the event will be black tie, have free drinks and chock-a-block with celebrities. Unfortunately it doesn't actually say what sort of organization LAB is (something to do with animals, I should imagine).

I've always wanted to be one of those celebrities that supports good causes, so I really think I should go.

23 MAY

This morning I was watching *2Early4Talk*, Channel 4's 'outrageous' early morning breakfast show. It's only been on air for a couple of months but it's already one of those shows that everyone's talking about.

It's presented in the style of a radio show, with the host, Paddy McCourt, sitting behind the decks and basically insulting the celebrity guests. Paddy is a former shock-jock from Belfast who really doesn't give a damn. With his caustic comments and wild dress sense, the papers have labelled him 'The Man You Love To Hate'. Last week, he reduced Donna Keyes the game-show hostess to tears with his constant jibes about her reported weight problems. It made the front page of every single tabloid and for that very reason celebrities are queuing up to be insulted by Paddy. *2Early4Talk* is *the* show to appear on.

'Right, it's time for the weather now,' barked Paddy in his broad Northern Irish accent. He sounded like a cross between Frank Carson and Ian Paisley, only louder. 'I'm afraid I had to sack the last weather girl because she wouldn't suck my knob.'

I glanced at the clock on the wall. It was 7.33 a.m. Even I was shocked by this.

'When I say "*my knob*", I'm referring, of course, to the knob that controls the volume on the monitor here.'

In the studio, 'Paddy's Posse' whooped and hollered. Paddy's Posse whoop and holler at everything Paddy says.

'It's quite a big knob for the size of the monitor, wouldn't you agree?'

'Yessss,' shouted the posse in unison.

'I'm sorry, I'm digressing here, what was I saying?'

'Weather,' shouted a lackey from the back of the studio.

'Oh yes,' said Paddy. 'We've got a brand-new weather girl for you this morning, and let me tell you she is going to be a big star.'

Paddy took a deep breath and turned to another camera. They immediately cut to a close-up of him.

'If I could be serious for one moment,' he said. 'I've worked in broadcasting for a few years now, and I've never met anyone with such a deep understanding of meteorological studies, climate control and the processes and phenomena of atmospheric changes.'

The posse were quiet, stunned by the seriousness of Paddy's speech.

'And if you're not interested in the weather, you can just stare at her titties for the next two minutes.'

The studio erupted into cheers and wolf whistles.

'By Jesus, they're a sight to behold, so they are. Here she is, the lady with two warm fronts forming over the Bristol area, it's Pippa.'

And there she was.

Pippa.

Pippa the Weather Girl.

Pippa the Girl I Loved.

God, I fancied her. She was standing on the roof of the television studio in front of a brick wall that was covered in graffiti. She looked even more beautiful on television. Her hair had been chopped short, emphasizing her big blue eyes. She wore a sleeveless, tight black T-shirt with the slogan 'TART' in large gold letters across her chest. She held a can of spray paint in each hand and began to tell the viewers all about the high pressure coming in from the Atlantic. I realized that the graffiti on the wall was in fact a map of the British Isles and it was Pippa's job to tell us about the weather and then spray paint the sun where it was going to be sunny and the clouds where it was going to be cloudy.

As she spoke, I simultaneously felt a pinch of pride and a twinge of jealousy.

It had been a month since I'd last seen her in Max's office. Within that month, Max had got her a job on one of the hottest shows on television. To be the weather girl on *2Early4Talk* is just one step away from national stardom. How did Max do that? How did *she* do it? I don't resent her success in any way but it just seems to have been so easy for her. She seems to have glided to the top like a knife through butter. I know things are going well for me at the moment, but it's always as if my butter's been in the freezer for three months. Pippa's doing a similar sort of job as me, but on a show that's a million times cooler.

Something inside me wanted her to be terrible.

But she wasn't.

She was actually rather good. She presented the weather as if she had a degree in meteorology and her artwork wasn't too bad either. Not that I was paying attention, of course. I spent the full two minutes staring at her titties.

'And with that, it's back to you in the studio, Paddy.'

She said it as if she'd been saying that sort of thing all of her life. It cut back to Paddy, who was pretending to button up his trousers.

'Thank you . . . erm . . . Pippa . . .' he said, throwing some Kleenex into the bin. 'The . . . erm . . . Graffiti Goddess there.'

Everyone in the studio gave a spontaneous round of applause.

'Now, let me tell you, that girl is going to be huge,' Paddy continued. 'Or at least she will be huge in nine months when she's expecting my baby.'

Everyone laughed, because that's what they were paid to do.

I have really mixed feelings about Pippa being on television. When she was just a dancer, I always thought I stood a chance with her. I thought that maybe, just maybe, she'd be impressed by the fact that I worked in television. Now she's not only working in television herself, she's working on one of the most talked-about shows on the box. Part of me keeps thinking, It won't last. She's only the weather girl. But another part of me knows it won't be long before she's so much more.

Deep inside I know that Pippa is destined for the celebrity super league.

24 MAY

I feel I should make more of an effort to keep in touch with Pippa. I know from experience that she'll need some real friends around her now, not just people who are interested in her because she's drop-dead gorgeous and might be really famous soon.

I thought maybe she would like to accompany me to the LAB charity ball on June first. I called her number and, surprise surprise, her answer machine was on. I thought about hanging up but the machine beeped and I started telling her all about the ball and how great it would be if she could be my guest. That would have been OK if I'd just left it there, but before I knew it I was gushing with praise about her performance on *2Early4Talk*. I said how good I thought her graffiti was and how, in my opinion, she's the best weather girl since Wincey Willis. I commented on the unusual weather we've been having for the time of year and started doing my impressions of Ian McCaskill and Michael Fish, which for some bizarre reason led on to my impression of Zippy from Rainbow. I eventually ran out of things to say, but still I couldn't put the phone down. I whistled for a while, hummed a little tune and then eventually hung up.

Why can't I just say, 'Pippa, it's Simon, call me,' and leave it at that?

Why can't I be cool?

25 MAY

The light on my answer machine was flashing and the LCD informed me I had three messages.

I couldn't wait to hear Pippa's voice again. Would she come to the ball with me? Had she finished with Manky Mancini? Would there be any sort of future for the two of us? I held my breath and pressed the play button.

'Hello, it's Archie Rimmer here,' said the voice in a thick Yorkshire accent. 'I hope you don't mind me phoning, lad. A nice young lady at the television studio gave me your number and said it would be all right to call.'

It would be Charley's idea of a very funny joke to give Archie Rimmer my home phone number.

'I just wanted to say thank you, thank you very much.

And if there's anything I can do for you, just call me. I mean it, lad . . . call me . . . thank you.'

His voice started to break up and he was obviously getting very emotional. Either that or he still had a bit of gristle stuck in his throat. I pressed the delete button and the next message started to play.

This one had to be Pippa.

'Hello Sshhhimon, it's Vince Envy here. Howareyou, my old pal?'

My heart sank a little lower. Vince was really drunk this time.

'You're my besht friend, you are,' he slurred. 'No, I take that back. To me you're more than a beshht friend . . .'

He started to sing 'The Son I Never Had' again and then finished his call with, 'Give me a call Sshimon . . . I've got no-one . . . no-one.'

I pressed the delete button, completely uninterested in the drunken ramblings of a sad old has-been.

The last message had to be from Pippa.

'Simon, it's Mimi. Call me.'

Think of a five-year-old child learning to play a recorder while simultaneously scraping her nails down a blackboard and dragging a fork across an empty plate. That was the effect Mimi's voice had on me. She sounded hysterical and I was scared. I pressed the delete button but the message played again.

'Simon, it's Mimi. Call me.'

In my mind I heard the slow haunting cello from the *Jaws* soundtrack.

'dum dum, dum dum, dum dum, dum dum.'

I pushed the delete button again, this time a little harder.

'Simon, it's Mimi. Call me.'

'dum dum, dum dum, dum dum, dum dum.'

I pressed the button several times in rapid succession.

'Simon, it's Mimi. Call me.'

dum dum, dum dum, DUM DUM, DUM DUM.

'Simon, it's Mimi. Call me.'

Mixed in with the cello from *Jaws*, I heard the staccato violin notes from *Psycho*: dum dum, dum dum, dum dum, dum dum EEK, EEK, EEK, EEK.

BEEEEEEEEEEEEEEEEEEEPPPPPPPPP!

I pulled the plug out and the machine went dead. I was shaking, and to calm myself down I had to spend the rest of the day watching old episodes of *Simon Says*.

I do wish she'd stop calling me, and the same goes for the other two. All I did was talk to Vince, sleep with Mimi and save Archie's life. What is it with these people? Why can't they just leave me alone?

26 MAY

I left a message on Pippa's answer machine reminding her about the LAB charity ball and telling her all about the message Vince had left for me. I could only remember a couple of verses of 'The Son I Never Had,' but I'm sure she got the idea.

On *2Early4Talk* this morning, Pippa's breasts were trying to escape from a very revealing white top. When she handed back to Paddy, he had a great big grin on his face.

'If those puppies are for sale,' he said, 'I'm having the one with the pink nose.'

Pippa was still on the monitor and seized her opportunity.

'Paddy,' she said. 'If these were puppies, I would rather put them in a sack, tie them to a brick and throw them in the Thames than let you get hold of them.'

For the briefest moment the whole studio fell silent and

looked towards Paddy to see what his reaction would be. He started to roar with laughter and soon the entire posse were doing the same.

Pippa was officially '*in*'.

27 MAY

I keep having dreams that Pippa and myself are an item. The dreams seem to take the shape and form of paparazzi snapshots.

FLASH: Pippa and me stepping out of a limousine.

FLASH: Me in a tux looking tanned.

FLASH: Pippa in Gucci looking gorgeous.

We're in all the tabloids and on the front cover of every magazine. Our lives become a showbiz whirl of parties and premieres. 'Peters and Pips, The Ultimate Celebrity Couple.'

Why shouldn't this happen? Why shouldn't Pippa and I be together? We've got so much in common; we share the same agent and we both survived panto in Grimsby. If that isn't a bond I don't know what is. Everything else seems to be going so well for me at the moment, why can't I have the girl of my dreams as well? The more I think about it, the more I think it's meant to be.

If only she'd return my calls.

29 MAY

Midnight.

I dialled her number.

Once again the electronic voice informed me nobody was home. This time I was determined to leave just a short message to remind her about the LAB ball, quickly apologize for my last couple of messages and then hang up.

That was the plan, but there's something about Pippa's answer machine that draws me in. It's as if I'm caught in its evil spell. I start speaking and I can't stop.

I rambled aimlessly like a comedian with no punchlines. I stumbled from one topic to another with no common thread. It was a monologue of no meaning, a soliloquy of no sense. I glanced at the clock and realized I'd been speaking to her machine for a full thirteen minutes. I had to find a way to finish.

In the finest showbusiness tradition, I decided to end on a song.

I was halfway through my rendition of Norman Wisdom's seminal classic 'Don't Laugh At Me Because I'm A Fool,' when I heard a beep and a click, followed by a man's voice.

'Will you shut the fuck up!'

He sounded very angry. My first thought was that it was Manky Mancini. Maybe he'd moved in with Pippa?

'Who is this?' I asked snootily, quite upset that he'd interrupted my finale.

'Never mind who I am,' he screamed. 'Who the fuck are you?'

He didn't sound like Manky. This guy had a strong cockney accent, and in the background I could hear what sounded like a very big dog barking. Maybe Pippa had a 'bit of rough' living with her.

'Never mind who I am,' I said, trying to sound equally tough. 'Who the fuck are you?'

My 'fuck' didn't sound quite as convincing as his.

'Listen mate,' he said. 'For the past four weeks I've had to put up with your droning voice on my answer machine. I've had you choking, snoring and now singing, and I don't mind telling you, IT'S DOING MY SODDING HEAD IN.'

'Look,' I said, doing away with the tough-guy accent and replacing it with one of authority. 'Is Pippa there, please?'

'No!' he shouted, mimicking my northern accent. 'Pippa is not here.'

'Is that 0208 107 3410?'

'Yes, this is 0208 107 3410.'

There was a pause.

'Well, erm . . . can I speak to Pippa then?'

'No,' he screamed at the top of his voice. 'You cannot speak to Pippa. Pippa's not here. Pippa's never been here. I don't even know who Pippa is. Listen, mate, I'll spell it out for you, FOR THE PAST FOUR WEEKS, YOU'VE BEEN CALLING THE WRONG FUCKING NUMBER!'

I picked up the now tattered and torn piece of paper that Pippa had written her number on all those weeks ago in Max's office. When I studied it carefully I realized that the '1' could actually be a '7'.

Suddenly I didn't find it quite so difficult to hang up.

1.30 a.m.

I've started to feel guilty about having disturbed that guy all those times.

1.45 a.m.

I called him back to apologize. He swore at me and said he'd only just managed to get back to sleep again after I'd woken him up the first time. I said to make it up to him I could arrange for him to go to a TV studio to see a show being recorded. At that point, he threatened to come around and chop my legs off.

'What's your name anyway,' he demanded. ' I recognize your voice.'

I had no qualms about telling him.

'Ricardo Mancini,' I said and hung up.

30 MAY

My *Pulse Toner* still hasn't turned up.

There's nothing I like more than making a complaint, so I got myself in the mood for an argument and called up the *Going-Gone TV* switchboard.

'*All our lines are busy at the moment, please be assured that your call is important to us. An operator will be with you shortly.*'

That's when the music started playing. I was subjected to a distorted cover version of Blondie's 'Hanging On The Telephone,' played on what sounded like one of those Stylophones that Rolf Harris used to advertise in the 1970s. The music was interrupted every twenty-two seconds – I know because I counted them – by the same recorded message:

'*All our lines are busy at the moment, please be assured that your call is important to us. An operator will be with you shortly.*'

After thirty-five minutes I started to think my call probably wasn't that important to them at all and that an operator was never going to be with me. I started to get paranoid. The people at the call centre knew it was me calling them. They were all sitting there with their feet up, laughing at the flashing light that was my call. The longer I waited, the funnier it was to them. They hold a weekly competition to see who can keep a caller on hold the longest. It became a battle of wills. I was determined not to put the phone down. They *had* to take my call.

Forty-seven minutes and eighteen seconds later I was so angry I was ready to explode.

'*All our lines are busy at the moment, please be—*'

The recorded message cut off and I could hear the sound of a busy office.

'I'm sorry to keep you waiting, caller,' said the sexiest voice I've ever heard in my life. 'You're through to *Going-Gone TV*, how can I help you?'

Her voice was a hoarse whisper. It was breathy and husky, but best of all it was Welsh. A female Welsh accent gets me every time. The huskier, the better. It was so disarming, I completely forgot that just thirty seconds earlier I was positively apoplectic.

I told her that my *Pulse Toner* hadn't arrived yet and she began to explain there'd been a problem with the computer system that processes the orders. As she did so, I became lost in her voice. It had a guttural quality to it that sent shivers down my spine. She told me the computer had just been fixed that morning and that my *Pulse Toner* would be with me within three working days.

'Those Pulse Toners are ever so good,' she said. 'I'm wearing mine at the moment.'

I detected a slightly flirtatious tone in her voice and decided to pick up on it.

'Where are you wearing it?' I said, in a suggestive manner.

'In South Wales,' she said.

There was a pause.

'Yes . . . but where are you wearing it on your body?'

'Wouldn't you like to know.'

'Yes, I would.'

'I'm sure you would.' She giggled.

This was brilliant; I normally have to pay sixty pence per minute for this sort of phone call. That voice, oh that voice. There was something about the way she said 'Wouldn't you like to know?' that made me think I stood a chance with her. Maybe she could come to the LAB ball with me tomorrow? I hadn't been able to get in touch with Pippa and I couldn't think of anyone else to invite. A blind date might be fun.

'So where are you from in South Wales then?' I asked, easing my way in gently.

'The Mumbles in Swansea,' she said, knowing full well she was being chatted up. 'Have you heard of it?'

'Yes, I know it. It's where all the beautiful girls live.'

God, I was smooth.

'So what's your name then?'

'I'm not allowed to tell you that,' she answered with a nervous giggle.

'Oh, you can tell little old me.'

'It's against company policy to give out personal information.'

She was really playing hard to get, but I had an ace up my sleeve and I played it beautifully.

'You can trust me,' I said. 'I'm a television presenter.'

'Really?'

She was obviously impressed.

'What programme are you on then?'

'Oh, I host a game show called *Simon Says* and I'm one of the regular presenters on a little show called *Coffee Morning with Mike and Sue*.'

'Oh my God!' she screamed. 'Simon Peters. I know who you are.'

'Well, now you know who I am, the question is, who are you?'

'I'll get the sack if I tell you.'

'You can tell me your first name, surely that's allowed?'

'Just my first name?' She giggled.

'Just your first.'

There was a pause.

'Oh, all right then,' she said.

'What is it?' I said.

128

'Gareth.'

It took a moment for it to sink in.

Then my head started to spin.

I remembered all the times I'd heard *'Your call may be recorded for training purposes.'* I imagined them playing a tape of this conversation at every Christmas party for the next ten years.

I swallowed hard and gave a little cough.

'So when will my Pulse Toner be arriving, Gareth?'

'Within three working days, Mr Peters.'

'Goodbye, Gareth.'

'Goodbye, Mr Peters.'

As he hung up, I swear to God I heard him sniggering.

I wonder if Charley would come to the ball with me.

1 JUNE

We arrived at seven thirty sharp. I was wearing a black dinner suit (on hire from Moss Bros), a white wing-tipped shirt and my matching bright-pink waistcoat and bow tie. Charley looked absolutely stunning in a gold sequinned dress which I think she said came from *Karen Millen's*.

We were ushered into the VIP guest room for champagne and canapés. I quickly became very excited as I realized the calibre of celebrity in attendance. David Bowie was deep in conversation with Rod Stewart, and Shirley Bassey was in the corner chatting away with Tom Jones.

'I can't believe it,' I said to Charley. 'This is a definite A-list event. I've just seen Mick Jagger talking to Paul McCartney.'

'I know, it's really weird,' said Charley, with an ironic look in her eye. 'I've just seen Marilyn Monroe being chatted up by Charlie Chaplin.'

Then I saw the sign:

WELCOME TO LAB
THE LOOKALIKES ANNUAL BALL

I nearly screamed. These people weren't celebrities at all. In show business circles, lookalikes are the lowest of the low. Their only talent, if you can call it that, is that they resemble someone famous (I use the term resemble very loosely).

At that moment Sammy Davis Jr tapped me on the shoulder.

'Hey, nice to meet you,' he said in what was quite possibly the worst American accent I've ever heard.

What do you say to a Sammy Davis Jr lookalike?

'You look just like him,' I said.

'Thanks, I've been a Michael Jackson lookalike for years now.'

I felt like saying, Oh no you haven't, but I didn't want to appear rude. I know how these lookalikes like to mix with real celebrities, so I decided to humour him.

'You . . . erm . . . look just like him,' I said it again.

Maybe that's the only thing you can say to a lookalike. Maybe that's the only thing they want to hear.

'Hey, thanks, man,' said Sammy/Michael. 'Now, can I give you a compliment?'

'Of course you can,' I said, expecting him to mention *Coffee Morning* or even my early work on *Simon Says*.

He looked at me, his eyes full of admiration.

'You're the best Chuckle Brother I've ever seen,' he said, and Charley nearly choked on her chicken vol-au-vont. 'You look just like them.'

I was about to set him straight when the MC announced that dinner was served. We went through to the main ballroom and took our seats. On our table, there were three Freddie Mercurys, two George Michaels and one Adolf

Hitler. There was also an empty seat, which was soon filled by an old man with a large white beard.

'I'm Karl Marx,' he said in a thick Birmingham accent.

For some reason, lookalikes always introduce themselves as the person they're supposed to resemble.

'I'm the only Karl Marx in Britain,' he continued. 'And the good thing is, with this beard I can always double as Father Christmas.'

The rest of the evening was possibly the longest night of my life, although Charlie was in hysterics the whole time and said she hadn't enjoyed herself so much in years. She spent most of the night talking to Adolf Hitler, who turned out to be a part-time plumber from Basildon called Barry. He said there wasn't a lot of call for Hitler in Basildon. Charley told him he should consider invading Romford. I think the highlight of the evening for Charley was seeing Adolf arguing with Karl Marx over who should pay for the extra bottle of wine that had been ordered.

At one point, one of the Freddie Mercurys disappeared to the loo and a man with dark hair took his place.

'Hello,' he said. 'I'm Des Lynam.'

This was just ridiculous. Admittedly he'd got the voice and the moustache right but he looked nothing like him. It was the last straw.

'Oh, come on,' I exploded. 'How much work can a Des Lynam lookalike possibly get. Be honest, it's not exactly the first thing you think of when you're organizing a party, is it? '*Oh, I know what'll make this party go with a swing; lets' book a Des Lynam lookalike.*' It's just ridiculous, why book his lookalike in the first place? Surely you could get the real Lynam for a couple of hundred quid. I mean, no offence, mate, but you don't even look anything like him. You're much too old.'

That's when Charley pointed out that it was the real Des Lynam.

Apparently the organizers of LAB had invited lots of 'real celebrities' to attend but only myself, Des Lynam and Lionel Blair had actually bothered to turn up, and Lionel goes to everything so that doesn't count. Des left the table without saying another word and a small fat man immediately took his place. I couldn't tell who he was supposed to be, but his dress sense was appalling. He wore a bright blue suit that was clearly two sizes too small for him and looked like it had gone out of fashion at some point during the late eighties. He had thick wiry hair, which was long and curly at the back, a large hooked nose and he was slightly cross-eyed. He shook my hand enthusiastically.

'Hello,' he said. 'I'm Simon Peters.'

That's when I knew it was time to leave.

2 JUNE

4 a.m.
He looked nothing like me.

10.27 a.m.
He was completely overweight.

6.42 p.m.
I hope the *Pulse Toner* arrives soon.

4 JUNE

Still no Toner.

5 JUNE

It finally arrived in the second post.

I carefully unwrapped it from its packaging, but was slightly disappointed by what I saw. On *Going-Gone TV*, the *Pulse Toner* had a glossy sheen that seemed to glisten under the studio lights. It looked so much more sleek, professional and expensive. In real life it looked like a belt, a wire and two suction pads.

It's *The Young and the Brave* premiere tonight and I have to be there to film the exclusive insert for *Coffee Morning*. I have a car coming to pick me up in twenty minutes. With the memory of my fat lookalike hanging over me and with the New York trip and *Swizz Quiz* pilot just around the corner, I've decided to wear the *Pulse Toner* underneath the purple and green Hawaiian shirt (with palm-tree motif) I'm wearing for the evening. I haven't got time to read the instructions, but how difficult can it be?

2.15 a.m.
I've just returned home from the premiere and I'm in absolute agony. I've worn the *Pulse Toner* for eight hours solid and I've just had to cut myself out of it using a pair of scissors and a carving knife.

My plan was to switch it on for the cab journey to Leicester Square and switch it off while I did the interviews with the stars outside the cinema. I would then switch it on to watch the film and switch it off again for the duration of the party.

Problem Number One: Once I switched it on in the cab, I couldn't actually switch it off. To make matters worse, I had set the speed to 'high', which meant the Toner sent out a pulse that made my muscles contract once every fifteen seconds. At first this was a pleasant experience, but after twenty minutes my stomach really started to ache. After forty-five minutes the ache had turned to an unbearable pain, and by the time I arrived at Leicester Square I was doubled up in agony. I nipped into one of the phone boxes (which smelt of wee), unbuttoned my trousers, pulled up my shirt and tried to take it off.

Problem Number Two: The clasp on the Toner belt was buckled and the suction pads seemed to be welded to my stomach. I tugged, yanked, wrenched and pulled, but still my muscles kept on contracting. I tried ripping out the wires, but they just wouldn't budge. That's when I remembered that Tony Dobson had said the Toner was 100 per cent unbreakable. For once he wasn't wrong.

Becky, the *Coffee Morning* researcher, opened the door and found me rolled up on the floor with my legs in the air. She told me the stars of the film had started to arrive. She looked slightly embarrassed, but, like the true pro I am, I pulled my trousers up, grabbed my microphone and went to work.

Problem Number Three: I couldn't stop twitching. Once every fifteen seconds the device sent a shock wave through my system that made my whole body jerk. When I was interviewing the stars I had to time my questions to coincide with the gaps in between muscle spasms.

During the film, the convulsions seemed to be getting worse and I couldn't keep still. People around me kept tutting. At one point, Colin Farrell, who plays the part of Captain Kowalski in the movie, leant forward and tapped me on the shoulder.

'*Pulse Toner?*' he whispered.

I turned round and nodded.

'You shouldn't have it on such a high setting,' he said and gave me a little wink.

Or maybe it was a twitch.

The movie ended. I was in so much pain I really should have gone home, but Becky the researcher insisted we go to the party to try to get an interview with Cameron Diaz. Despite the hurting I'm pleased I went. If the Looka-likes Ball was full of people who looked like celebrities, this party was full of the people they were all pretending to be.

With the film crew, I twitched my way through myriad celebrities, grabbing a couple of interviews as we went. Charlie Dimmock said the film was 'wonderful' and Lionel Blair said it was 'the best party he'd been to this year'. I was in the middle of an interview with Dale Winton when I suddenly spotted Pippa standing at the bar with Manky Mancini.

I couldn't believe it was her.

Dale was saying how much he'd loved Kiera Knightly in the movie, but I couldn't concentrate. I looked over again and Pippa and Manky were deep in conversation. Dale was going on and on about how he'd 'recommend the movie to anyone' when out of the corner of my eye I saw Manky leave Pippa standing on her own. I stopped Dale in mid flow, thanked him for his time and made my way over to say hello.

'Pippa.'

She turned around and seemed genuinely pleased to see me. She looked absolutely stunning in a silver backless dress. There was so much I wanted to ask her.

How was she enjoying her new job?

What's it like getting up so early in the mornings?

Would she like to have my children?

Instead I asked her if she'd like to say a few words for *Coffee Morning* about what she'd thought of the film. She agreed, so I called the crew over and they set up for a take. The cameraman signalled he was ready and I went into action. I really wanted to show Pippa how good I was at this sort of thing.

'Joining me now is Pippa, the gorgeous graffiti goddess from Channel 4's *2Early4Talk*. So, Pippa, *The Young and the Brave*, a big hit or is it *2Early2Say*?' As she began to answer, The *Pulse Toner* kicked in, giving me an excruciating pain in my lower abdomen. The sudden jolt caused me momentarily to lose control of my upper torso. In that moment my head shot to the left, my hips to the right and the hand holding my microphone crashed into Pippa's face. Her nose seemed to explode into a fountain of blood and she crashed to the floor. I bent down to apologize and was just helping her to her feet when the Toner gave me another shock. The pain was unbearable and sent an involuntary shudder through my whole body. I dropped Pippa, my head flew back and my left arm shot out, catching a waiter in the stomach. To be honest, I think he overreacted slightly; he could have just dropped the tray of champagne glasses where he stood, but no, he was one of those waiters that's probably an out-of-work actor and he just had to make a meal of it, didn't he? He stumbled back three paces, bumped into Darren Day and threw the tray up in the air. As if in slow motion, ten glasses sailed through space, causing the champagne to cascade down onto the celebrities below.

As the bouncers escorted me out, I turned to see Pippa being helped to her feet by Manky Mancini. I noticed that he was absolutely covered in champagne, so at least some good came out of it

6 JUNE

WEATHER GIRL ASSAULTED
'. . . *a savage unprovoked attack* . . .'

CELEBRITY CAUGHT IN CHAMPAGNE CHAOS
'. . . *seriously injured* . . .'

PIPPA PUNCHED TO A PULP IN PREMIERE PANDEMONIUM
'. . . *might require plastic surgery* . . .'

TOO EARLY TO STALK!
'. . . *the attack was made by an unknown reporter with
a nervous twitch who had been stalking Pippa for
months* . . .'

Pippa is on the front page of every tabloid newspaper in
the country. The words *'seriously injured'* and *'might require
plastic surgery'* keep spinning around inside my head.

All the papers say that Pippa was assaulted by an *'un-
identified assailant'* or an *'unknown reporter'*. There are
paparazzi photographs of her being carried from the club
and being put into a waiting ambulance. Manky Mancini
manages to get his ugly mug in most of them, and underneath one of the photographs is a caption saying, *'Caring
boyfriend, Ricardo Mancini, is said to be "shocked" by this mindless
act of violence.'*

I called Pippa's number (the right number this time) to
apologize but once again her answer machine was on. All I
could say was I'm sorry over and over again.

7 JUNE

Front-page news again.

THE YOUNG AND THE BRAVE: PIPPA'S STORY

Underneath the headline was a large photograph of
Pippa with her nose and forehead covered in bandages. I

scanned the article, but once again there was no mention of me.

I spoke to Charley and she said the executive producers of *Coffee Morning* are obviously not very happy about the whole thing, but are relieved that at least the show isn't mentioned.

'They think it's a good thing that you're flying out to New York in a couple of days.'

Charley knew I'd be worried about that one. A wave of relief swept over me. I thought it might have been cancelled, or worse still they might have asked someone else to do it. I was off to New York, but that didn't change the fact that I'd ruined Pippa's life for ever.

'There's a beautiful young lady in hospital,' I said, 'who might need plastic surgery . . . because . . . because . . .' I could feel myself filling up. 'because of me.'

'Simon,' said Charley knowingly. 'I think you ought to speak to Max.'

She put the phone down, but I couldn't bring myself to call him. Max has a very nasty temper and I knew he'd be fuming about this. Pippa's his golden girl, and I know I've ruined it all.

8 JUNE

I finally plucked up enough courage to call him and immediately broke down in tears.

He listened patiently for five minutes as I told him how sorry I was about Pippa and how I feared I might have ruined her career for ever. When I finished, he burst out laughing.

'You *schmuck*,' he said. 'You don't get it, do you?'
'What?'

I was outraged at Max's casual attitude to the whole thing.

'This is a stroke of genius,' he said. 'We can't buy publicity like this. If people didn't know who Pippa was before, they certainly know who she is now. This sort of coverage is going to make her a star.'

'She needs plastic surgery!' I screamed.

'She doesn't need plastic surgery.' He laughed. 'She doesn't even need a plaster.'

'But I punched her in the nose.'

'You couldn't punch your way out of a paper bag. Pippa suffers with nose bleeds, she'd had one earlier that evening. You just caught her on the end of the nose and set it off again.'

'What about the ambulance?'

'That wasn't even for her. Some old *schlimazel* had a heart attack in the restaurant next door. Pippa saw the paparazzi, spotted the ambulance and decided to play it for all it was worth. She's a clever girl, that one.'

'What about *Pippa's Story? The Young and the Brave?* The photographs of the bandages?'

'All a set-up,' said Max. 'Genius. Absolute genius.'

I sometimes feel as though there's a whole side of showbusiness I know nothing about.

'Well, if it's all such good publicity, why did they say I was an "unknown reporter"?'

'We had to keep you out of it,' said Max dismissively, 'otherwise people would have thought it was a scam. Anyway, this story will be dead and buried when they realize there's nothing really wrong with her. The newspapers of today line the cat litter trays of tomorrow, always remember that. There'll be a whole new story tomorrow and everyone will forget about this one.'

I just hope he's right.

9 JUNE

MIMI LAWSON PREGNANT!

I was standing outside the WH Smiths at Heathrow Airport and wherever I looked there was a headline about Mimi. I picked up a copy of *The Sun* and read the front page in disbelief.

DADDY'S LITTLE GIRL'S EXPECTING
A LITTLE ONE OF HER OWN!
But Who's The Daddy?

Former child star Mimi Lawson (25) confirmed yesterday that she was expecting her first child, but she's keeping MUM about who the father is. Mimi, who is nearly five months' pregnant, confessed she and the father were no longer a couple. 'I'm hoping news of the baby will reunite us,' said Mimi, speaking from her rented flat in East London. 'We are soulmates and we're meant to be together. I can't wait for the three of us to be a family.' Mimi would not reveal the identity of the father but admitted that 'people would know who he is'.

MYSTERY FATHER

'I don't want to say his name because I haven't had the chance to speak to him yet,' she said. 'But I will tell the world when the time is right.'

Mimi Lawson first found fame as a five-year-old, when her hit single 'I'm Daddy's Little Girl' sold over thirty million copies worldwide. The burning question now is Who is the daddy of daddy's little girl's little girl? (or little boy), and what would the daddy say about it?

I'm not sure if it's jet-lag, but I can't seem to think straight. It took seven hours and fifty-six minutes to fly to New York and for the entire flight I seemed to be lost in a state of paternal shock.

I travelled with Becky, the researcher who directed the item we shot at *The Young and the Brave* premiere. She's like a little mouse and I get the impression she thinks I'm a little weird. Although I was quiet for the entire journey, she was probably relieved that at least I wasn't twitching. Once we were at JFK Airport, she handed me the itinerary for the two-day shoot.

Tomorrow, I get some free time while Becky meets up with the American film crew and goes off to shoot some B-roll (footage of generic New York action, which will be used to help set the scene). We film the interview with *4Real!* on the morning of the eleventh and then fly back later that evening in time for me to record the pilot for *Swizz Quiz* on the twelfth. I'm not sure I'll be in any fit state to do that.

We checked into the hotel very late, by which time I was in a complete daze. My thought patterns were all over the place and my attention span was zero. Once every ten seconds I almost forgot I was going to be a father, but then an image or a word would set me off and I'd immediately start thinking about Mimi and the unborn baby.

We're staying at The Chelsea Hotel, which is on 23rd Street, halfway between Greenwich Village and Times Square. It has a real rock 'n' roll pedigree, and in the Sixties and Seventies, anyone who was anyone stayed here: The Rolling Stones, The Grateful Dead, Jimi Hendrix, Janice Joplin and Mama Cass to name but a few. Leonard Cohen wrote a song about it and Bob Dylan's child was conceived here.

'*Conceived!*'

You see, there I go again.

'*Bob Dylan's child was conceived here.*'

My child was conceived in a Travel Lodge in Grimsby.

10 JUNE

It's always been my ambition to come to New York, but now that I'm here I just can't seem to get excited about it.

I spent the day sightseeing but I didn't really *see* any of the sights at all: the Empire State Building, the Chrysler Building, the Flat Iron Building, Central Park, Madison Avenue, Broadway, the neon lights, the theatres, the bars, the cops, the yellow cabs, the hot-dog vendors, the skyscrapers, the subways and the sidewalks with steam coming out of them. I've grown up with these images and have seen them in every TV show from *Kojak* to *Friends*. Today, the day that I get to see them for real, they were just a blur.

It's strange, but in all those TV shows I never noticed how many babies there are in New York. There are babies everywhere. Babies in buggies, babies in cars, babies in restaurants, babies in elevators, babies on the television, babies in magazines, babies on the subway, babies in the park, there was even a baby in the hotel lobby. I'm staying at the most famous rock 'n' roll hotel in New York and all I can think about is babies.

4.16 a.m.

I'm not sure which is worse, the fact that I'm going to be a father or the fact that I'm going to be the father of a child who's mother is Mimi Lawson.

11 JUNE

11.16 a.m.

4Real! are massive here in the States. There are pictures of Troy Coral everywhere and everybody seems to be talking about him. My big interview with the band was scheduled to take place at eleven o'clock at the Yankee Stadium in the Bronx, where the band are performing in concert later this evening. The idea was for the boys to give me a guided tour backstage and show me the dressing rooms, wardrobes and costumes etc. I was then going to join them on stage for the sound check and they would teach me one of their dance routines. All of this would be inter-cut with footage from their latest video and a montage of shots of New York.

At quarter to eleven, *4Real!*'s manager called and said we'd have to push the interview back until two in the afternoon because Troy was suffering from 'exhaustion'. We all knew this meant 'hangover', but what can you do? Troy is the star and we have to have him in the film. Our flight is at four thirty this afternoon, which means it will be tight but the guys in the crew have assured us it's 'do-able'.

I have to be back in London for the *Swizz Quiz* pilot tomorrow morning. If it wasn't for that, I think I'd be tempted to stay in New York for a little longer.

Fifty years longer.

2.35 p.m.
No sign of Troy.

2.56 p.m.
Troy and the band are on their way and we'll record the interview as soon as they get here.

3.17 p.m.
Still no sign of Troy.

3.36 p.m.
There is now no way we can make the four-thirty flight.
Becky has cancelled those seats and booked us on to the
flight that leaves at eight o'clock this evening. With the time
difference, that flight doesn't get into Heathrow until nine
in the morning. I start shooting the *Swizz Quiz* at ten.

6.06 p.m.
4Real! have just arrived.

6.22 p.m. (in the back of a cab)
Harvey Welbertstien is the band's New York manager.
He's a fast-talking Brooklyn Jew with a bald head and the
eyes of a gangster; I was pretty sure that somewhere along
the line he must be related to Max. He told us there was no
way the boys would have time for the interview and said we
would have to reschedule it for tomorrow. I told him I was
shooting a pilot for the BBC tomorrow, but he didn't seem
that interested. Becky looked worried and the crew started
to talk amongst themselves. I decided to give Welbertstien
the Old Peters Charm.

'Harvey,' I said, putting my arm around his shoulders
and flashing him my winning showbiz smile. 'You probably
don't realize this, but I was the first person *ever* to interview
4Real! on live television.'

'Gee, I'm really impressed,' he said sarcastically. 'Now
get your filthy paws off me before I sue your sorry ass, you
friggin' Limey faggot.'

Becky told him she would lose her job if she didn't film
the interview today, but he just shrugged his shoulders and
handed her a silver coin.

'Here's a dime, go call someone who gives a fuck.'

I began to think this guy had a little bit of an attitude problem. Becky was crying and using her mobile phone to call the *Coffee Morning* office in London. The crew had started to pack the equipment away.

'Look,' I shouted in desperation. 'I've just discovered that I'm going to be a father for the first time. I am desperate to get back to England to see the woman who is carrying my child. WE HAVE TO DO THIS INTERVIEW NOW!'

I looked round to see Becky staring at me.

'I'll call you back,' she whispered into her phone and quickly hung up.

It had been a dramatic outburst and Welbertstien looked at me for what seemed an eternity. Suddenly his hard expression softened.

'Hey, I know what you're going through, buddy,' he said. 'I've just become a father myself. Wait here.'

He went into a room, only to reappear a moment later.

'You've got five minutes with the band.' He pointed in the direction of the dressing room. 'Make it snappy.'

We did the interview in one take.

Troy is everything you would expect an international pop star to be. After spending five minutes in his company I can totally understand why the female population of the world has fallen in love with him. He exudes an air of confidence and you can't help but be swept along by his personality. He is handsome, charming, intelligent and witty.

God, I hate him.

I think the main reason I hate him is because he once slept with Pippa, and as we were packing up and saying our goodbyes, I mentioned that I knew her.

'You want to watch that one,' he said in his posh scouse accent. 'She's only interested in one thing.'

'What's that?' I asked innocently.

'Fame,' he said with a knowing wink.

Just then Welbertstien and two minders came in and swept Troy away. Just as he was leaving the room, Welbertstien looked back, pointed at me with his index finger and then bent his thumb as if he were cocking a gun.

'Hey, look after that baby,' he said, sounding like Robert De Niro the gangster.

'Oh, I will,' I said, sounding like Terry Thomas the cad.

We're currently on our way to JFK. The flight leaves in one hour and forty minutes. We have to make that plane. Back to England. Back to the *Swizz Quiz*.

Back to fatherhood.

12 JUNE

This was the worst day of my professional career. The *Swizz Quiz* could have been the show to make me a star; it could have been *The* One.

But I blew it.

Big Time.

Becky and I managed to make the eight o'clock flight. As we were boarding I noticed that Ian Botham, the famous cricketer, was on the same flight. My first thought wasn't Ooh, that's Ian Botham the famous cricketer. It was Oh no, if this plane crashes Ian Botham will get all the headlines and I won't even get a mention. I realized these were not the thoughts of a normal sane person and put it down to tiredness, emotional fatigue and concerns over my unborn baby.

We were flying through the night and I knew I'd have to get some sleep. *Coffee Morning* had only paid for us to fly economy so the seats were really small and I couldn't get comfortable. I was so restless. I fidgeted and fiddled and tossed and turned, but I just couldn't get to sleep. I loosened my collar, unfastened my belt and took my shoes and socks off. I tried talking to Becky, but she didn't seem very interested. I'm sure she was just pretending to be asleep to avoid talking to me. I think the sight of me fumbling to undo the top button of my jeans while wearing earplugs, an eye mask and an inflatable neck support was too much for her. I tried reading but couldn't concentrate, so I decided to watch the in-flight movie instead.

It was called *Maybe Baby*.

It was all about a couple that find it difficult to have a child. It's supposed to be a comedy, but I cried all the way through it.

I was totally exhausted and tried to relax by letting my mind drift. It seemed to do the trick, but I was just dozing off when the captain's voice came over the intercom and informed the cabin crew there were ten minutes to landing.

We eventually touched down at Heathrow at twenty past nine this morning. There was a car waiting to pick me up which took me straight to BBC Television Centre.

I've never been jet-lagged before and it's a very strange experience. Every little movement seems to take so much longer than usual, as if there's a time delay between your brain sending out a message and the rest of your body receiving it. Your normal personality is suppressed and you feel as though the inside of your head has been covered in treacle. Your mind switches off without any warning. People speak to you and it takes an age for you to reply. In conversation you use completely the wrong words.

With hindsight, these are not the ideal circumstances in which to be presenting a pilot for a prime-time quiz show.

Swizz Quiz is a clever idea where contestants have to swizzle their fellow contestants out of the prize money.

There are ten contestants in total. The host asks them general knowledge questions, and if they get the answer right, they're asked a question about their personal life. The catch is that only one of them is telling the truth, the other nine are allowed to lie and cheat in order to swizz their fellow contestants and the viewing public into believing they are who they say they are. The more lies they manage to tell, the more money they can win. The studio audience and viewing public at home have to vote for which contestant they think is telling the truth, and the winner is the person who gets the most votes.

The format has plenty of opportunity for the host to interact with the contestants. From a presenter's point of view this is a real chance to show what you can do. I certainly showed what *I* could do. I stumbled over the questions, fluffed the pieces to camera and forgot the contestants' names. In normal situations like this *The Other Me* automatically takes over, but today I think he was still in New York.

There was a moment when one of the contestants said his name was Mr Bridge. This was a glorious opportunity to show how sharp and quick-witted I could be.

'*Mr Bridge? You shouldn't let people walk all over you.*'

This would have been a guaranteed woofer from the studio audience. But no, the line I came up with was a real gem.

'Mr Bridge? . . . Erm . . . good luck in the show.'

Blank look to camera. Silence from the studio audience. To use an old showbiz adage, 'I died a death.'

13 JUNE

'*Mr Bridge? My advice to the other contestants is not to cross him.*'

Maybe the skill of a true game-show host is to come up

148

with a witty line actually in the studio, not twenty-four hours later when he's lying in bed.

14 JUNE

'*Mr Bridge? I know your brother Severn.*'
I wonder if Bob Monkhouse used to do this to himself.

15 JUNE

I know I didn't do a very good job on the pilot, but hopefully the powers-that-be will see past that. Surely they'll see my potential. I called Max to ask him what he thought, but Scary Babs said that he was 'in a meeting'.

I called back an hour later and he was 'out to lunch'.

I called back again and he was 'with a client'.

This was Max avoiding my calls. To use his analogy, I could suddenly feel the bathwater getting very cold. I asked Scary Babs if she'd heard whether *Swizz Quiz* was going to be commissioned. She said we probably wouldn't hear anything for a couple of months or so. She then told me that she'd seen an edited version of the pilot.

'What's it like?' I asked.

'Well, the show's good,' she said.

She seemed to emphasize *the show's*.

'Anyway, don't worry about it, dearie, at least you've got *Coffee Morning*.'

That's something I suppose.

16 JUNE

Quentin, one of the executive producers on *Coffee Morning*, called me this morning. He said they'd been happy with my items on the show but felt that maybe I'd been overworked recently. He said they'd had a production meeting and had decided to 'rest' me for a couple of weeks. He apologized, told me not to worry as this was only a temporary measure and they would still honour my contract and pay me until the end of July.

When he hung up I immediately called Charley for the real story, but she seemed distracted. I asked why I was being 'rested'. She said that Becky the researcher had complained that I was 'ignominious', and on two separate occasions had tried to expose myself to her, once in Leicester Square and once on the aeroplane. I explained to Charley how I was wearing The Pulse Toner on the night of the premiere and how, on the aeroplane, I couldn't get comfortable.

Charley didn't say anything.

'You believe me, don't you, Charley?'

'Of course I believe you, that's not what I'm worried about.'

'Well . . . can't you do anything to help me?'

'Like what?'

'You're in a good position there. Maybe you could say something to the execs.'

'Simon, you've got to stop using our friendship just to further your career.'

Fifteen love to Charley.

'Friendship? Is that what you call it?'

Fifteen all.

'What's that supposed to mean?' she asked indignantly.

'You're never there for me when I need you.'

Of course, this was grossly unfair, but I had to take out my anger and frustration on somebody. It was all about point scoring now and that little statement made it *thirty-fifteen* to Peters.

'You claim to be my friend,' I continued, 'but the first time I really need you you don't do anything to help.'

Forty-fifteen and going for match point.

'Simon?'

'Yes, Charley?'

'Fuck off.'

She slammed down the phone.

Game, set and match to Charley.

3.06 a.m.

In five years of friendship Charley has never slammed the phone down on me.

3.32 a.m.

I must check in the dictionary to see what ignominious means.

17 JUNE

I know that I should try to contact Mimi Lawson and talk to her about the baby but I think I'm going through something called denial.

19 JUNE

I spent the whole day in bed. I think I'm suffering from exhaustion.

20 JUNE

At what point does exhaustion become depression?

21 JUNE

Maybe it's a nervous breakdown.

22 JUNE

Mimi, Pippa, Charley, Max, *Coffee Morning, Swizz Quiz*. My whole life seems to be collapsing around me. What else could possibly go wrong? Surely I'm due some good news.

23 JUNE

SINGER DIES

Sixties crooner Vince Envy died yesterday, aged 68. Married four times but with no children, he will be best remembered as 'The Man With The Tan'. Police say his death was 'drink related.'

Sixty-eight years of life and that's all they could write about him.

I was stunned and read the article over and over again. There was something so desperately sad about how short it was. After all the things Vince did in his career, he'll be *'best remembered'* for an advert he did in 1973. What about the time he spent with Sinatra in Vegas? What about the charity work? The West End shows? The pantos? What about the Number One single in Albania? None of that seemed to matter. They thought it was more important that he'd been *'married four times but with no children'* and that his death was *'drink related'*. According to them, that was Vince's life.

Why didn't they just write LOSER DIES and be done with it:

'Vince Envy died yesterday . . . and, to be honest, no-one really cares.'

Maybe I could have done something. Maybe I could have been there for him and helped him through what was obviously a very difficult period. When I appeared in panto with Vince, I always liked him and considered him a friend, but I feel almost hypocritical saying that now. With hindsight it was a showbiz friendship: paper-thin and superficial; empty, cracked and shallow, like a children's swimming pool in winter. When he needed a real friend I didn't even return his calls, and the truth is I didn't even want to. I was so preoccupied with my own problems that I couldn't be bothered with those of a sixty-eight-year-old alcoholic.

I sat and cried for two hours. I started off crying for Vince, but ended up crying for myself. When I'm old I don't want to be like Vince, bitter and twisted about the breaks I never got and ungrateful for the ones I did.

What did Vince dream of when he was young? Happiness? Contentment? Growing old gracefully, surrounded by adoring grandchildren? Or did he do a deal with the devil and trade it all in for a shot at fame and fortune? When Vince was having hit singles, appearing in the West End and jetting off to Vegas, he must have thought, Everything's going so well at the moment . . . nothing can go wrong. But it did go wrong, it went horribly wrong and Vince died a sad and lonely death.

Fifty years in showbusiness bought him three lines in the *Daily Mirror*, telling everyone what a failure he'd been.

25 JUNE

When I die I want so much more than three lines. I want it to be reported on the *Six O'Clock News*; if not the lead story, then at least the second. I want them to show highlights from my career and have a montage of celebrities saying what a sad loss it is to the world of light entertainment. I want the BBC to clear the schedules to make way for a homage to me.

'And now on BBC1, as a change to our advertised programming, we present *Simon Peters, a Tribute to the Game-Show King.*'

28 JUNE

As I was coming out of my flat this morning, I saw a taxi dropping off a passenger. I noticed the driver looked old and haggard and had a very red face, as if he suffered from high blood pressure or a drink problem, or both. There was something vaguely familiar about him. At first I thought it was somebody I knew personally, but when I looked again I realized I recognized his face because he was famous, or at least he used to be. It was Walter Payne, or 'Wally' as he was known to millions of kids in the mid-Seventies. He used to present a children's show called *Wally's World,* where he was the only human in a world full of puppets. He used to wear outrageous tank tops and brightly coloured flares, and although I didn't realize it at the time, the show had a bizarre, almost surreal sense of humour.

Wally's World is now considered retro-cool and it always gets a mention when people in pubs start talking about classic TV. Someone will start to hum the distinctive theme tune and then everyone will attempt to name all the puppets. No-one can ever remember the name of the pig, though. Some people think it was *Pink,* others insist it was *Plank,* but I know for a fact that it was *Planks,* as in '*Thick as two short . . .*'

That was the humour of the show.

Wally Payne was a hero of mine. He was the reason I wanted to be a television presenter. I used to watch his show and think, He's having so much fun, that's what I want to do when I'm older.

Wally Payne holds a special place in the heart of anyone between the ages of twenty-five and forty. When you think of children's television, you think of him. He was an icon and a national treasure.

Now he's a taxi driver.

29 JUNE

I wonder if I'll ever be retro-cool?

Will people sit in bars in thirty years' time and say, 'Yeah, but do you remember *Simon Says*?'

'Oh man, that was a classic. What was it again? "The show where you do what I do, not say what I say."'

'"Say what I do, not do what I say."'

'"Do what I say, not say what I do."'

'Something like that.'

'What was that guy's name again?'

'Peter Simon?'

'No, that was the other bloke.'

'Simon Peterson.'

'That's the one.'

'I wonder what ever happened to him?'

'Didn't he marry that Pippa bird, and then go to Hollywood and become a massive star?'

'No, that was that Ricardo Mancini.'

'Lucky git.'

'I heard Simon Peterson stacks shelves at Tesco.'

'Poor bastard.'

30 JUNE

Why do I have this obsession with being remembered

by people who don't even know me? My brother's an accountant and he doesn't want people to be sitting around in twenty years saying, 'Yes, but that David Peters was the greatest accountant I ever saw . . . no-one could fill out a tax return like that man.'

What is celebrity? And why do I crave it so much?

5 JULY

I'm thirty years old in exactly five months and all I can think about is death and failure.

What have I got to show for my existence on this earth? A couple of panto posters with my picture on them and a videotape of my appearance on the *Celebrity Squares Christmas Special*.

10 JULY

I was in the park today and I saw a little three-year-old boy flying a kite with his mum and dad. The little boy was wearing a red coat with bright yellow Wellington boots. Every time a gust of wind took the kite higher, the boy shrieked with pleasure. The dad was showing his son how to do a loop-the-loop. When the kite crashed to the ground, the boy would run to it as fast as his little legs could carry him and launch it again with a countdown.

'Three . . . two . . . one . . . FLYYYYYY!'

I watched them for forty-five minutes. The child giggled the whole time and never tired of playing with the kite. The look of pride on his mum's and dad's faces was enough to make me have to choke back the tears.

I've never felt that proud of anything.

12 JULY

I can't stop thinking about the family in the park. They seemed so *complete*.

If the devil came to me and offered me the chance of a loving wife and adoring children in one hand or a celebrity death and tribute programme in the other, I think I'd have to plump for married life and babies. I never thought I'd think like that.

What made me want to be a *somebody* in the first place? I'm sure John Goff, who I used to walk to primary school with, is very happy as a nobody.

At least he's a nobody with a wife and three children.

15 JULY

I knew there was only one person I could talk to about the way I was feeling. I called Charley's number and waited. I hadn't spoken to her since we'd fallen out over the *Coffee Morning* job. Her answer machine cut in and I began to speak.

'Hi, it's me . . . erm . . . Simon . . .'

I heard Charley snatch up the receiver.

'Hello, you ignominious bastard,' she said.

'Ignominious.' I said. 'Adjective, causing or deserving ignominy. Disgrace. Humiliation.'

Silence.

'Are we still friends?' I asked, sounding like a seven-year-old schoolboy.

'Well that depends.'

'On what?'

'On whether you're calling up to apologize for being such a complete git or calling because you've got one of your self-obsessed monologues to get off your chest.'

I told Charley I wasn't self-obsessed. I then went on to

157

tell her how I feared I was developing a fixation with death and how I felt Vince Envy's death was a warning to me. I told her my 'Ian Botham on an aeroplane' story and how terrible it was when I saw Wally Payne driving a taxi. I told her the story of the little boy with the kite and how proud his parents were. I told her how inane and meaningless my existence felt and how I dreaded ending up stacking shelves in a supermarket, or, worse still, being a presenter on a shopping channel. Once I started I just couldn't stop. The words just tumbled out. I was the patient and Charley was the therapist.

'There must be more to life than showbusiness,' I said and began to weep uncontrollably.

Once again there was silence at the other end of the line. I wasn't sure if she was still there.

'Charley?'

'There's a special guest on tomorrow's show,' she said pointedly.

'I don't want to talk about your special guest. I want to talk about *me!*'

'I think you'll want to talk about this one.'

'Who is it?'

'I don't think you'll like it, Simon.'

'Who is it?'

'It's someone you know.'

'WHO?'

'Mimi Lawson.'

The name hit me like an articulated lorry.

'But Mimi Lawson's pregnant.'

I nearly added 'with my child', but managed to stop myself just in time.

'Yes, Simon, that's why we're having her on. In case you hadn't noticed, "Who is the Father of Mimi Lawson's Baby?" is the biggest news story there is.'

Her words hung in the air.

'Simon?'

'Yes, Charley?'

'It's not your baby, is it?'

Her voice was distant, almost matter-of-fact.

'What do you mean?'

'Mimi Lawson's baby. It's not yours, is it?'

'No!'

I said it with real indignation, as if the idea of Mimi Lawson carrying my baby was absurd. Which of course it was. Or at least it used to be.

'You had a one-night stand with her during panto, didn't you?'

Charley had such a good memory for that sort of thing.

'Yes . . . no . . . I don't know . . .'

'Simon?'

'Yes, I had a one-night stand with her and yes it's my baby . . . at least I think it is.'

There was a pause.

'Have you spoken to her?' she asked, sounding more upset than I expected her to.

'Not exactly . . .'

'What do you mean, *not exactly*?'

'Well, I've sort of avoided talking to her. She used to hang around my flat, but I just ignored her. I didn't know she was pregnant then.'

'Simon, you have to speak to her and find out if it's your baby. When are you going to stop living in this self-indulgent fantasy world of yours and face up to your responsibilities, you egotistical little shit?'

There was a pause.

'I take it we're still friends then?' I said.

'Yes, we're still friends, but sort your life out.'

And with that she put the phone down.

She didn't slam it down, though, so I knew we were OK.

Charley's right.

Charley's always right.

I have to sort my life out and stop being such a depressive. Things aren't so bad. Career wise I still have the possibility of a prime-time game show with *Swizz Quiz* and maybe bringing up a child would give me the fulfilment I've been looking for.

4.42 a.m.

Please don't let Mimi mention I'm the father on live television; it would ruin me.

16 JULY

This was the first time I'd watched *Coffee Morning* since they decided to 'rest' me. When I was working on it I didn't quite realize how empty, insincere and futile it is.

Mike and Sue did a cookery item, talked to a woman who had the longest tongue in Britain and then set up the phone-in competition (calls cost 50p per minute) where the viewer could win £1,000 in cash by answering this question:

What is the name of the TV programme you are currently watching? Is it:

a) *Coffee Morning*

b) *Coronation Street*

c) *EastEnders*

That was so ridiculously easy and so obviously a way of conning people into calling up lots of times. I'm not that stupid though, I only entered twice.

Mike turned to the camera and said, 'Now on *Coffee Morning*, a true legend from the world of entertainment . . .'

I broke into a cold sweat as the instrumental version of

'I'm Daddy's Little Girl' began to play. They showed a montage of clips of Mimi as a child star, playing the trumpet with Roy Castle, tap dancing with Bruce Forsyth and performing the famous 'lollypop sketch' on *The Morecambe and Wise 1976 Christmas Special.* There was a clip of her on *Top of the Pops* and then another one of her singing live at the London Palladium. It ended on the well-known black-and-white footage of her as a six-year-old meeting the Queen. Instead of curtseying she gave the Queen a great big cuddle and said, 'I love you the most, Queenie.' The Queen famously replied, 'I thought you were Daddy's Little Girl', and everyone laughed really loudly, as they always do whenever a member of the royal family says anything remotely amusing.

They cut back to the studio and I began to feel a little nervous. Mike introduced Mimi and then Sue started asking her about her career to date. She asked her what it was like working with Eric and Ernie and what she remembered of that famous encounter with the Queen.

Mike interrupted.

'Mimi, is it true that your mother told you to give the Queen a cuddle instead of curtseying, just to get the publicity?'

'Absolutely not,' said Mimi emphatically.

'Tommy Cooper used to tell a very funny story. He said before being introduced to the Queen, he heard you rehearsing that line with your mother in the dressing room.'

'Mike, I was six years old and just said what I felt at the time.'

'Is it true that you no longer speak to your mother?'

'We haven't spoken for some time now, but I sincerely hope that one day we'll be reconciled.'

She flashed Mike a 'dancer smile', but her eyes warned him that was the end of this particular line of questioning.

I'd seen Mike and Sue's interview technique a million times before. It's very much a good cop/bad cop routine. Sue asks all the 'nice' questions while Mike, who fancies himself as a little bit of a Jeremy Paxman figure, prides himself on asking the questions no-one else would dare to. It's like watching a boxing match. Sue does the jabs and upper cuts while Mike waits until the opponent is on the ropes, then comes in with the killer punch.

I knew the viewing public would be on the edge of their seats, begging Mike to ask the big question about who the father of her baby is. He opened his mouth to speak, but Sue asked Mimi about all the charity work she was involved in and you could almost feel the nation breathe a huge sigh of disappointment. Mimi started to talk about being heavily involved with a charity for blind donkeys.

I glanced at the clock on the wall. It was two minutes to midday and I knew they'd have to hand over to the news at twelve o'clock on the dot.

Mimi was talking about a blind donkey orphanage in Budapest and I could sense Mike getting restless.

They're running out of time.

'I think donkeys really are the most beautiful creatures,' continued Mimi.

They're not going ask it.

'Do you do any other charity work?' asked Sue.

I might just get away with this.

'Well, I also do a lot of work with children.'

Oh bugger.

Mike had spotted his chance, but Sue beat him to it.

'Talking of children, Mimi, everyone here at *Coffee Morning* would like to say congratulations on being a mum-to-be.'

'Thank you very much.'

Surely it's time for the news now?

'So, Mimi,' said Sue, beating Mike to it again. 'Would you like to reveal who the father of your child is here on national television?'

Please don't say my name. Please don't say my name. Please don't say my name.

Mimi smiled sweetly and turned to the camera.

Please don't say my name. Please don't say my name. Please don't say my name.

'I think that's my business actually, Sue.'

She didn't say my name. She didn't say my name. She didn't say my name.

'The tabloids have been saying he's a well-known public figure, is that right?'

Oh for God's sake, Sue, leave her alone, she doesn't want to say.

'The public will be aware of him, but it has to be said that his talent hasn't been fully recognized.'

That's very sweet of her.

'But can you tell us his name?' said Sue, giving it one last shot before the news.

No, just say no.

'All I will say, Sue, is this. The father's name . . .'

Is not Simon Peters. Is not Simon Peters. Is not Simon Peters.

'. . . will be revealed when I feel the time is right.'

YEESSSSSSSS!

Sue ended the interview by thanking Mimi. She then did the link into the news while Mike continued to give her the dirtiest of looks.

I have to say Mimi wasn't half as bad as I expected her to be. She seemed switched on and rational, less highly strung and more like a real person.

Pregnancy really suits her.

She looked . . . radiant.

18 JULY

I remember Vince Envy offering me some advice at the panto company meal. In his drunken stupor he said '*have children*'. The more I think about it, the more I think having a baby isn't such a bad idea after all. Maybe all this is meant to be.

I think I'll make a very good father.

I'll stay at home and change the nappies while Mimi goes out and carves herself a career as a successful television personality. My little boy will be the cutest kid in the street and I'll carry him on my shoulders and buy him lots of sweets. I'll take him to the park and we'll play on the swings and the slides and the seesaw. We'll wrestle on the grass and I'll teach him how to fly a kite and ride a bike without stabilizers. We'll play football and cricket and tennis and golf and rugby. We'll hunt and fish and swim and climb trees and tie knots and skim stones and mend punctures and row boats and paint pictures and read poetry and listen to jazz. He'll come to watch me perform and he'll sit at the side of the stage and laugh at all my jokes and think I'm great. I'll teach him how to play the guitar and the piano and the saxophone and the harmonica and the drums and he'll grow up to be a world-famous pop star, more successful than Troy Coral.

We'll call him Vince.

2.29 a.m.
Why do I automatically assume he's going to be a boy?

2.48 a.m.
Why does he have to end up as a famous pop star?

3.16 a.m.
Maybe we shouldn't call him Vince.

19 JULY

I have to talk to Mimi face to face.

20 JULY

Surely she'll want to discuss the future with me.

21 JULY

I'm going to find out where she lives and go to see her.

22 JULY

I'll do it tomorrow.

27 JULY

There's something desperately sad about seeing the reality of where Mimi lives. Every person in the country knows the name Mimi Lawson, and I'm sure most people would imagine she lives in a large country mansion.

She lives on a council estate in Hackney.

It's the part of Hackney that isn't considered trendy and probably never will be. Charley found Mimi's address in the *Coffee Morning* production files. She gave it to me and persuaded me that going to see her was the right thing to do.

When I arrived I was shocked at what I saw. The whole estate had a feeling of misery and desolation. As I looked around I saw piles of rubbish, burned out cars and young teenage mothers pushing prams, their babies constantly screaming, voicing their disapproval at what they were born into.

I parked Ringo in the communal car park and sat and listened to the radio. Is it just me or is Radio Ace rubbish these days? I grew up listening to Radio Ace – the whole country grew up listening to it – but these days it's gone downhill and doesn't seem to cater for its audience. The DJs all seem to be about twelve, they have absolutely nothing of relevance to say and, without wanting to sound like my father, the music they play is atrocious: BOOM-BOOMtittlytittlyBOOMBOOMtittlytittlyBOOMBOOM-tittlytittly . . .

I sat there and listened for two hours as they played the same song over and over again, at least that's what it sounded like. I eventually turned it off and sat there in silence for another hour. I was just starting to snooze when I saw Mimi walking up to the block of flats. At first I wasn't sure it was her. She was wearing a baseball cap, a pair of dark glasses and was carrying a couple of Pound-Saver shopping bags. As she stopped to press the button for the lift, I could see that she was wearing a *Jaws, The Musical* 1983 tour jacket. I knew that she'd played the daughter in that production. It had done so badly at the box office it had made the well-known theatrical producer Sir Douglas Beaumont bankrupt. One critic famously wrote of the show, 'What a pity the shark didn't eat Mimi Lawson sooner . . . when she was eight years old perhaps.'

As Mimi got into the lift she turned round, and I could see her bump was really starting to show. I couldn't get over the fact that that bump was my baby. The doors closed and I noticed that it went up to the seventh floor. I should have got out of the car and followed her to the flat. I should have told her I was ready for a relationship and happy to accept responsibility for the child and that he or she would be brought up in a loving family home.

I should have done that, but of course I didn't. I started Ringo and drove home.

Maybe I'll go back tomorrow.

28 JULY

I sat outside Mimi's flat, this time with the radio tuned to Radio Easy 'Where the music's so easy it hurts', as the jingle informed me once every thirty seconds. I hope it's not a sign of me getting old but I actually rather enjoyed it. The DJs seem to have pleasant personalities and nice voices, not just attitude.

I've always thought I'd make a good DJ. Charley thinks my voice is too squeaky, but I think it's all about personality. I'd be in the mould of Dave Gold and Mike Prince. They were big DJs with big personalities, that's what the listening public want.

Radio Easy played songs I knew the words to. I sang along for four hours and didn't hear the same song twice.

I didn't actually go up to see Mimi, but I did catch a glimpse of her taking the rubbish out.

29 JULY

I sat in my car from eight in the morning until six in the evening. In that time she went to the newsagent's once and received one visitor. He was a really shady-looking character, unshaven and wearing a dirty brown overcoat. I've always been a good judge of character and there was something decidedly dodgy about this man. I felt quite protective towards Mimi. I don't think the mother of my child should be associating with people like that.

31 JULY

Mimi didn't go out all day, but Mr Shady turned up in his dirty brown overcoat at around three thirty and then left again about half an hour later.

There's something really strange about watching someone's movements and being so close to them without them knowing. I felt as though I was on a secret mission deep undercover.

1 AUG

With hindsight, I shouldn't have gone deep undercover in a vehicle painted the same colour as Noddy's car.

The police arrived this morning and accused me of 'stalking Miss Lawson'. Mr Shady turned out to be Detective Constable Dave Green of Scotland Yard. I tried to explain to him that Mimi actually stalked me for two months, but he didn't seem interested.

'The best thing you can do, Mr Peters,' said DC Green of the Yard, sounding like a bad actor in a TV cop show, 'is move along quietly and not come near Miss Lawson again.'

'But I'm the father of her child,' I screamed.

He laughed, as if to say I was the second person that week to have made that claim.

My exit had to be swift and dramatic. I wanted to wheel-spin away and leave the fascist pig choking on the smell of burned rubber. I slammed the car into first and revved the accelerator. I fixed him with a steely glare.

'You ain't heard the last of me, copper.'

I let out the accelerator and promptly stalled the car.

It wouldn't have been quite so bad if I'd started it straight away and then made a speedy getaway, but I couldn't. I turned the key in the ignition. Nothing. I tried again. Still nothing. Ringo had died and DC Green of the Yard ended up getting his jump leads out to get it going again.

I must find another way of speaking to Mimi.

4 AUG

My contract with *Coffee Morning* is now officially up, so I'm not earning any money at the moment. I'm not too worried because I feel very confident *Swizz Quiz* will be commissioned to be a series. It's a really strong format, and even though I wasn't on form I just know it's going to happen. It's like a small light at the end of a very long tunnel. The one thing that's keeping me going through all this is the thought that within a couple of months I, Simon Peters, could be presenting my own prime-time light-entertainment game show on BBC1.

In the past I wanted this so I would be famous and invited to lots of film premieres. Now I've put it into perspective and realized the real reason I want it so badly is so I can provide the very best for Mimi and our child.

7 AUG

I was flipping through the channels and something made me stop on Channel 5's *Talking Point with Mary Matthews*.

'Who is the father of Mimi Lawson's child? is fast becoming the biggest mystery since Who shot JR?' said Mary, squinting at the autocue from beneath her heavily lacquered bouffant hairstyle.

Mary Matthews is a legend in the world of television and seems to have been broadcasting since the year dot. She looks like a sexy grandmother and is a real cult figure among students, especially since she posed for a 'Sexy at Sixty' photo shoot for *FHM* magazine. Her interviewing technique is tough but motherly, and she has a knack of making her guests tell the truth whether they want to or not.

She announced that Mimi Lawson would be appearing later in the show.

'We'll be attempting to unravel the mystery of who the father is . . .'

I quickly switched the television off. I knew *Talking Point* was two hours long and broadcast live from The Magnet Television Studios on Tottenham Court Road. I decided to go along and speak to Mimi there.

When I arrived at the studio there was a security guard on the main desk. I decided to try to bluff my way in.

'Hello, I'm a guest on *Talking Point with Mary Matthews*.'

'Name?' said the security guard without looking up.

I glanced down at his clipboard and saw a list of the guests he was expecting. One name immediately caught my attention and I couldn't believe my luck.

'The Chuckle Brothers,' I said.

He looked up and studied me for what seemed an age. Then he looked behind me. I gave him my best Chuckle smile.

'I thought there were two of you?' he said suspiciously.

'We've split up.'

'Sorry to hear that, Mr Chuckle,' he said, stamping a visitor's pass. 'Me and my kids never miss your show.'

He handed me the pass, but didn't let go of it. I tried snatching it but still he managed to maintain a firm grip. I pulled it towards me but he immediately pulled it back again.

'To me, to you . . . to me, to you,' he said bursting into a fit of giggles and finally releasing the pass.

'Very funny,' I said, desperately hoping he didn't know any more of The Chuckle Brothers' comedic repertoire.

'Right, Mr Chuckle,' he said. 'I'll just call them and tell them you've arrived and a researcher will come down and take you to your dressing room.'

For the briefest moment I panicked.

'Oh, no need for that,' I said, moving away from the

desk and giving him a cheery wave. 'I know exactly where it is.'

I walked over to the lift and pressed the button.

'Stop,' shouted the guard.

My mouth went dry and I swallowed hard.

'Studio One's on the ground floor,' he said.

I smiled at him and walked back past his desk.

'To me, to you,' he said and burst out laughing again.

I found the studio, but the red 'On Air' light was flashing. Next to the light was a monitor showing the pictures being transmitted and I could see Mary had already started her interview with Mimi. I couldn't hear what was being said, but I could tell from Mary's face that she wasn't getting the answers she wanted. I decided to find Mimi's dressing room and wait for her there.

All the dressing rooms had silver stars on them with the guest's name written in black felt tip. As I walked past The Chuckle Brothers' room, a worried-looking researcher came out and started talking into a walkie-talkie.

'I've asked security and they say one of them has definitely arrived . . . he's got to be here somewhere . . . apparently they've split up . . . no . . . no . . . split up as in never working together again . . . yes . . . it's an exclus- ive . . .'

I kept my head down and said nothing. I found Mimi's dressing room at the end of the corridor. The door was unlocked. I opened it and slipped inside. Mimi was certainly getting the star treatment. It was the Number One dressing room and it looked more like a hotel suite. There was a red velvet couch, a bed, a shower, a fridge, a big bowl of exotic-looking fruit and several bouquets of fresh flowers. In the corner was a large television set. I turned it on just in time to hear Mary finishing the interview with Mimi.

'Now promise you'll come back when you're ready to tell us who the father is,' said Mary.

'I promise,' said Mimi.

'Thanks for coming along today and good luck with the birth. Ladies and gentlemen, the beautiful and very secretive Miss Mimi Lawson.'

The studio audience burst into applause and, as it subsided, the shot cut back to Mary, who looked slightly worried.

'Our next guests were to have been children's favourites The Chuckle Brothers, who were about to embark on a nationwide tour. Now we have some very sad news for any children watching, apparently The Chuckle Brothers have split up, and I'll be finding out why when I interview one of them. He's in the building somewhere, but we . . . erm . . . just don't seem to be able to find him at the moment.'

There was nervous laughter from a couple of members of the studio audience.

'So what are we going to do instead?' asked Mary, doing the old trick of putting her finger to her ear and letting the viewing public know it wasn't her fault.

Silence.

Mary looked embarrassed.

Nobody seemed to know what to do next.

A member of the studio audience coughed and you could actually hear him say sorry.

There's nothing more fascinating than watching live television go horribly wrong. It's like watching a car crash; you know it's wrong to look but you just can't help it.

I heard a noise outside the dressing-room door. Mimi was telling a researcher that 'yes, she'd enjoyed doing the show' and 'no, she hadn't seen Barry Chuckle anywhere'.

She walked into the room and I stood up.

'Mimi.'

'Simon.'

For a moment she seemed pleased to see me.

'What are you doing here?'

'I thought we ought to speak.'

She seemed to hesitate.

'No . . . I . . . I can't.'

'But we've got a lot of things to discuss.'

'We've got nothing to discuss.'

'I thought you wanted to talk to the baby's father.'

'It's impossible . . .'

'You said in a newspaper interview that you wanted to discuss the future with him—'

'You don't understand.'

'Well I'm here to tell you that I'm ready to face up to my responsibilities. I'm here to talk about the future.'

'You don't get it, do you, Simon?'

'Sorry?'

'You just don't get it.'

Mimi shook her head. She turned round, walked to the door and slowly opened it.

'SECURITY!' she screamed at the top of her voice.

She turned back to face me and her personality completely changed. Suddenly she was fierce and intense.

'Look, Simon,' she screeched with pure venom. 'Keep the fuck out of this. Me having this baby is the best thing that's happened to my career since 1972. The fact that no-one knows who the father is makes it even better. SECURITY! My publicist told me to string this out for as long as possible, so the last thing we need is for you to start shouting your mouth off and trying to steal some of the limelight. SECURITY!'

'I wasn't trying to steal the limelight, I'm just trying to do the right thing.'

'Don't give me that shit, Simon. When I really needed

someone to talk to you wouldn't even return my calls. For three months I tried to get in touch with you, but you didn't want to know. I was desperate to speak to you for a reason and a very good reason, but all you did was ignore me. Now that I'm hot you suddenly want to know me again. Well I'm sorry, you selfish bastard, it doesn't work like that. Now if you'll excuse me, I have to leave because I'm doing *Parky* tonight. SECURITY!'

A security guard burst into the room. When I say 'burst', he actually just hobbled in (why do all security guards walk with a limp?). I agreed to leave quietly and, as I was making my way to the exit, caught a glimpse of the real Chuckle Brothers talking to the security guard on the front desk. I made a dash for the door, but it was too late, the security guard had already seen me.

'Hey,' I heard him shouting.

This is it, I thought. *This is the moment I get into serious trouble.'*

'Hey.'

My whole career flashed before my eyes and still it wasn't very exciting.

So this is how it ends. Arrested as a Chuckle Brother imperson-ator.

I ignored him and carried on towards the door.

'Mr Chuckle, sir,' shouted the security guard, and I realized he was actually talking to me. I spun around and could see he was holding The Chuckle Brothers in a headlock, one under each arm.

'These blokes were pretending to be you,' he said.

I flashed him my best showbiz smile, gave him a friendly little wave and ran through the door as quickly as I could.

It's strange, but I never thought The Chuckle Brothers would know that many swear words.

8 AUG

Following her appearance on yesterday's *Talking Point*, Mimi was in several of the tabloids again this morning. In *The Sun*'s 'Bizarre' column was the headline:

Mini Mimi, The Prime Suspects!

They'd compiled one of those jokey charts of all the possible candidates who could be the father and then given odds as to who they thought it was most likely to be. They mentioned ten names, including the host of *2Early4Talk*, Paddy McCourt (at 10 to 1), and Troy Coral (at evens). Tony Blair was at 25 to 1 and even Dale Winton was a rank outsider. ('We said *rank*,' joked the journalist.)

Maybe it's my ego raising its ugly little head, but I was slightly disappointed I didn't get a mention.

10 AUG

The *Daily Mirror* ran a story about one of The Chuckle Brothers being spotted in Mimi Lawson's dressing room at the recording of *Talking Point with Mary Matthews*.

Without actually saying it, the journalist hinted that Barry Chuckle could be the father.

11 AUG

ARE YOU THE DADDY? screamed the headline.

The *Daily Star* has offered £25,000 to the man who can prove he's the father. This, I feel, is a scandalous piece of tabloid journalism; it's an outrageous intrusion into private lives, morally and ethically unjust and a shocking indictment on the society in which we live.

4.02 a.m.
I must stop thinking about what I'd do with the money.

12 AUG

Being the father of the most famous unborn baby in the country is bad enough. No-one knowing I'm the father is even worse.

3.19 a.m.
I could buy a new car with £25,000.

13 AUG

I can't switch on the television without seeing Mimi's face. She seems to be appearing on every single TV show, and even when she isn't appearing herself, someone else is talking about her.

'. . . Mimi's birth . . . just 100 days to go . . .'

'. . . And on Ian's team tonight, former child star Mimi Lawson . . .'

'. . . Mimi Lawson today rejected claims that the father of her child was, in fact, a member of royalty . . .'

'. . . is rumoured to be a member of the England football squad . . .'

'. . . a well-known comedian . . .'

'. . . an actor in one of our top soaps . . .'

'. . . and in *Countdown Corner* today, please welcome Mimi Lawson . . .'

I can't help feeling a little jealous. She's getting so much publicity, so much work and what I imagine is so much money from what is ultimately the birth of *our* child.

14 AUG

I called Charley and told her about the offer in the *Daily Star*. She said selling my story would be like selling my soul. I said I'd already done that the day I started working in television. She said if I did sell my story, she'd never speak to me again.

2.03 a.m.
I'm not going to sell my story.

2.46 a.m.
I'm proud that I value my relationship with Charley at more than £25,000.

3.36 a.m.
It's strange that I didn't value my relationship with the mother of my child quite so highly.

17 AUG

One of Mimi Lawson's ex-husbands, Kevin Pearson, has come forward and told the *Daily Star* he's the father of Mimi's baby. Pearson is no stranger to tabloid headlines. He and Mimi were married in the summer of 1996 at a big showbiz wedding with no expense spared. He'd told her he was an oil baron and property tycoon from Monte Carlo. Their marriage ended four months later when *The Sun* revealed to Mimi he was actually a part-time Elvis impersonator from Wolverhampton who'd stolen £250,000 from a building society in Dudley. He went to prison and Mimi went to rehab. Now he's been released, he's claiming he and Mimi were never officially divorced and are currently in the process of trying to patch up their marriage.

He says the child is his and he's willing to take a DNA test live on *Trisha* to prove it.

21 AUG

Kevin Pearson has confessed to the *News of the World* that he's *not* the father of Mimi's baby and only said he was to try to claim the money offered by the *Daily Star*. A friend of Charley's at the *News of the World* told her they'd paid Pearson double the amount to admit he's not the father just to keep the story going.

24 AUG

The phone rang just before midday and I picked up the receiver. All I could hear was an unusual panting sound. This quickly became a strange wheezing noise, which built to a crescendo of choking, coughing and spluttering. Anyone else would have thought they were the victim of a dirty phone call, I knew straight away it was Scary Babs calling from Max's office. It was a full two minutes before she actually spoke.

'Sorry about that, dearie,' she said. 'I'm really suffering with my phlegm this morning.'

She made a strange noise from the back of her throat. The sort of noise builders make just before they spit.

And then she spat.

It must have been into the waste-paper bin and all it needed was a comedy sound-effect '*ting*' to complete the image.

'That's better,' she said. 'Now then, do you want the good news, the bad news or the so-so news?'

For a moment I was thrown. My mind couldn't move on from the image of Scary Babs gobbing into a bin.

'Erm . . . I'll have the so-so news please, Babs.'

'Right,' she said with a voice that sounded like gravel. 'The producers of the panto in Grimsby have offered you the chance to go back there again this Christmas, playing the part of Buttons in Cinderella. You'll be joint top of the bill with The Grumbleweeds.'

The thought of having to spend another Christmas in Grimsby filled me with dread. I can't go back there. To go full circle and not to have progressed at all would be the final nail in the coffin of my career.

'How much are they offering?' I said.

'Two grand a week.'

'I'll think about it.'

I wanted to know what the good news was. For Scary Babs to call it good news I knew it was something special.

'What's the good news?'

'The good news is they've commissioned a series of *Swizz Quiz*.'

'YEEEESSSSSSSSSSSSSSS!' I screamed, jumping up and spontaneously punching the air.

This was the call I'd been waiting for my entire career, the realization of all my dreams and ambitions. Stuff *Simon Says*, stuff *Coffee Morning*, stuff panto in Grimsby. This was The Big One. This was my chance to prove myself and be up there with all the greats.

A thousand images flashed through my mind.

Me hosting *Swizz Quiz*.

Me being interviewed by Parky.

Me collecting the Lifetime Achievement Award at The BAFTAs.

179

I took a deep breath and tried hard to contain my excitement.

'What's the bad news?' I said with tears of joy rolling down my cheeks.

Whatever it was, nothing could take away this moment.

There was a pause and I could hear Scary Babs lighting another cigarette.

'They want a different host,' she said.

I laughed, thinking it was Scary Babs's legendary sense of humour. Then I realized Scary Babs doesn't have a legendary sense of humour. Scary Babs doesn't have a sense of humour full stop.

'Pardon?'

'They want a different host . . . they don't want you.'

'*THEY DON'T WANT YOU.*'

The words echoed inside my head and pierced me at my most vulnerable point, my ego. In this profession you get used to rejection, but the further one goes up the showbiz ladder, the harder it is to take.

'Why?' I pleaded, the tears of joy quickly turning to tears of pain.

'They say they want a bigger name,' wheezed Babs, and with that she started to cough again.

'But how do you become a bigger name if they don't let you host the shows that *make* you a bigger name?'

I was in floods of tears and realized I was starting to sound a little frantic.

'Who is it?' I cried. 'Who've they chosen instead of me?'

By this point Scary Babs was in the middle of another coughing fit.

'I'm going to have to go, dearie,' she spluttered. 'I've left my inhaler in the bog.'

'WHO IS IT?' I shouted, but it was too late, Scary Babs had hung up.

25 AUG

I've been in situations like this before and I know the thing to do is to keep my head together. If there's one thing I'm good at, it's that I never overreact and I don't let these things get to me.

26 AUG

My life has imploded, my career lies in tatters and it's not an understatement to say my world is crumbling all around me. The light at the end of the tunnel has been extinguished and I can feel the heavy mists of depression closing in on me.

29 AUG

I'm not sure which is worse, not getting to do the series of *Swizz Quiz* or the thought of having to go to Grimsby again this Christmas.

Swizz Quiz was the thing that kept me going. It didn't matter what else was happening in my life: being fired from *Coffee Morning*, my unrequited love for Pippa, impending fatherhood, there was always the thought at the back of my mind, Well, at least I've got *Swizz Quiz* to look forward to.

Now all I have is Grimsby.

I wonder who the new host is. If it's someone older than me, someone I admire and respect, someone who is genuinely a bigger name, then maybe I won't feel quite so bad.

2 SEPT

You cannot begin to understand the pain I feel inside just writing these words . . .

I'd called Max's office to talk about the Grimsby offer. I was expecting to hear Scary Babs's harsh tones, so it came as something of a shock when a pleasant-sounding young lady answered the phone. She explained she was from a temping agency and was standing in for Babs who was off for a couple of days with 'women's problems'.

The thought of Scary Babs having 'women's problems' made me feel queasy.

'Oh, right. Can I speak to Max then, please?'

'I'm really sorry but he's out at lunch,' said the new girl, sounding genuinely apologetic.

'Who with?' I enquired, seizing the opportunity.

I wouldn't have dared ask that if it was Scary Babs I was talking to.

'One moment please . . . let me just see . . . erm, yes, here it is. He's out with the host of a new show called *Swizz Quiz.*'

I swallowed hard.

'Oh really.' I tried to sound nonchalant, but my voice was three octaves higher than usual. 'Who's that, then?'

'Let me see . . .'

I could hear her rustling some papers.

'Here it is . . . Ricardo Mancini.'

The name thundered into my mind like a freight train and the cargo it was carrying was rage, fury, jealousy and resentment.

'What's Max doing with him?' I screamed incredulously, not even trying to hide the fact that I was fuming.

'I think he's just signed him to a three-year exclusive contract,' said the girl, totally oblivious to my mood.

Max never signed me to a three-year exclusive contract; come to think of it, he's never even taken me to lunch. Is Ricardo Mancini going to keep destroying my life like this? Is he always going to be one step ahead of me? Always getting the girl, the agent and the job that should be mine. He is talentless, insincere and smarmy. Why on earth would they choose him as a game-show host?

5 SEPT

'Is that Simon Peters?'

'Yes it is. Who's calling please?'

'Ah, you don't know me. I'm a friend of Michael Clarke's; he gave me your number and suggested I give you a call.'

'Oh, hello.'

'How's everything going?'

'Great,' I said, still not knowing who I was talking to.

'Are you doing pantomime this year?'

It seemed like a fair question. Maybe it was a theatre manager or a panto producer wanting to hire me. Anything would be better than Grimsby.

'I've had some interest, but I'm always open to offers.'

'I understand you worked with Mimi Lawson last Christmas?'

The alarm bells started to ring. If it's possible for bells to talk, these were chiming the word 'journalist!'

'Who did you say you are?' I asked.

'I'm a friend of Michael Clarke's,' he said, before quickly adding, 'So you worked with Mimi in . . . erm . . . Grimsby was it?'

It suddenly struck me that I've never met Michael Clarke; in fact, I've never even heard of him. It just sounds a familiar name.

'Yes, I worked with Mimi,' I said slowly, choosing my words very carefully.

'You were very close, weren't you?'

There was a pause.

'. . . hello?' I said.

'Hello, Simon. How did you get on with Mimi Lawson?'

'. . . hello?'

'Simon, can you hear me?'

'. . . hello? I'm sorry, I can't hear you.'

I was impressing myself with my performance.

'Simon?'

'No . . . I'm sorry, I've lost you. I'm going to have to go now.' I gave him one final parting shot. 'If you see Michael Clarke, say hello from me.'

I quickly put the phone down.

7 SEPT

I haven't been able to sleep for the last couple of nights for worrying about the journalist. That, coupled with the fact that Ricardo Mancini has stolen my career, made me pluck up enough courage to make an appointment to see Max. Initially Scary Babs said his first available date was 17 December but she called back two minutes later to say he'd had a cancellation and would see me today if I 'got my arse into gear and got over here sharpish'.

I managed to get to the office in forty-three minutes, which is a personal record for me.

'He's in a meeting,' said Scary Babs, her breath smelling of fresh mint and stale alcohol.

'But you said to get over here sharpish.'

It was no good; Scary Babs was already taking another call. I sat down on one of the leather seats and decided to wait.

Three hours and twenty-six minutes later, Max walked in wearing a Pringle sweater and carrying a very expensive set of golf clubs. He began to tell Scary Babs how he'd just thrashed Ricardo Mancini and McGovall the Shovel at golf, but as he was saying it, Scary Babs coughed a not very subtle cough and nodded in my direction. Max looked over at me and, for the briefest moments, I thought I saw a look of panic flicker across his face, but just as quickly it was gone.

'Peter!'

'Simon.'

'Whatever. Come into my office.'

Why doesn't Max ever ask me to play golf?

We went into his office and sat down, Max in his large executive leather swivel chair, me opposite him on a small wooden stool.

'What can I do you for then?' he said, and then immediately started playing with his Palm Pilot.

I wanted to build up slowly to the question of Manky Mancini and the *Swizz Quiz*. I told him I didn't have much work at the moment and wasn't sure whether to accept the Grimsby gig again.

'Well, people aren't exactly kicking the door down to offer you work, are they? The phone isn't ringing off the hook, is it? Maybe you should accept.'

Well thanks for that then, Max.

I told him about the journalist calling me and asking me about Mimi Lawson. He looked up and suddenly appeared very worried.

'Has he spoken to Mimi?' he snapped.

'I don't know.'

'Does he know who the father is?'

'I'm not sure . . . I think he thinks it's me.'

Max seemed to regain his composure 'You don't think you're the father, do you?'

'Of course I don't,' I lied.

'Shame,' he said. 'It would have been great publicity.'

Once I had his attention, I didn't want to let go. I told him how upset I was about not getting *Swizz Quiz*.

185

'Crap show anyway,' he said dismissively.

I asked him who the new host was going to be, but he looked uncomfortable and asked me if I knew how to set the time on a Palm Pilot.

'I've heard it's going to be Ricardo Mancini.'

'I think you have to hold this button down and press this other button twice.'

'Somebody told me you're representing him now.'

Max let out a sigh and rubbed the bridge of his nose with his forefinger and thumb.

'Yes, Mancini's got *Swizz Quiz* and yes, I'm representing him, but that doesn't create a conflict of interest with what we're trying to do with your career.'

'Max,' I said, with tears filling my eyes and more than just a hint of desperation in my voice. 'I haven't got a career!'

He studied me long and hard, like an eagle watching its prey. After what seemed an age, he raised his hand and slowly nodded his head as if to say, *Don't worry, I can solve all your problems with just one phone call.*

He picked up the phone and started dialling. He made a gesture with his thumb, which suggested I should leave the room. I waited in reception and watched Scary Babs reapply her make-up for what looked like the twelfth time today. It was as if she'd been playing paintball and everyone had used her face for target practice.

Two minutes later, Max called me back in.

'I've got you an audition,' he said.

I said, 'If it's that easy why don't you get me an audition every day? Or do you forget about me the minute I walk out that door?'

Of course I didn't say that at all. What I actually said was, 'That's brilliant, Max, what's the show?'

'It's a new science programme for the Beeb called *Raison D'Être*.'

My immediate reaction was fear.

'I don't really know much about science.'

'*Oi gevalt*, you're so negative, already. You've got a science O level, haven't you?'

'Yes, but that was domestic science.'

'Well there you go, then, you're perfect for it. You can bluff it, can't you? That's what you presenters do for a living, isn't it?'

Maybe he's right, I thought. At least I'd have some time to prepare for it, read some books, do a little homework etc.

'When's the audition?' I said.

'Tomorrow at three o'clock.'

I went home and looked up what '*raison d'être*' means.

8 SEPT

Being a television presenter, the two most important soldiers in your infantry are confidence and the ability to communicate. One might have other armed forces fighting alongside them: personality, charm, charisma, universal appeal and a modicum of modesty bringing up the rear, but it's ultimately confidence and communication that will win the battle for you. If one of these goes missing in action, it isn't long before all the others go AWOL as well.

I arrived at the audition and the producer introduced himself as Tarquin. Producers are like policemen, you know you're getting older when they start to look younger and this guy looked about twelve. I took an instant dislike to him. He seemed to have real intellectual pretensions, and when he explained what *Raison D'Être* was about I only understood every third word. He asked me which shows I'd presented in the past, and when I told him about *Simon Says* and *Coffee Morning* he just stared at me blankly.

'God, they sound *awful*,' he said and burst out laughing. It was a real public schoolboy laugh, a repetitive, high-pitched snort.

I smiled weakly. That's when the 'confidence' soldier in my regiment took a little bit of shrapnel and started to withdraw.

'The mainstay of the programme will be theological experimentations – scientific, mathematical and theoretical. It's a new spin on the science versus religion debate. We're saying if God was one of us, he'd probably be a scientist.'

That was obviously meant to be a joke because he laughed that laugh again. I had this overwhelming urge to punch him.

'We're not expecting the presenter to be an expert,' he continued in his patronizing manner, 'but obviously we can't have a complete idiot, either, so what we're going to do is make sure you have a basic grasp of science and mathematics by asking you to solve a very simple mathematical problem for us on camera.'

My mouth went dry and I started to panic. Confidence had done a runner and the ability to communicate was hard on his heels. All I had left now was personality and charm, and somehow I knew they weren't going to be enough.

Tarquin switched on the video camera and asked me to stand in front of it.

'Don't worry,' he said. 'It's very, very easy.'

I wish he hadn't said that. I had a strange feeling he knew I wasn't going to be able to do this, but he seemed to be taking a sadistic pleasure in seeing me suffer. He handed me a *Thomson's Local Directory* and a ruler.

'Right,' he said. 'Can you give me the measurement of the thickness of a single page in that directory and explain to the camera exactly how you do it. Take your time . . . and coming to you in five seconds. Five . . . four . . .'

At the back of my mind, I heard a bugle rallying the troops and sounding the 'call to arms'. Suddenly confidence and the ability to communicate came thundering through the mists of my insecurities, riding to the rescue on their large, powerful white stallions.

'. . . three . . . two . . .'

They joined together and formed the mighty army that is *The Other Me*.

'. . . one and cue.'

'Welcome to *Raison D'Être*,' I said with so much poise and self-belief it was hard to understand why he didn't just offer me the job there and then. 'Today we're measuring the thickness of a single page of a *Thomson's Local Directory*, because, let's be honest, you never know when knowledge like that is going to come in handy.'

I gave a cheeky little wink to the camera; as far as I'm concerned you can never have too much irony. I was really starting to get into my stride and could genuinely imagine myself as the host of this show. I could wear a white coat with some pens in the breast pocket and maybe they'd even call it *Simon Peters' Raison D'Être*.

'All you have to do is take a ruler, then place the ruler next to a page and, as you can see – can you get a close-up of that? – It's not quite a millimetre, is it? That, my friends, is how you measure the depth of a page of a *Thomson's Directory*. Until the next time on *Raison D'Être*, goodbye.'

I stood there, beaming into the camera, genuinely pleased that I'd managed to pull it off.

'Very good,' said Tarquin emerging from behind the camera with an unusual smirk on his face. 'But can you be more precise than "not quite a millimetre"?'

'Well you'd have to get a more accurate ruler to do that,' I said knowingly.

Tarquin tried unsuccessfully to stifle a snort.

'How would you go about solving this problem mathematically?' he said. 'Coming to you in five seconds . . . four . . . three . . . two . . . one and cue.'

I tried to speak but I couldn't. This time, the bugle sounded a hasty retreat and one by one my armies deserted me. *The Other Me* had become a conscientious objector and I was suffering a humiliating and crushing defeat on all sides. I was stripped bare and drowning in a sea of stupidity. I knew that Tarquin could see me for what I was, somebody who just likes showing off for a living but doesn't have any real depth of knowledge. He could see that I was paper-thin, thinner than a page of the *Thomson's Directory* itself (however thin that was).

'In your own time,' said Tarquin.

There was just one option available to me. I did the showbiz equivalent of waving the white flag. I grabbed my coat and ran out the door as fast as I could.

9 SEPT

I called Charley to tell her all about yesterday's disaster and she couldn't stop laughing.

'If you're so clever,' I said, 'how would *you* measure the depth of a page?'

'Measure the depth of the whole book and divide it by the number of pages,' said Charley, quick as a flash.

To change the subject, I tried explaining my 'television is war' analogy, but by that point she was in hysterics.

'I've got to go, Sergeant Major,' she said through tears of hysterical laughter. 'I'm on a secret mission deep undercover to try to find three grannies who want to have a make-over done on tomorrow's *Coffee Morning*. Over and out.'

I realize, of course, that television is nothing like war; it's just that yesterday's audition has left me battle-scarred and shell-shocked. I can definitely call it a career low point, and the only good thing to come out of it is the fact that I know things can't get any worse.

10 SEPT

'*Going-Gone TV* is looking for new presenters.'

It was Scary Babs's dulcet tones ringing the final death knell of my career. 'I don't know if you've seen it or not, it's one of those crappy auction channels. Tony Dobson, who used to work on *Coffee Morning*, is one of the presenters. People have to call in and bid for stuff.'

'Yes, I've seen it.'

'We sent them your showreel and they're really keen to use you. Actually, I think you're perfect for it.'

I didn't like to point out that she'd just called it crappy.

'When do I have to let them know?' I said, finding it hard to disguise the feeling of failure.

'They need an answer by the end of September,' she said, before hanging up.

It is now a race against time. Twenty days to save my career.

12 SEPT

My answer machine informed me I had one message.

Please let it be a job. Please let it be a job. Please let it be a job.

I pressed the play button.

'Hey up lad, it's Archie Rimmer here. I don't know if you remember me, but you saved my life on live television. Can you give me a call, please? I've got some news you might be interested in.'

191

I pressed delete. The last thing I need at the moment are the ramblings of a senile old man.

13 SEPT

The journalist called again and this time he didn't try to pretend to be a friend of a friend. He told me his name was David Mulryan and that he was an investigative journalist on a new television programme called *The Sword of Truth*. He said he was interested in finding out what really happened with Mimi Lawson in Grimsby.

'Simon,' he said, his voice soft and mellow. 'I will find out what happened, so if you know anything you may as well tell me now.'

'I don't know anything,' I shouted.

'It's OK, Simon, there's no need to get upset.' He sounded smug and superior, as if I'd somehow admitted something by my outburst. 'I'm going to go now, but if you think of anything, give me a call.'

'I don't think there will be anything,' I said, trying to compose myself.

'Think about it, Simon. *The Sword of Truth* is going to be a prime-time television show. It would get your name in the papers and give your career a much-needed kick-start. And let's be honest here, your career certainly needs it.'

I so nearly asked him what time on prime time, but managed to hold my tongue.

'I'm close to the truth,' he whispered and hung up.

16 SEPT

'Hello. It's Archie Rimmer again. I left you a message the other day, but I'm not sure if you got it or not, I'm hopeless with these bloody machines. Can you give me a call, please?

I've got some really good news for you. It's Archie. Archie Rimmer. You probably don't remember me, but you saved my—'

Beeeeeeeeeeeeeeeeeeeeeeeeeep.

Once again I pressed the delete button. What good news could Archie Rimmer possibly have for me? He's probably had his bunions done or something.

18 SEPT

I have just had a crushing thought. I've obviously been aware of it for some time but I didn't want to admit to it. I kept sweeping it under the carpet of my brain in the hope that if I didn't think about it, maybe it wouldn't happen. Today it finally seeped through to the forefront of my mind and now I can't think of anything else.

Yes, in 78 days I'm going to be 30 YEARS OLD.

If I'm going to be thirty, how come I still feel like a 16-year-old schoolboy?

If I'm going to be 30, how come when I meet somebody and they tell me they're 30, I think that sounds really ancient.

If I'm going to be 30, what happened to all the things I'd promised myself I'd do by the time I *was* 30? What happened to the successful career, the big house, the flash car, the wife and child? (Mimi and the unborn baby don't count). What have I got? A rented flat, panto in Grimsby and the offer to sell tat on a crappy auction channel.

21 SEPT

I told Charley my worries over my forthcoming birthday (it was actually a subtle way of reminding her of the date, just in case she'd forgotten). Charley said to be positive about it, as thirty is a great age. She would say that, though, she's only twenty-five and already has a successful career as a television producer.

'You're right,' I said. 'I have to look on the bright side. At least men reach their sexual peak at thirty.'

'That's women.'

'What?'

'Women reach their sexual peak at thirty.'

'Really?' I said. 'When do men reach their sexual peak?'

'Eighteen.'

'Shit.'

'Look,' she said. 'It's the big Three O. You have to embrace it, not fear it. Why don't you organize a party, hire a bar or something and invite everyone you know?'

I thought about it for a moment.

'That's a brilliant idea.'

I can see it now, A-list celebrities eating canapés and drinking champagne, top DJs providing the music and an eight-page spread in *OK* magazine with the headline, THE SHOWBIZ EVENT OF THE DECADE.

22 SEPT

So far I can only think of eleven people to invite.

23 SEPT

I keep putting my dad on the list and then taking him off again. I want him to be there, I just can't imagine calling up to invite him.

24 SEPT

I've booked the venue for my thirtieth birthday party.

I wanted to hold it in a really trendy West End bar like the Met Bar or The Cosmo but they all wanted to charge a fortune for the hire of the place and the drinks seem to me to be extortionate. So instead it's going to be in the upstairs room of the Red Lion pub at the end of my road. They were a little bit reluctant at first because the dominoes team were going to hold their Christmas party on that date, but in the end they relented because I told them there'll be some celebrities turning up. They said I could have the room for free as long as they take over £1,000 at the bar. The worrying thing is, even with my distant relatives I can only think of thirty-six people to invite, which means that each person will have to spend £138.88 on alcohol. Although, knowing some of my relatives, that won't be a problem.

I can't believe I only know thirty-six people. Maybe I should invite the dominoes team as well.

1.24 a.m.
I've just finished writing the invitations, and rather than the usual 'bring a friend', I wrote 'bring two friends'. I hope that doesn't sound too desperate.

26 SEPT

'Hello, lad, Archie Rimmer here . . .'

I do wish he'd stop leaving messages. Yes, I saved his life and yes, he probably feels he owes me a great deal, but he has to realize that beyond that, we haven't got a great deal in common.

2.17 a.m.
I wonder if Archie would like to come to my party?

27 SEPT

MIMI'S BABY IS AN ALIEN

Mimi has released (or sold) a picture to the *Sunday Sport* newspaper of her recent ultrasound scan and they've blown it up and published it on the front page.

Looking at it brought a tear to my eye.

The picture is black and white and grainy, but you can clearly make out the shape of a baby's head. The *Sport* said it looked like an extra-terrestrial.

I couldn't help thinking it looked like me.

28 SEPT

David Mulryan, the journalist, was waiting outside my flat. If you had to cast someone as an investigative journalist, you'd cast this man. He was handsome in a newsreader sort of way, had dyed black hair and wore a large brown overcoat. I noticed a red light over his shoulder and quickly realized it was a camera and that I was being filmed. My first thought was that I wasn't wearing any make-up and hadn't brushed my hair.

Mulryan asked if he could have a few words. I ignored him and hurried to my car.

'This sort of thing is just a joke,' he shouted, holding up a copy of the *Sunday Sport*. 'I'm a serious investigative journalist and what we're interested in on *The Sword of Truth* is exactly that, the truth. The truth about what happened in Grimsby.'

I quickened my pace but he hit me with a dozen quick-fire questions. His tone was sneering and aggressive and all I could do was mumble vague monosyllabic answers.

'What was your relationship with Mimi like?'

'Erm . . . OK.'

'What happened during the last week of pantomime?'

'Erm . . . nothing.'

'How did you get on with Ricardo Mancini?'

'OK.'

'How did Mimi get on with Ricardo Mancini?'

'Erm . . . Fine.'

'Were you upset when Vince Envy died?'

'Yes, Vince was a truly great professional who—'

'Did your agent, Max Golinski, go to see the show?'

'Yes but—'

'Did Mimi have an affair with anyone during the pantomime?'

'No . . . I don't think so.'

'Who do you think is the father of Mimi's child?'

'Erm . . . I don't really know.'

By this point I was in my car and he was shouting the questions through the window. I put the key in the ignition and prayed.

Please let it start. Please let it start. Please let it start.

It started.

The engine roared into action and I left Mulryan and his cameraman choking on Ringo's exhaust fumes.

As I sped away, I couldn't help feeling the net was closing in on me.

29 SEPT

Charley really is the best friend in the world. She intuitively knows when I'm down and need a metaphorical and sometimes literal shoulder to cry on. Last night she popped around to the flat with a pizza and a signed photograph of The Chuckle Brothers – they'd been guests on *Coffee*

Morning to try to stop the rumours they were splitting up. She also brought with her a great big bottle of vodka.

'You're not going to bed until we've drunk that and sorted your life out.'

And that's exactly what we did. We talked for hours, mainly about me, which made it all the more enjoyable. I asked her what she thought about the *Going-Gone TV* offer and she said I shouldn't take it.

'In television, careers and reputations are built on the jobs you turn down. The ones you don't do are more important than the ones you do.'

Charley was really good at administering little nuggets of advice.

'It's a cliché,' she said, 'but you're only as good as your last job. Your last job was *Coffee Morning*, which had some kudos attached to it. If you do *Going-Gone TV*, you're on a slippery slope, and once you start going down it's an awfully long way back to the top. Or in your case, the middle.'

I knew she was right, but to use another cliché, beggars can't be choosers.

I changed the subject and told her about David Mulryan asking me questions about Mimi's baby. Charley said not to worry about it as she had a funny feeling I wasn't the father anyway. She then went off on a bit of a tangent and said she'd like to settle down one day and hopefully have children of her own. She started to waffle on about how she desperately wanted to feel more fulfilled and how she thought television was ultimately vacuous and full of egotistical idiots. She went on like this for a while, but luckily I managed to steer the conversation back onto the subject of me.

I asked her what she thought of Manky Mancini hosting the *Swizz Quiz*.

'Wanker,' she said.

God, I love Charley. She has an acute way of telling me exactly what I want to hear.

'Just because he's got the gig, it doesn't mean he's better than you. It just means one television executive thought he was more suitable for this job, but what do television executives know?'

'Nothing,' we said in unison.

'And what do we call television executives?'

'WANKERS!' we shouted at the tops of our voices.

'Exactly. That's what they and Manky Mancini have in common, which is why he got the gig and you didn't. End of story.'

She told me not to lose any sleep over it, as I was bound to get another gig.

'You were born to be a game-show host,' she said and started giggling, but I took it as a compliment anyway.

'I ought to have that tattooed on my arm,' I said, joining in with the laughter. "Born to Be a Game-Show Host!"'

'Yeah,' giggled Charley. 'With a big picture of Ted Rodgers and Dusty Bin underneath it.'

We spent the next half-hour talking about how Ted Rodgers did that 3-2-1 thing with his fingers and saying how much fun it would have been if the show was called 10-9-8-7-6-5-4-3-2-1.

By this time we'd drunk a lot of vodka, you understand.

It was around two in the morning and I offered Charley a coffee. As I was making it she took hold of my hand and looked me in the eye. She said she didn't want to start sounding like an old hippy but she was a big believer in positive energy and the fact that things seem to happen in cycles. A person will have a run of bad luck and then suddenly there'll be some good news and it will come from the most unusual source. She said if I stayed positive and believed in myself then one day good things would start to happen. I like it when she says things like that.

By the end of the night, Charley was too drunk to go home.

'You can stay here if you like,' I offered.

'Where am I going to sleep?'

'In my room . . . er . . . I'll sleep on the couch.'

'Is there a lock on the door?' she asked.

'It's OK, I trust you.'

She laughed and we looked at each other for a moment longer than we should have. Then she went to bed.

I always feel a better person and things never seem quite as bad when Charley's around.

30 SEPT

There was an article in the *News of the World* today about what Mimi's baby would look like if certain celebrities were the father. There were several different pictures of male celebs, which they'd morphed with Mimi's face and then superimposed it onto a baby's body. The Michael Jackson picture was very funny, but I couldn't help feeling a stab of jealousy when I noticed they'd done the same with Ricardo Mancini.

1 OCT

Scary Babs called to say that *Going-Gone TV* had been on the phone again asking me for my decision. She said they're desperate for me to join their team as I have all the right qualities to be one of their presenters.

That really depressed me.

They've given me another five days to decide whether to

take the job. I can't believe it's come to this. I'm just five days away from becoming a failure.

On one shoulder sits Charley saying, 'Television is all about the jobs you don't accept,' and on the other shoulder is my landlord saying, 'Your rent is eight hundred pounds a month.'

2 OCT

I normally let the answer machine kick in and screen my calls, but when the phone rang this morning something told me to answer it. I was hoping it was going to be Charley with some ideas for the party or Max with some good news about work. I snatched up the receiver.

'Hello?'

'Ooh, thank goodness I've found you, lad, it's Archie Rimmer here.'

My heart sank, but I knew I had to be polite.

'Hello, Archie,' I said through gritted teeth. 'I'm sorry I didn't get back to you sooner. What have you been up to?'

There followed a long, rambling one-sided conversation in which Archie told me how he'd recently climbed Ben Nevis, run the London Marathon and broken the world record for balancing beer crates on his head.

'Not bad for a seventy-two-year-old, eh, lad?'

'Not bad at all, Archie,' I said, desperately trying to hide the boredom in my voice.

'And to think, I wouldn't be here if it wasn't for you.'

A small part of me was proud I'd saved his life, but a large part wished I hadn't bothered.

'Now, I suppose you want to know the reason I've been calling you all these times?'

Not really, I thought.

'Yes please,' I said.

'I don't think I mentioned it before, but my son works for ITV.'

I had an image of Archie's son working behind the counter in the canteen.

'What does he do then, Archie?' I said, humouring him.

'I can't remember, but he's got some fancy title . . .'

Head of Washing Up? I thought.

'Controller of Programmes or something.'

The Controller of Programmes at ITV Network Centre is Michael Rimmer, the straight-talking no-nonsense Yorkshireman who has revolutionized independent television.

'Michael Rimmer is your son?' I said, not quite believing what I was hearing.

'Aye, he's doing rather well for himself, isn't he?'

I saved Michael Rimmer's dad's life.

Michael Rimmer is the most important man in television.

'So how are you then, Archie, my old mate?' I said with sudden sincerity. 'How's everything since I saved your life? We really ought to speak more often, you know.'

'Aye, we will do, lad. But listen, it's because of Michael I'm calling. He came up here to visit me a couple o' weeks ago an' I reminded him of what you did for me. I said to 'im "You ought to gi' that young lad a show." He said, "I'll see what I can do, Dad." Anyway, he wants you to give him a call at his office first thing in the morning. That's what I've been trying to get in touch with you for.'

I couldn't quite believe this seventy-two-year-old record-breaking beer-crate balancer was the man who was giving my career the kiss of life.

'I really appreciate that, Archie.'

'Don't mention it, lad.'

There was a pause.

'Archie?'

'Yes, lad?'

'Do you want to come to my birthday party?'

He said he'd think about it.

3 OCT

Michael Rimmer *is* the ITV network. Television programmes don't get made without his say so. He has the power to make and break people's careers, so I couldn't believe I was going to speak to him personally.

I didn't want to appear too keen, so I left it until five past nine to call. The automated machine told me the offices didn't open until nine thirty. I called back at nine thirty-one and got through to Rimmer's secretary. She explained that Michael – surely she should call him 'Mr Rimmer' – was in a meeting.

'What time will he be out of this meeting?' I said, trying to sound like the sort of person who calls the likes of Michael Rimmer every day.

'About ten thirty,' said the secretary.

'I'll call back later.'

At ten thirty-one, I dialled the number again. The secretary informed me he was still in a meeting. I think she recognized my voice from the earlier call because she asked me if I wanted to leave a message.

'It's all right, I'll call back later.'

At five past eleven I called again, then again at twenty past eleven and again at quarter to twelve. Each time I spoke to the same secretary and each time she told me he was in a meeting. Finally she told me he was unlikely to be free until one o'clock. When I called back at five past one she told me he was at lunch.

Then she asked me the dreaded question.

'Who's calling please?'

I felt trapped.

If you leave your name and number, you put the onus on the other person to call you back. If they don't return your call within a couple of hours, paranoia sets in and you wonder how long you can leave it before you call them again. Giving her my name was only one step away from her telling me she'd pass on my message and ask him to call me back.

'My name's Simon Peters,' I said.

'I'll pass on your message and ask him to call you back.'

'I saved his dad's life,' I shouted quickly just so she wouldn't think I was mad.

'I'll pass on your message and ask him to call you back.'

That was three hours ago and so far he hasn't called.

5.32 p.m.
I've just called again to check I'd given her the right number. I had. When I asked if he was available, she said he was in a meeting, but assured me she'd passed on my message.

10.47 p.m.
I don't think he's going to call back.

4 OCT

No call from Michael. I feel like a spurned lover.

5 OCT

I have to say that I'm very disappointed that Michael Rimmer values the life of his father so cheaply. Not even a courtesy call to say thank you. I'm thinking of taking a stance and never working for ITV again.

2.16 p.m.
Called the operator to check the line is working properly.

3.42 p.m.
I keep calling 1471, just to make sure I haven't missed the call.

4.27 p.m.
Called the operator to check my 1471 is working properly.

4.46 p.m.
I think I'm suffering from a rare form of tinnitus where I keep thinking I can hear the phone ringing.

5.15 p.m.
The phone really did ring and I snatched up the receiver. This is it, I thought. This is where I find out my destiny.

It was Scary Babs. *Going-Gone TV* need an answer by tomorrow.

6 OCT

It's night-time. I'm climbing Mount Everest and I've nearly reached the peak. Archie Rimmer is at the top with twenty-two beer crates balanced on his head and he's lowering a telephone towards me. I stretch out my hand but can't quite reach it.

The phone starts to ring.

My fingertips creep nearer but the closer I am to it, the further away it seems. *Ring Ring*. I glance up at Archie, and from out of the darkness behind him I see the un-mistakable orange glow of Tony Dobson's perma-tan. He's smiling at me menacingly and seems to be willing me to fall. In an unbelievable act of bravery, Archie throws his beer crates at him, but Dobson pulls out a knife. ***Ring Ring***. I know I have to answer the phone, but suddenly I feel a vice-like grip around my ankles. I glance down and Dobson is hanging on to my legs and violently trying to pull me off (off the rock face, that is). ***Ring Ring***. Using all my strength, I kick him off and make a gigantic leap for the phone. I grab the receiver but still it continues to ring. ***Ring Ring***. I'm dangling in mid-air and I can feel the phone slipping through my fingers. I look up, only to see Dobson at the peak laughing manically. ***Ring Ring***. I see the moonlight bounce off his knife as he slices through the telephone wire. ***Ring Ring***. I start to fall. ***Ring Ring***.

I woke up in a cold sweat and the phone next to my bed was ringing. I picked up the receiver and glanced at the LCD on my alarm clock. It read 6.58 a.m. I'm grumpy most mornings, but to be woken up at six fifty-eight didn't put me in the best of moods.

'Hello?' I said sharply.

'Hello, lad,' said the gruff Yorkshire voice at the other end of the line.

What on earth was Archie doing calling me at that time of the morning?

'Bloody hell,' I said, wanting him to know I wasn't happy about this. 'It's a bit early, isn't it?'

'It's Rimmer here.'

'Yes, I know,' I said impatiently. 'Whatever it is, can't it wait?'

I added the words *'you old git'* under my breath, knowing full well that his hearing wasn't what it used to be.

'It's Michael Rimmer.'

'Oh God.'

'Close, but not quite. I'll be quick 'cos it's early and I've got a game of golf to get to. Listen, I've just commissioned a new show called *Slebs*, a live Friday-night prime-time show – showbiz gossip, celebrity lifestyles, you know the sort of thing. I've told Cat's Eyes, the production company making it, that I want you to be one of the presenters, doing the sort o' stuff you did on *Coffee Morning*. What do you think?'

'Oh my God.'

'I'll have a word with your agent,' he said. 'By the way, lad, just in case I don't get time to say it again, thank you for what you did for my father . . . the old git.'

He laughed, so I laughed too. In our shared moment of hilarity, I seized my opportunity.

'Would you like to come to my birthday party?'

'No.'

I suppose when you get to his position there isn't a lot of time for socializing. We said goodbye and it slowly dawned on me that I wasn't going to have to work on *Going-Gone TV*. I lay back on the bed and wrapped myself in a blanket of total euphoria.

Michael Rimmer had said the magic words, '*PRIME TIME.*'

7 OCT

'I've got you a job,' said Max.

I'd been expecting this call.

'*You've* got me a job?' I said.

'Yes, I've been working really hard on this one for months, putting a lot of hours in.'

'Really?' I said.

'Yes, I even called Michael Rimmer himself about you.'

'*You* called *him*?'

Maybe it's impossible for an agent to tell the truth.

207

Maybe the very nature of their work means they can't be honest. The trouble is, even though I knew I'd got the job myself and that Max was lying through his teeth, I ended up believing him. Max told me all about *Slebs* and said the show would go out live at 8 p.m. on ITV1 every Friday night for six weeks.

'I can't believe they're letting me be the main host,' I said enthusiastically.

'They're not,' said Max, bursting that bubble immediately. 'Claudia Mix is.'

Claudia Mix is sexy and sassy, streetwise and hip. She's the sort of girl who could be on the front cover of *Loaded* magazine, but you still wouldn't mind introducing her to your mother. She's a darling of the tabloids, respected by the broadsheets and adored by the public. Men fancy her and women want to be her. In the world of television, she's red hot and had been the face of Channel Four for over two years. She started off presenting her own mid-afternoon chat show *Claudia*, and went on to play the lead role in the popular late-night sit-com *Mix It*.

Max said that ITV had stolen Claudia from Channel Four and signed her to a multi-million-pound golden-handcuff deal. I could tell this made Max feel slightly bitter. A couple of years ago he used to represent her, but 'let her go' because he didn't think she had a future. That was about a month before she landed the *Claudia* show.

Max told me I was going to be one of two co-hosts and my job would be to report live from the set of a different TV show every week. I'll be getting a thousand pounds a show, and while that might not be the big money Claudia will be earning, it's more money than I've ever earned before, and it'll certainly pay the rent for a few months. I told Max about my thirtieth birthday party and he said he was busy on that date.

Strange, because I didn't actually tell him which date it was.

9 OCT

Everything's happening so quickly and I suddenly seem to be playing in a different league.

Tomorrow I've got a meeting with Lizzi Rees-Morgan, the producer of *Slebs*. She's something of an eccentric in the television industry, famous for her warped sense of humour and the fact that she doesn't suffer fools gladly. She is undoubtedly one of the best in the business, having devised and produced the controversial *Stalkers Inc.*, where ten contestants had to stalk ten different celebrities for ten weeks without being detected. The show was a massive ratings winner and the format sold all over the world, making her a multi-millionaire. While *Stalkers Inc.* was universally condemned for the subject matter, it won critical acclaim for the look of the show and the way it was shot. Rees-Morgan is famous for her mottos, '*It doesn't matter what the show is as long as it looks good*', and '*Style, style, style. If you've got that you can get away with murder*', or attempted murder in the case of one of the contestants on *Stalkers Inc.*

I have to admit, I'm a bit nervous about meeting her. She only produces big shows and Claudia Mix only presents cool shows, so the fact that they're working on this show together means *Slebs* will be big and cool.

I can't help thinking I'm a little out of my depth.

10 OCT

Because I know Lizzi Rees-Morgan is such a style guru, I made a real effort with my clothes. I wore my turquoise and cerise Hawaiian shirt (with parrot motif), my two-tone purple slacks and my brand-new lime-green Converse baseball boots. To my face I applied just a hint of Boots No. 7 beige tinted moisturiser.

I felt pretty good.

I arrived at the office in Beak Street and at first I thought I had the wrong address. It was a big empty room with a few wooden crates scattered across the floor. Eventually the secretary emerged through a side door and explained that Lizzi was running late.

'Take a seat,' she said.

'I think somebody already has,' I said, but my joke fell flat.

The secretary explained that the decor was the latest in Nepalese minimalist art. Apparently it was v. chic and v. expensive. I sat on one of the crates and waited. After thirty-five minutes Lizzi Rees-Morgan swept into the office. She was dressed from head to toe in black. She wore black sunglasses, black nail varnish, black lipstick and she was holding a long black cigarette holder. She had a very powerful presence, which I found intimidating but at the same time strangely alluring. At first, she totally ignored me and just read through some papers on the secretary's desk. After a couple of minutes, she turned dramatically and shook my hand firmly.

'Welcome to the show,' she said, sounding as if she didn't really mean it.

I immediately tried to win her over and gave her my best Simon Peters Showbiz Smile®.

'Thank you very much, I'm really looking forward—'

'Come into my office,' she snapped.

Maybe it was the old paranoia setting in, but I couldn't help thinking she'd taken an instant dislike to me. I followed her into her office, which once again had several crates and packing cases strewn across the floor. She pointed at what looked like a tea chest and indicated I should sit on it.

'I'm going to be honest, because that's what I always am.'

'Shoot,' I said, imagining that was the sort of expression she used all the time.

She looked me straight in the eye.

'I didn't want you for this job.'

'Right,' I said, the Simon Peters Showbiz Smile® starting to wilt at the edges.

'Personally I think you're cheesy and belong on *Challenge TV*.'

Her words pierced the thin layer of armour that protected my already fragile ego.

'I wanted to use Pedro, the guy who won *Stalkers*,' she continued. 'I'm sure you've seen him in the papers, Spanish-looking ex-model, very sexy, very 'now'. Ironically enough, he's got a stalker of his own these days. Anyway, I digress. The Network Centre has insisted I use you; it seems Michael Rimmer is a very big fan of yours.'

'Yes, apparently he loved my work on *Simon Says*,' I said, lying through my teeth and finding it difficult to disguise the emotional quiver in my voice.

She seemed to be able to see through my gossamer-like veneer. The silence was heavy in the air. I wasn't sure I was going to be able to work with this for two months. Surely she couldn't get away with talking to people like this. I swallowed hard and tried to blink away the tears of humiliation.

Suddenly she started to laugh hysterically.

'You stupid bugger,' she said. 'I'm winding you up. Your agent said you'd be easy to get. God, I wished we'd filmed that.'

While I sat there, drowning in a sea of degradation, she took out a Dictaphone and spoke into it

'Idea for a new hidden-camera show . . . we wind up celebrities . . . the public vote on who they think will be the first to cry . . . it could be called *Star Tears* or *Celebrity Cry Babies* . . . Ant and Dec to host . . .'

She switched the machine off.

'I'm sorry, Simon, you're going to have to get used to my sense of humour.'

'What's *Slebs* going to be like, then?' I said, changing the subject and finally managing to compose myself.

'Fucking great,' she said, growling the 'r' and sounding like Tony the Tiger from the Frosties adverts. Suddenly she was a totally different person, animated and passionate. 'Think of it as *OK* magazine for the MTV generation. Lots of fast cuts, flash frames, slow mo, strobe lights, digital effects and back-projection animation. It's never been done on a live prime-time show before – thirty different cameras using different film stock: digi-beta, VHS, Hi8, black and white etc., plus 8mm and 16mm inserts. You name it, we'll use it. Claudia's going to be in the studio, you're going to be on location and the other presenter will be interviewing all the Hollywood stars.'

'Who's the other presenter?' I said.

'Pippa,' said Lizzi, not really appreciating the effect the name would have on me. I was shocked. I haven't seen Pippa since the little accident in the club back in May. It's strange to think she's famous now. Lots of appearances on the right TV shows, lots of articles in the right magazines, lots of partying with the right people. Max had certainly managed to fulfil his promise. Like Davina, Brucie and Dale, she was famous enough to be known by just the one name. I don't think that will ever happen to me, Simon just isn't a sexy name, and besides, people might think you mean Cowell or Mayo. Or worse still Bates.

Lizzi told me there was a launch party for the show on

1 November and the first transmission was the following Friday.

'Now, have you got any skeletons in your cupboard?'

'What do you mean?' I asked innocently.

'Anything the press can get hold of and use against you, because, believe me, once this show starts transmitting, they'll start digging for stories.'

I nearly told her about Mimi Lawson, the baby, the journalist who knew too much, my obsession with Pippa, the lap-dancing club I went to in 1996 and the fact that I'd only got this job because I'd saved the life of the Controller of Television's father.

'Nothing I can think of.'

'Good,' she said. 'We can do without any negative press.'

She looked me up and down and shook her head.

'We're going to have to sort out your fucking image,' she said.

I laughed out loud, thinking this was another example of the famous Rees-Morgan sense of humour. I looked up but she wasn't laughing, she wasn't even smiling.

'You look like you've been trapped in Timmy Mallet's wardrobe since 1984. I'll get our top stylist to sort you out. This is the big time, Simon, we can't have you looking like a sack of shit.'

The fact that she said I looked like a 'sack of shit' didn't really register. The fact that she said, 'This is the big time' did.

12 OCT

Lizzi Rees-Morgan made me an appointment at LaForret's hairdressing salon in Soho, and Daniel LaForret himself cut my hair. He chopped into it with two pairs of scissors at the same time and then gave it the famous LaForret 'Hint of

Tint'. When he'd finished, it looked absolutely brilliant. I know for a fact that it cost £450 – Donna at 'Hairs and Graces' usually only charges me a fiver – but Lizzi said it was all in the budget as long as he got rid of my 'fucking mullet'.

13 OCT

Lizzi sent me to Mirage beauty salon, where I had my eyelashes and eyebrows tinted. I had a manicure, pedicure, sauna, jacuzzi, facial, aromatherapy massage and deep-cleansing seaweed wrap. I was waxed, plucked, pummelled, buffed, kneaded, slapped and pinched.

I've made another appointment for the same time next week.

14 OCT

Today it was the The Bronze Goddess tanning salon, where I had a Cote D'Azure all-over tan applied. I had to strip down to my pants – I wish I'd worn my best ones – and two young girls in white uniforms covered me in a warm, sticky brown liquid. I'm sure it would be illegal in some countries and I've seen photos of a similar sort of thing on the Internet.

It doesn't smell as good as Mr Bronzer's Self-Tanning Lotion, but it's certainly a lot more fun having it applied.

15 OCT

The bill for my clothes came to £6,365.81, which is more than I'm getting paid for presenting the show. I'd told the stylist I believed presenter's personalities should be reflected in the clothes they wear on screen and that the public like to see their stars wearing bright colours. I told her I used to admire Noel Edmonds; he really made that patterned-sweater look his own, and what he did for the knitwear industry has never been fully recognized. I told the stylist I saw myself in vivid-sports-casual, but I don't think she was listening because this is what I ended up with:

Two Prada suits (both black)

Two Ozwald Boateng suits (both grey)

Two Dolce & Gabbana shirts (one black, one grey)

Two Gucci shirts (one black, one slate grey)

Two Alexandre shirts (one black, one gunmetal grey)

One Jean Paul Gaultier shirt (bright pink and yellow with a picture of Jesus smoking a joint and playing a Fender Stratocaster guitar.)

I chose that last one.

I took the clothes home and tried them on again. One of the Ozwald Boateng suits had a shiny red lining. I've always wanted a suit with shiny red lining and I keep casually pulling the jacket open and catching a glimpse of red. I can't stop looking at myself in the mirror (even more than usual). With the suit, the lining, the hairstyle and the tan, I look different.

I look sharp.

I look cool.

I look like a star.

6.42 p.m.

I've just built a bonfire in the garden and burned all my Hawaiian shirts. I can't believe I used to wear that stuff.

19 OCT

It's suddenly hit me what a big show *Slebs* is going to be. It doesn't start airing for another two and a half weeks, but the ITV network have already started running trailers for it on heavy rotation.

The promo looks like a movie trailer. In grainy black and white, it shows a montage of famous celebrities who have passed away over the last five years.

In a deep guttural American accent, the voice-over said '*Slebs*. The show the celebrities are dying to be on.'

Personally I thought it was in slightly bad taste, but at least the network seems to be getting behind it.

Shame they didn't mention me.

24 OCT

'Congratulations on your new job.'

It was David Mulryan. The cameraman was over his left shoulder and once again they followed me to my car.

'*Slebs* is going to be quite high profile,' said Mulryan, sounding pompous and superior. 'You're going to have to get used to questions about your private life.'

'I don't have a private life. There's always some idiot following me around with a camera.'

I thought that was really cool and made me sound like a Hollywood film star who's always being hassled by the press.

'Just answer me one question,' he said.

This is it, I thought, this is where he accuses me of being the father of Mimi's baby and then shows me the evidence to prove it: CCTV footage of us entering the Travel Lodge, a taped interview with the night porter, receipts for the minibar, DNA samples taken from the sheets.

Was this the end of my career? I had an image of Lizzi firing me from *Slebs* before I'd even started. I would never work again and would always be known as the 'nearly' man.

I noticed the cameraman zooming in for a close-up on my face. I knew I had to remain calm.

'Shoot,' I said. I quite like saying that at the moment. 'I've got nothing to hide.'

I turned my head slightly and made sure the camera was favouring my best side. I felt ready for anything he could throw at me. I knew that the trick was to deny, deny, deny.

'Did Vince Envy ever give you advice about having children?'

That wasn't quite the question I was expecting. Was he trying to trick me? Was it just a gentle jab before the killer punch? To honour the memory of Vince I felt compelled to tell the truth.

'Yes,' I said. 'He said to me if there is one piece of advice I can give you, it's to *have children.*'

'Thank you, Simon,' said Mulryan with a self-satisfied smile on his face. 'Good luck with the new show. We'll see you at the press launch.'

The cameraman switched off his camera and they both turned round and headed for their car.

Was that it? Where was the big confrontation? Where was the 'J'accuse' and the 'I put it to you . . .'?

I stood there, stunned and unable to move. Mulryan drove past, pipped his hooter and gave me a smug little wave. I gave him the finger.

26 OCT

I saw another trailer for *Slebs*.

Once again it was in grainy black and white, and this time it showed a montage of fight scenes from different British soaps over the years. The same American voice-over said,

'Coming Soon . . . *Slebs*. The show celebrities are fighting to appear on.'

Still no mention of me.

27 OCT

I went to the *Slebs* office for a meeting and was introduced to the rest of the production team. I thought they'd be excited about meeting me, but to be honest they didn't seem overly impressed. We were all sitting around drinking coffee when Claudia Mix swept in, looking every inch the star. Suddenly there was a buzz in the room. Claudia oozed the kind of confidence that you can only get from a public school education, but she played it down with a cool self-effacing charm. It was the first time I'd met her in person and she was exactly what I'd expected her to be: charming, witty, sexy, funny and stunningly attractive. She seemed to have this aura around her. If there's such a thing as 'X' factor, Claudia definitely has it, and sitting next to her made me realize for the first time that maybe I don't.

She introduced herself to me.

'Simon Peters,' she screamed enthusiastically. 'Oh God, I used to love *Simon Says*.'

This is something I've noticed about really famous people. To put you at ease in their presence they'll say something complimentary about you, something you wouldn't expect them to know. It's their way of saying, 'Hey, I'm just a normal person.' I knew Claudia was employing this tactic, but I didn't care, she was gorgeous and I was totally smitten. The only other person I've ever met who's had the same effect on me is Pippa. Pippa wasn't at the meeting because she was in a jacuzzi with Russell Crowe. She was only filming an interview with him, but I couldn't help feeling a twinge of jealousy.

218

Lizzi Rees-Morgan stood up and told us the Network Centre had received 547 complaints about the 'dead celebrity' trailers for *Slebs*. She told us this was a record number of complaints for a programme that hadn't even been broadcast, and every newspaper in the country had commented on it. I started to worry that maybe the Network Centre would try to pull us, but Lizzi said the advertising space during the show was being sold at a premium rate and Network Centre were 'over the moon'.

She told us all about the first show and it sounded very exciting. Claudia was going to be interviewing Teri and Chantelle from The Foxy Girls live in the studio. This was quite a coup. Teri and Chantelle are big stars with big egos and it's a well-known fact that they haven't spoken to each other since July, when The Foxy Girls split up amid rumours of catfights, backstabbing and all-round general bitchiness.

'Why don't we do the interview in a boxing ring?' said Claudia and everyone laughed.

Why can't I come up with ideas like that? I felt I was making no impact on the production meeting whatso-ever.

'That's a fucking great idea, Clauds,' said Lizzi. 'Teri can be in one corner, Chantelle in the other. Clauds, you act as the referee in the middle. Derek, we need a boxing ring.'

Derek the production designer nodded his head and was already doodling designs for a boxing ring on his A4 sketchpad.

'Emily dah-ling, we want a sexy male model to walk around the ring holding up cards with numbers on them.'

Emily, a pretty young junior researcher immediately picked up the phone and started dialling the number of a modelling agency.

'Tell the agency I want a Spaniard with a great arse,' said

Lizzi and a few members of the production team started to snigger.

'Tell them to make mine an Italian,' said Claudia and everyone was suddenly helpless with hysterical laughter.

This was my opportunity to make an impression. Riding the wave of hilarity I timed my line beautifully.

'I'll have a Chinese if there's one going,' I said. 'No prawn crackers with mine.'

Vurrrrrrrpppppppp.

The classic comedy sound effect of a needle being removed from a record. Everyone in the office stopped laughing and stared at me. The silence was deafening. All that was missing was the tumbleweed and howling wind. My joke hadn't just died a death; it had been murdered, cut up into tiny little pieces and dissolved in a bath full of acid. I knew I was blushing and I could feel the beads of sweat trickling down the back of my neck.

'I thought that was a great joke,' said Claudia, riding to my rescue like a damsel in shining armour. Everybody looked at her.

'It wasn't funny in the conventional sense,' she continued as everyone started to giggle, 'but it was still a great joke. An unfunny great joke – Ben Elton does them all the time.'

This got a big laugh. Claudia leant over and gave me a hug and I knew I was off the hook.

'The only thing we haven't got yet is a story for Simon,' said Lizzi, getting the meeting back on track.

Tamsin, one of the associate producers, put her hand up. Lizzi pointed at her.

'What have you got, Tams?'

'We've asked Mimi Lawson for an exclusive interview,' she said.

I suddenly felt very faint.

'I thought we could do some sort of sketch where Mimi's giving birth and Simon's pretending he's the father of her baby.'

The room started to spin and the inside of my mouth turned to sand.

'That's a fucking great idea, Tams,' said Lizzi.

I grabbed hold of the table and began hyperventilating.

'Unfortunately, she turned us down.'

I breathed a huge sigh of relief.

'She's not doing any more interviews until after the baby's born.'

'When's she due, Tams?' asked Lizzi nonchalantly.

'Any time during the next week or so.'

The news exploded in my head and I started to hyper-ventilate again. I hadn't realized she'd be giving birth quite so soon. Of course I realized it would be about nine months after the dirty deed, but I hadn't realized the nine months had gone by so quickly.

'That's what we've got to work on, then,' said Lizzi. 'Ideas for Simon. Are you OK, Simon? You look a little shaken.'

'I'm fine,' I said.

At that moment I wished I could have come up with a brilliant suggestion like Claudia's boxing idea.

'*Fucking brilliant idea, Simes,*' Lizzi would say. '*Let's run it up the flagpole and see who salutes it.*'

But of course I didn't come up with an idea. I didn't say anything. Instead I went home and felt more than ever that I was in at the deep end without my inflatable armbands.

29 OCT

Panic attacks.

Since the production meeting, I've had what feels like a

221

great big knotted ball in the pit of my stomach and I haven't been able to eat anything at all. I called Charley and she said it was nerves, but I think it's more than that. I think that as well as the worry over Mimi and the imminent birth, career wise, I have a genuine fear of failure. In the past I've always had the excuse that the powers that be have never given me a shot at 'The Big Time'. Now they're giving me the chance, what if I'm not cool enough? What if I'm not smart enough? What if I'm just not good enough? What if the entire nation sees what Tarquin saw at the audition for that science programme? That I'm a fake and a fraud and just some ordinary guy who got lucky.

2.16 a.m.
I put the Ozwald Boateng suit on and just spent two hours looking at myself in the mirror. I might be some ordinary guy who got lucky, but boy I look sexy with red lining.

30 OCT

My birthday is just thirty-six days away and so far only two people have said they're coming to my party. One of them is Charley, who doesn't really count because she has to come, the other is Archie Rimmer. Archie Rimmer is seventy-two years old and probably wears incontinence pants. What a swinging party that's going to be. The Red Lion will never have seen anything like it.

Actually it probably has.

3.02 a.m.
Why did I invite Archie Rimmer?

3.56 a.m.
I really want to invite my dad.

1 NOV

I have a sense of nervousness the whole time and still seem unable to eat anything. Tonight is the big launch party for *Slebs*. Lizzi Rees-Morgan has hired the Velvet nightclub in Leicester Square and invited journalists and photographers from every newspaper and magazine in the country. She also sent invites to over 150 A-list celebrities, and most of them have said they'll be there. The idea is for Claudia, Pippa and me to mix 'n' mingle with everyone and 'press the flesh' as much as we can.

'I want your photograph in every paper and your name mentioned in every gossip column,' she told me. She also told me to wear one of the new suits the stylist had bought for me, not one of the 'disasters' I usually walk around in. I told her I'd burned all my old shirts and she said, 'The fashion police will be pleased.'

The party will be the first time I've seen Pippa in four months. The last time we met I nearly broke her nose, so I'm not entirely sure how she'll react.

I must remember tonight's party is work and that I'm not just going there to enjoy myself. I have to be professional. I have to be focused, mentally alert and aware that the press will be watching every move I make.

2 NOV

Before I was even fully awake I knew I was suffering from a hangover. There was a dull aching pain inside my head, as if someone were tweaking my brain with an industrial-sized pair of tweezers. As I fought my way towards consciousness, I had a sense things weren't quite as they should be. I slowly opened my eyes and looked around the room. The four-poster bed, the big soft pillows, the creamy-white linen sheets. I stared at these things for a full thirty seconds before it dawned on me that I didn't actually own a four-poster bed, big soft pillows and creamy-white linen sheets.

Panic set in.

I turned to the right and saw the face of a sleeping woman. She looked familiar, but I couldn't quite place where I knew her from.

Who was she? And what was I doing in her bed?

Memories of last night's party started to crawl across my mind: the press, the photographers, the celebrities, the champagne . . .

I think the launch will be considered a great success, but I don't remember too much of it. I hadn't eaten all day and the free glasses of bubbly went straight to my head. The club was wall-to-wall celebrity, and everywhere you turned there was a recognizable face. There were so many stars there, none of the journalists paid any attention to me. I tried to do some networking, but no-one seemed interested, so I just drank more champagne.

I only saw Pippa once and that was at the official photocall at midnight. She looked even more beautiful than I remembered and I couldn't stop looking at her. Once again she'd had a complete change of image. She was tanned and wearing an all-in-one white leather catsuit, and her hair was straight and jet black, which served to accentuate her deep blue eyes. She was pleasant towards me, but that was about it; a casual onlooker wouldn't have been able to guess we'd worked together before. Pippa and Claudia hardly spoke to each other and I detected a real tension between them, but they did what was required and smiled together for the photographs. The paparazzi only seemed to want shots of Claudia and Pippa. They started off by taking photographs of all three of us, but pretty soon they were shouting at me to *'just step to your left there, mate'*, which translated as *'just move out the way'*. Standing there next to the two of them I felt ugly and uncool. I'd tried to make up for it by flashing a bit of red lining, but even that didn't work.

I was determined not to get depressed about it and went to the bar and drank more champagne. I'm not sure how much I drank, but I do remember having a bizarre conversation with Christopher Biggins about Joan Collins's film career. I said *The Bitch* and *The Stud* were her best work, but he was insistent *Annie II* was her finest hour.

That's where the rest of the evening becomes a bit of a blur and I could only recall snapshot images: champagne, beer, wine, tequila, dancing, flirting, stumbling, taxi, large Georgian house, four-poster bed, leather straps, chains, handcuffs, whips . . .

The sleeping woman opened her eyes and stared deep into mine.

'If you breathe a word of this to anyone, dah-ling, I'll cut your fucking balls off.'

It was Lizzi Rees-Morgan.

She didn't even offer me breakfast.

3 NOV

Why do I get myself in these situations? Why am I only attractive and *attracted* to older women? And why does it only happen when I'm blind drunk? What makes it worse is that I'm scared of Lizzi. Really scared. She's powerful and domineering and I have terrible images of her turning me into her sex slave. She'll dress me up in a rubber suit, put me on a lead and make me parade around on all fours with an orange in my mouth.

I don't like oranges and rubber brings me out in a rash.

I think the best thing to do is wait and see how she plays it and we'll take it from there.

4 NOV

For the last three days I've bought every single tabloid newspaper and celebrity magazine there is. *Slebs* has been getting lots of press but it's all '*Claudia's New Show*' and '*Pippa's Big Break*'. There hasn't been one single mention of me being at the party. Not one photograph. Not one interview. Not one single column inch in one single publication. What does one have to do to get some coverage? I'm seriously considering telling David Mulryan the truth about Mimi and me.

2.24 a.m.
I wonder if Mimi's had the baby yet?

5 NOV

I know I'm a bit of a worrier and a glass-is-half-empty kind of guy, but *Slebs* will be broadcasting live to the nation in two days' time and so far nobody has told me where I'm going or what I'm doing.

I would call the office, but I'm scared of talking to Lizzi.

6 NOV

'Dah-ling, we've found you a story.'

It was Lizzi.

'Brilliant,' I said.

I didn't want to give too much away and waited to see if she'd say anything.

226

'You're going to be broadcasting live from the set of a new game show the BBC are making.'

Her tone was cool, direct and to the point.

'Excellent,' I said, swallowing hard.

The image of her in a basque and thigh-high boots filled my mind.

'You'll be making television history; this will be the first time a live ITV show has broadcast from the set of a Beeb show.'

She was being very professional about this.

'Great.'

All I could think of was whips and chains, manacles and handcuffs.

'Tams has come up with an idea where you pretend to be a game-show host and you ask the real host questions about the show. It sounds like your sort of thing, doesn't it?'

She was speaking as if our night of passion had never even happened.

'It's very much my thing,' I said.

If that's the way she wanted to play it, fine by me.

I started to focus on what she was saying and it really did sound like a good idea. Maybe I'd get the chance to show the nation, and more importantly the TV execs, my skills as a game-show host.

'What's the show?' I asked casually.

'It's called *Swizz Quiz*, hosted by Ricardo Mancini.'

I felt physically ill.

'Tams is faxing over some info on Mancini and the show. You have to be at the Beeb at three for rehearsals. We're live on air at eight.'

That's all she said. No '*thanks for a great night*', or, '*Let's do it again sometime*', or '*You're the best, big boy*'.

She just hung up.

227

I'm not sure whether I'm more upset about that or the fact that my first interview on prime-time television is with the man I despise the most.

7 NOV

6.45 a.m.
I couldn't sleep at all. Today's the day I find out if I'm good enough to play in the premier league.

8.30 a.m.
The post has just arrived and there was a good-luck card from Charley; she's brilliant at things like that. The card was in the shape of a large gold star and inside Charley had written:

> *This is for you because you are one!*
> *Good luck tonight.*
> *Love, Charley XX*
> *PS Have you considered punching Manky live on air? That would make great television!*
> *PPS I'm joking, of course.*

6 p.m.
I'm in a dressing room at the BBC and we're live on air in two hours.

Swizz Quiz is being shot in Studio One, the Beeb's biggest studio. The set is very impressive, all plush red velvet and chrome, and much larger than the one we used for the pilot. The Beeb have invested a lot of money in *Swizz Quiz* and it's obvious they think it's going to be a hit show.

I can't help thinking it should be *my* hit show.

So far I haven't had a chance to speak to Manky Mancini,

as he was 'in make-up' the whole time we were rehearsing. I'm slightly worried I won't be able to disguise my contempt for him once we start broadcasting.

I have to put all of these negative feelings to the back of my mind. This is still a big break for me.

7.45 p.m.
Fifteen minutes to go. I have to remain professional, focused and sharp.

7.47 p.m.
Charley has just texted me a message:

> **JUST ON NEWS. MIMI L. BABY GIRL. NAME JESSICA. EVERYTHING FINE.**

Oh my God.

10.03 p.m.
In the words of W.H. Auden 'Stop all the clocks, cut off the telephone.'

My career officially died at eight twenty-two this evening. Few will mourn its passing, but the ten million people who witnessed its demise will agree that it was shot down in quite spectacular fashion . . .

I watched the beginning of *Slebs* in the scanner (a large mobile gallery where the director and vision mixer sit during outside broadcasts. It's usually in a car park and today was no exception). Claudia seemed to be on sparkling form and the interview with The Foxy Girls in the boxing ring was getting a huge response from the studio audience. It all seemed to be going very well, although I was finding it difficult to concentrate.

'Coming to you on location in ten minutes,' said the PA back in the main studio.

'Good luck,' whispered Peter the director, looking over his shoulder at me.

'Cheers,' I said vacantly.

'Remember there are twelve million people watching this.'

He gave me a big thumbs up. I genuinely believe he was trying to make me feel better.

I exited the scanner and walked the short distance to Studio One. Outside, I paused and took a deep breath to steady my nerves. I then swung open the big heavy doors and walked across the studio floor. The audience were just taking their seats and the knot in my stomach tightened its vice-like grip.

Suddenly there was a hive of activity around me.

A make-up girl applied powder to my face, a wardrobe assistant brushed non-existent fluff from my suit and a stressed-out floor manager (floor managers are always stressed out) reminded me of my start position.

Despite being in a state of shock about Mimi, I loved all the attention I was getting. The only thing that upset me slightly was when I looked over and saw Manky Mancini surrounded by even more people than I was.

God, I hated him.

He was wearing a purple velvet suit, had a deep tan and looked a complete poseur. He spotted me, waved as if he were royalty and flashed me a great big cheesy smile (I'm sure he's had his teeth done). I gave the slightest nod of recognition in his direction. He was obviously expecting me to go over and go through my questions with him, but I decided to make him suffer. There was still a good five minutes before we were live on air and I planned to casually saunter over to him with about a minute to go.

A sound man with particularly bad breath fixed a small microphone to my lapel and then handed me my earpiece.

'Hey, man,' he said. 'Do you want your talkback open or switched?'

He sounded like a hippy from the 1970s. He smelt like one too.

'Open,' I said nonchalantly.

I actually wanted it switched but open is definitely the more professional answer.

'Cool,' said the Halitosis Hippy.

Having the talkback open meant I'd hear everything from the scanner as well as everything from the main gallery back at the *Slebs* studio. I slipped the small piece of moulded plastic into my ear. The Halitosis Hippy pressed a button on the receiver and I heard a high-pitched beep followed by the sound of Claudia introducing Pippa's jacuzzi interview with Russell Crowe. I could also hear the PA counting down to the VT, and in the background I could just pick out Lizzi telling everyone they were *'fucking marvellous, dah-lings'*.

There was something very comforting and reassuring about having these noises transmitted straight into my ear. It made me realize I wasn't alone and reminded me there was a team of highly trained professionals supporting me.

Suddenly the voices stopped.

There was a crackle, a hiss and then silence.

I looked around for the Halitosis Hippy but he was nowhere to be seen. I looked towards the stressed-out-floor-manager, but he was deep in conversation with Manky Mancini.

I gently tapped the receiver.

Nothing.

I tapped it again slightly harder.

Still nothing.

231

I gave it a great big whack and this time there was a deafening burst of static and the voices returned.

I breathed a sigh of relief but immediately realized all was not as it should be. I could hear panic in the gallery. From what I could make out something had gone wrong with Pippa's VT and they'd had to return to the studio. I could just make out the sound of Lizzi telling everyone they were fired when the sound went dead again. I tapped the receiver and it seemed to do the trick, but the signal kept breaking up and I could only hear every other word.

The PA in the studio was obviously trying to get my attention.

'*Coming to y—Simon—location—in—econds*'

'How many seconds?' I said, desperately wiggling the wire that connected the earpiece to the receiver.

'*Five—fo—thr—*'

I looked up to see the stressed-out-floor-manager sprinting across the studio towards me and frantically gesticulating towards a camera, which was quickly being aimed in my direction.

The only thing I could think of was that a fifth of the population had just watched the show go horribly wrong and now they would all see me rescue it.

Well, not me exactly. *The Other Me.*

'*—two—ne—and cue, Simon.*'

The red light flashed and *The Other Me* was on.

'Thank you very much, Claudia. We seem to be having a few technical difficulties up your end.'

The Other Me paused just long enough to let the studio audience know he expected a laugh on this double entendre. Right on cue, they roared their approval, as if it was the funniest thing they'd ever heard.

'Who wanted to see Russell Crowe in a jacuzzi anyway?

I'm here on the set of a brand-new BBC quiz show called *Swizz Quiz.*'

'*Very—ood—S mon—eep it goin—*'

It was Lizzi talking in my ear, sounding remarkably like comedian Norman Collier when he used to do his old broken-microphone routine.

The Other Me was feeling confident and, as rehearsed, I showed the viewer around the set, had a quick chat with a couple of the contestants and then walked over to where Mancini was standing pretending to go through his questions.

This was where I made the first mistake of the evening. I actually introduced Ricardo as Manky Mancini but it was one of those situations where the adrenalin was pumping and I didn't even realize I'd done it. Sub-consciously I probably did it on purpose, but when all this ends up in court, I will swear to God that I didn't.

The idea was for me to act as a game-show host and put Mancini on the spot by asking him questions about the show, his career and his personal life mixed in with general-knowledge questions (which he'd already been given the answers to).

Manky and I stood face to face on separate podiums. In true game-show style the lights were taken down, leaving us lit by two single spotlights. The tension was increased by the music, which was one long synthesized note played underneath the sound of a heartbeat that gradually quickened as the questions got harder.

I have to admit I took a sadistic pleasure in the power I was exerting over Manky and couldn't resist a little twist of the knife.

'Now ladies and gentleman,' said *The Other Me*, addressing the viewers at home. 'Ricardo has very kindly agreed to donate £1,000 of his own money to charity for every question he gets wrong or refuses to answer. Isn't that right, Ricardo?'

This, of course, came as a complete surprise to Manky, but he knew that we were broadcasting live.

'Yes . . . erm . . . that's right, Simon,' he said with a hint of uncertainty in his voice. The studio audience took their cue from the stressed-out-floor-manger and gave Manky a spontaneous round of applause. This obviously gave him some confidence and he acknowledged their applause with that self-assured grin of his.

At this point he obviously thought he was going to know all the answers.

'What's the capital of Peru?' asked *The Other Me*.

Manky looked shocked. He stared at me as if to say, 'That wasn't one of the questions in the script.'

'I'm going to have to hurry you, I'm afraid.'

Beeeeeepppp!

'There's the time-up buzzer. The answer to that is, of course, Lima. Ladies and gentlemen, that's one thousand pounds Ricardo has to donate to charity.'

Once again, the studio audience gave him a round of applause.

I couldn't help but smile and went on to ask him several other questions I knew he wouldn't know the answer to, including, 'Who won the FA Cup in 1952?', 'What is the dictionary definition of the word pemphigus?' and 'Who wrote the French classic *Les Fleurs du Mal*?'

Before long, Manky was £7,000 down and I was really starting to enjoy myself as a game-show host, a role I felt was rightly mine anyway.

Suddenly my earpiece burst into life and amongst all the static I could just about make out Lizzi saying, '*You're—oing a—great job—imon. Now ask—im some—ifficult qu—stions*'

'What is the cubic capacity of a proton when infused

with the polarity of a sub-atomic particle?' asked *The Other Me* as quick as a flash.

'*Not tha—sort of—uestion you—upid f—king—unt*,' screamed Lizzi in my ear. '*Ask—im—uestions abou—his—ersonal life.*'

I touched my earpiece with my finger and nodded my head to let her know I understood.

'Let's forget that one, shall we, and move on. Here's your next one and it's a personal question.'

'Ooooooohhhhh,' said the audience in true game-show style.

Manky looked worried. For the past two months, press speculation had been rife about Ricardo Mancini's sexuality. Some papers claimed his on/off relationship with Pippa was very much on again, while others claimed he was bisexual and dating an Argentinian waiter called Paulo.

'Have you got a girlfriend at the moment?' *The Other Me* asked pointedly.

Mancini hesitated and seemed uncertain.

'No . . .'

'A boyfriend then?'

This got a big laugh from the studio audience.

'Of course not, I'm straight.'

From out of the darkness I could hear a murmur of derision. This was great, even the studio audience were turning against him.

'I'm a red-blooded heterosexual male,' he shouted.

'Methinks the gentleman doth protest too much,' said *The Other Me* with a cheeky little wink to camera. This got another big laugh from the studio audience and I felt I was on a roll. Manky glared at me with hatred in his eyes, but he suddenly seemed to remember twelve million people would be watching this and took a deep breath and composed himself.

'I can prove I'm straight,' he said quietly.

'What are you going to do? *Not* sleep with me?'

Maybe I didn't time the line quite right because it didn't get a laugh from the audience at all. I think they were more interested in what Manky was going to say.

'I'm going to be a father,' he said calmly.

His words hung in the air and my first reaction was one of shock. I knew he'd been dating Pippa again. Did this mean she was pregnant and she'd never be mine? I felt the camera cut to me, but I couldn't think of anything to say. *The Other Me* had disappeared as quickly as he'd arrived and I was totally deflated.

'Congratulations,' I mumbled.

'Thanks.'

Then there was silence.

'*A—k him who th—kin mother is,*' screamed Lizzi into my ear.

I went onto autopilot.

'Who's the mother of your baby?'

Please don't let it be Pippa. Please don't let it be Pippa. Please don't let it be Pippa.

I was aware of the music and the sound of the heartbeat. I glanced at the monitor. The camera was tightening in on a close-up of Manky and you could clearly see the beads of sweat forming on his forehead. He was feeling the pressure.

'*Tell—im—e has to f—ing tell us,*' shrieked Lizzi.

'I must remind you that any question you refuse to answer is another £1,000 to charity. Ricardo, who is the mother of your baby?'

Please don't let it be Pippa. Please don't let it be Pippa. Please don't let it be Pippa.

'Mimi Lawson,' he said.

'What?' I shouted, echoing what was being shouted in every living room in the country.

'It's true,' he said. 'Mimi Lawson is carrying my child.'

There was a stunned silence from the studio audience.

'F—kin' ye—sssss!' screamed Lizzi.

Manky said '*is* carrying my child'. He obviously wasn't aware she'd already given birth.

'*You're* the father of Mimi Lawson's baby?' I asked slowly.

'Yes, and I'm ready to face up to my responsibilities.'

'*You're* the father of Mimi Lawson's baby?'

I repeated the question, still not quite believing he'd said it.

'Yes, Mimi and I met in panto, the panto you were in actually, Simon. We had a brief affair and this baby is a result of that affair. I'm the father.'

This was an obvious ploy by Manky to try to get some publicity and I wasn't going to let him get away with it. I suddenly felt very defensive about the baby.

'Oh no you're not,' I said dramatically.

'Oh yes I am.'

'Oh no you're not,'

'Oh yes I am.'

'"For f—cks sake—imon, this isn't a—uckin pant—m—me. If he wants to—ay he's the f—ther let—im say he's the f—kin father. Th—s is—ucking great—ele—vision.'

Great television.

An image of Charley's card and the words she'd written on it flashed into my mind.

'*Have you considered punching Manky live on air? That would make great television!*'

Something inside me snapped.

The years of pent-up anger and bitter jealousy I felt towards Mancini quickly bubbled to the surface. Acting purely on impulse, I let out a banshee wail and launched myself towards him in the style of a Hollywood stuntman. Unfortunately I misjudged the distance slightly, tripped up the step of the podium and landed in a crumpled heap on the floor. He was obviously surprised by the speed of my attack and, as he took a step backwards, I noticed he was caught slightly off balance. I grabbed him around his ankles and wrestled him to the floor. We rolled off the back of the podium, screaming, thumping, kicking and biting. It was at this point that we both realized we were no longer lit and the cameras couldn't actually see us. We released each other, clambered back onto the podium and, once we were back in shot, continued where we'd left off.

'You're not the father,' I shouted, holding him in a headlock and poking him in the eye.

'Yes I am,' he said, pulling my hair and managing to get a finger up each of my nostrils.

'You're not,' I shouted, glancing at the monitor and waiting for them to cut to a close-up of me.

Out of the corner of my eye, I noticed the red light on camera three. I managed to wrestle our bodies around to ensure it was capturing my best side.

'*You're* not the father of Mimi Lawson's baby,' I said, pausing for dramatic effect, 'BECAUSE I AM!'

If it had been an episode of *EastEnders* this is the point where the drums would have come in.

Dummm . . . Dummm . . . Dummm Dummm Du Du Dudummm

I knew straight away I'd made a mistake.

'*S—mon*,' screamed Lizzi in my ear. '*You'll never—uck—work in television again. Throw to a comme—cial break.*'

'We'll be right back after this break,' I said automatically.

The stressed-out floor manager tried to cue the audience to applaud, but they were too stunned to react. The lights came up and an eerie silence fell upon the studio. Manky and I stood up and started to dust ourselves down.

'You could have killed me,' he said through gritted teeth. 'My agent's going to sue you for this.'

The fact that Manky's agent is also my agent didn't stop me worrying. I certainly wouldn't put it past Max to try to sue me. Two members of the production team then helped Manky down from the podium. For what seemed an age I was left standing alone in the middle of the studio floor trying to come to terms with what I'd just said and done.

I didn't want to speak to anyone and left the studio with Lizzi's words ringing in my ears.

11.14 a.m.
I've just tried calling Mimi's mobile, but all I heard was the no-such-number tone.

2.18 a.m.
I'm the father of a baby girl whose mother doesn't want to know me. Someone else who claims to be the father of said baby girl is going to sue me for attacking him on a live television show, and as a result of said attack I will now lose my job as host of said live television show.

4.16 a.m.
I can feel the clouds of depression gathering on the horizon.

5.02 a.m.
I wonder if the *Going-Gone TV* job is still going?

8 NOV

I spent the whole day in bed and only got up once to get a

glass of water. When I did, I noticed the light on my answer machine was flashing. I looked at the LCD and it informed me I had nineteen messages.

I pressed the play button.

'Simon, it's Max—'

I quickly pressed the delete button.

For Max to call me Simon and not *schmuck* indicated it would have to be something serious. Manky was obviously going ahead with his plan to sue me.

The next message started to play.

'Simon, it's Lizzi, I didn't get chance to speak to you after the show, you seemed to disappear quite quickly—'

Once again I pressed the delete button. Maybe I'm in denial, but I didn't want to hear Lizzi firing me and repeating her threat that I'd never work in television again.

'It's David Mulryan from *The Sword of Truth*,' said the next message. 'I really think we ought to speak about what happened last night, I've got some really important news—'

Delete. Whatever he had to say, I didn't want to hear it.

'It's Max again—'

Delete.

'It's Lizzi—'

Delete.

'It's Max—'

Delete.

'Simon, it's Charley. I know you've probably spent the whole day in bed and you've just got up and realized you've got hundreds of messages and you're just deleting them without even listening to them but—'

Delete.

In all there were eight messages from Max, five from Lizzi, three from David Mulryan, two from Charley, and there was even one from Pippa. I deleted them all without listening to them and went straight back to bed.

4.26 a.m.
I wonder if Jessica looks like me.

9 NOV

The first thing I noticed was the ringing, then the banging and then the shouting. I realized somebody was pressing my doorbell and knocking on my window at the same time. My telephone started to ring and then my mobile too. I glanced at the clock by the side of my bed and saw it was three minutes past seven in the morning.

That's three minutes past seven on a *Sunday* morning.

Still half asleep, I got out of bed, crossed the room and looked out of my bedroom window. I couldn't quite understand why there were about fifty people standing in my front garden looking up at my flat. I quickly closed the curtains.

My mobile started to ring again and I could see that it was Charley.

'Charley, you won't believe this, there are loads of people outside my—'

'Press,' said Charley flatly.

'What?'

'They're the press outside your door.'

'But there are hundreds of them.'

I peeped through the curtains and this time I could see they looked like reporters and paparazzi. At the back of the throng I noticed David Mulryan and his cameraman. One of the paparazzi spotted me and immediately started snapping away. As soon as he did, a thousand flashbulbs exploded and my front garden lit up like a firework display.

'Why are they here?' I asked.

'Simon, have you seen the papers?'

'No, why?'

'Your fight with Manky is on the front page of every Sunday newspaper.'

'Do I look good in the photos?' I asked.

'I'm coming over, don't speak to anyone else, they may have bugged your phone.'

Twenty minutes later she arrived clutching a large bundle of newspapers. She marched straight through the mêlée, totally ignoring the barrage of questions being fired at her. I opened the front door to let her in.

'Have you spoken to Mimi yet?' shouted one of the journos.

I slammed the door shut.

'This is mad,' said Charley.

I made her a coffee and we looked through the newspapers. Charley hadn't been lying. I was on the front page of every single one (broadsheets as well as tabloids).

SLEBS STARS SCRAP OVER MIMI'S KID!

PUNCH-UP PETERS SAYS HE'S THE DADDY

TV'S SIMPLE SIMON SAYS 'I'M THE ONE'

'I MADE LOVE TO HER IN PANTO,' SAYS MANCINI . . . 'OH NO YOU DIDN'T,' SAYS PETERS

TV BRAWL GETS RECORD VIEWING FIGURES

Apparently eleven million people were watching when the fight started, but that rose to fifteen million people by the time it ended.

There were lots of photographs taken from the actual footage of the fight. One photograph showed me holding Manky in a headlock and another showed a big close-up of Manky's fingers shoved up my nostrils.

Reading through the papers, every journalist seemed to have something to say about it. Someone in the *Mail on Sunday* called for me to be arrested, whereas the TV critic in the *News of The World* called the fight '*The greatest comedy moment in television history.*' Every newspaper reported that Mimi and the baby were '*in hiding*' and some speculated she'd even left the country, although Charley thought this was unlikely.

'You do realize that everybody in the country's talking about this?'

'I hadn't really thought about it,' I said, and that was true.

I told Charley that Lizzi had said I'd never work in television again and that I was scared she was going to fire me.

'They won't fire you,' she said. 'This is the biggest news story this year.'

I told her I wasn't too sure.

'Simon,' she said, suddenly getting serious. 'Are you absolutely one hundred per cent sure you're the father?'

'Yes,' I snapped, but I knew I sounded unconvincing.

'Well, you've got what you've always wanted. Every person in the country knows who you are and you won't be able to go anywhere without being recognized. You're famous Simon, or better still you're INFAMOUS.'

Vince Envy's words came back to me: '*You can't just be famous these days, you have to be infamous.*'

The trouble is I'm infamous and unemployed.

5.40 p.m.
Lizzi has just left a message asking me if I'd meet her for

lunch at The Holly tomorrow afternoon. (The Holly is *the* restaurant to be seen in.) She said she'll send a car for me and a minder to help me avoid the reporters. He'll arrive at twelve noon tomorrow. I feel like a condemned man going for his last supper. Why can't she just fire me over the phone?

10 NOV

I woke up at 7.36 a.m. to discover Max had left me another message telling me it was urgent I call him. He and Manky have probably hired a team of top lawyers to tear me apart and take me for every penny I've got. How much longer can I avoid him?

I looked outside my window at the press who were gathered below and couldn't help feeling slightly disappointed there were only half as many there as yesterday.

At twelve noon on the dot my minder arrived to pick me up. He looked exactly like a bodyguard should look. He was a 6' 6" black guy with a bald head and no neck. He wore black shades, a black suit, black shirt and black tie. He didn't say much, but when he spoke he sounded like Barry White in a Quentin Tarantino movie.

'Mr Peters,' he said, in a low, whispered American accent. 'I'm Tank. I'm going to be helping you out of this situation.'

I hadn't realized I was in a situation, but Tank obviously thought I was. He threw a blanket over my head and bundled me past all the reporters. From the security of the blanket, I could hear them firing questions at me thick and fast.

'Will you have a DNA test?'

'Why is the baby called Jessica?'

'Have you been fired from *Slebs*?'

'Is it true Ricardo Mancini's suing you?'

'Have you ever slept with a donkey?'

I didn't understand the relevance of that last question, but guessed the reporter was from the *Sunday Sport*.

Tank threw me onto the back seat of a large silver Mercedes with soft leather seats. It looked like the sort of car that should have a celebrity in it, then I realized that today the celebrity was me. Twenty photographers surrounded the car, shouting my name. The car had tinted windows, so I wound them down to make sure they could get a good shot of me. Tank jumped into the front seat, slammed it into first gear and wheel-spun away. If it wasn't for the fact I was on my way to be fired I would have thought this was one of the most exciting moments in my life.

We arrived at The Holly only to be met by more paparazzi. Tank dealt with this by throwing himself in front of me and acting as a human shield. I was dying to ask him if he'd 'take a bullet for me', but thought better of it. I dived inside and came face to face with the Maître d'. All my insecurities came flooding back and I knew that he knew I didn't belong in a restaurant like The Holly. I expected him to take one look at me, tell me that my sort wasn't welcome here and then have three waiters escort me back outside and dump me unceremoniously on the pavement.

But he didn't.

'Ah, Mr Peters,' he said, shaking my hand as if I were his favourite regular customer. 'We've been expecting you.'

He whisked me into the main section of the restaurant, straight past a queue of people who'd obviously been waiting to be seated for some time. As we entered an electric buzz seemed to shoot through the room, as if someone special had just walked in. I looked behind me but there was no-one there. In my peripheral vision I was aware of diners nudging each other and nodding in my direction.

'*Simon Peters*,' I heard them whispering in hushed, almost reverential tones.

As I passed one table, Elton John stood up and shook my hand as if he'd known me for years.

'Simon,' he said, with a big smile of familiarity. 'Great to see you. Congratulations on the baby and hey . . . loved the fight.'

This was *the* Elton John. Not a lookalike. I was stunned he knew my name. So stunned that at that moment I couldn't remember his.

'Hi . . . mate,' I said.

I mumbled the word 'mate', and tried to make it sound like as many names as possible, the way you do when you're not sure of someone's name. Partly out of embarrassment, I released his hand and quickly moved on without saying another word. To a casual onlooker it probably looked as if I was far too busy to be seen talking to the likes of Elton John.

'Dah-ling,' screamed Lizzi from the far end of the restaurant.

'Hello, Lizzi.'

'I've taken the taken the liberty of ordering for you,' she said, air-kissing me on both cheeks. 'They do great fish and chips here.'

Fish and chips are *the* thing to order at The Holly. They serve them in yesterday's newspaper and charge forty quid a time for the privilege.

I sat down and Lizzi leant across the table towards me. At first I thought she was going to hit me, but she didn't. She grabbed hold of my cheek and gave it a playful tug, the way a mother might to a cute-looking baby.

Did I really sleep with this woman?

We started our meal and for most of it Lizzi just made small talk. If she was going to fire me she was certainly drawing out the process. We were just finishing off our dessert of deep-fried Mars bar (another Holly speciality) when Lizzi cleared her throat and looked me squarely in the eye. *This is it,* I thought. *This is when she fires me.*

'Is there anybody else you don't get on with?' she asked.

'I'm sorry?'

I didn't understand the question.

'We're thinking of making what you did into a regular feature. You fight a different celebrity each week. I think the reason it worked so well was because you genuinely hated Ricardo Mancini. Are there any other famous people you don't like and want to have a fight with.'

'I'm not fired then?'

'Fired? Of course you're not fired,' she said. 'What you did on Friday was the best piece of television I've produced in twenty years. We've already sold the clip to sixteen different countries, and at least five territories are interested in buying the format rights to *Slebs*. There might even be a spin-off show in it for you: *The Peters' Punch-up*, that type of thing.'

'But you said, "*You'll never fucking work in television again.*"'

There was a pause.

'I said, "*You'll never look for work in television again.*" You won't have to, dah-ling, the work will always find you. Don't you realize this has made your career?'

I could have kissed her, but thought better of it in case it gave her the wrong impression.

We finished our meal and, as I left the restaurant, Elton waved at me, but I felt too embarrassed to wave back, so I just ignored him.

11 NOV

The bathwater is officially '*hot*'.

Max has just called me and told me he's been inundated with offers of work for me. He said I've been invited to be a guest on over thirty-five different television shows, including *Lorraine*, *Kilroy*, *Trisha*, *GMTV*, *2Early4Talk*, *Talking Point with Mary Matthews* and *Countdown*. I've even been invited onto *Question Time* to take part in a debate about violence on television and a Radio Four programme about fathers who are denied access to their children.

'What about Mancini wanting to sue me?' I asked.

'I managed to talk him out of that,' said Max dismissively. 'At first I thought it might be good publicity, but on reflection I think a legal battle would be more trouble than it's worth.'

I chose to ignore the fact that Max had obviously contemplated suing me just for the publicity. I also couldn't help noticing that he seemed really pleased that Manky and I were both claiming to be the father.

'What do we do now then?' I asked.

It was at this point that I was hoping Max would unveil his strategic five-year career plan, which he'd hopefully spent the last three days mapping out for me.

'We do absolutely nothing,' he said triumphantly. 'I've told all the shows you're far too busy to appear. Mimi Lawson's got the right idea; you have to lay low for a while. We don't want to over-expose you.'

Doesn't he realize I've been waiting my whole career to be over-exposed? I got the impression Max thought this was a masterstroke. I find it slightly annoying that when I was a struggling presenter, Max never did anything for me, and now I've supposedly made it, he still isn't going to do anything.

'Now be honest, Simon,' said Max sincerely, which took me by surprise because I've never heard Max be sincere before. 'Are you the father?'

'Yes,' I said with a hint of indignation. 'Of course I'm the father. Definitely. One hundred per cent. I think. I'm not sure. Maybe I'm not. I don't know. Why? What does Mancini say?'

'He's convinced he's the father,' said Max flatly.

There was a pause.

'Has he had any job offers?'

'He's had a little bit of interest,' said Max, but he wouldn't be drawn further.

12 NOV

YES! I'M THE DADDY
RICARDO MANCINI: A FATHER'S STORY!

Manky has sold his exclusive story to *The Sun*. In it, he said he hasn't spoken to Mimi since the birth but is hoping to 'meet up with her soon'. He claims he had a fling with Mimi in the last week of the pantomime in Grimsby and the baby is a result of that fling. Interestingly, he claims that after the panto finished Mimi stalked him for a couple of months, but only every other day.

Manky said that following my attack on him he bears no malice towards me and, quote, '*To be honest, I feel quite sorry for him.*' He said this whole experience has made him spiritually stronger and he's now more mature and ready to face the responsibilities of fatherhood.

Personally I think it's disgusting that Manky's sold his story like this and it's obvious he's only doing it to get some publicity for *Swizz Quiz* (which, incidentally, is struggling in the ratings). He really shouldn't be washing his dirty linen in public.

How shallow can you get?

13 NOV

I've been offered £150,000 to tell my side of the story.

The *News of the World* has promised a front-page splash and a six-page pull-out special if I'll spill the beans. Max is really keen for me to do it, but I'm not so sure.

'I thought you said it was best not to over-expose me.'

'Yes, but this is for one hundred and fifty grand, you *klutz*.'

He did have a point, I suppose.

Ever since I was a kid, whenever anybody mentions a large sum of money to me I always visualize it in materialistic terms. I see the apartment, the clothes, the Porsche, the villa and the yacht. These are the things you have when you're rich, when you're successful, when you've made it, and these are the things I've wanted for as long as I can remember. Of course, £150,000 wouldn't buy *all* these things, but it would certainly be a healthy start.

I called Charley and told her about the offer.

'Don't do it.'

I knew she'd say that.

'Give me ten good reasons why I shouldn't.'

'Because it's cheap, crude, sordid, dirty, grimy, grubby, nasty, tacky and tawdry.'

'That's only nine.'

'You want a tenth reason?' she said. 'Jessica.'

And with that she put the phone down.

I kept seeing the money and all the things I could buy with it, but then Charley's words would come back to me and I'd see an image of what I imagine Jessica to look like.

I called Max and told him to turn down the offer.

14 NOV

Tonight was the second episode of *Slebs*, and after what happened in last week's show we were told to expect an audience of around eighteen million.

Lizzi said we had to top what happened last week, so I was sent to Leicester Square to broadcast live from the premiere of the new Hank Wells film *The Pugilist*. Lizzi's idea was for me to try to pick fights with as many celebrities as possible as they walked along the red carpet. This *might* have worked, but by the time Claudia threw to me, most of the celebs had already gone into the cinema. The only person still outside was Burt Kwouk, who played Kato in the *Pink Panther* films (I think he's currently in *Last of the Summer Wine*). Thinking Burt would play along, I thought it'd be quite funny to aim a Kato-style karate kick at him, but just miss him by a few inches.

With my cameraman in close pursuit, I climbed over the safety barrier and leapt into action. Maybe I should have done my research, as one thing I didn't realize was that Burt Kwouk is a genuine kung-fu master. He certainly moved quickly for an older man. He span around, dropped to his knee and, in one fluid movement, kicked my legs from underneath me while simultaneously rabbit-punching me twice in the kidneys. As I bent forward, he grabbed my wrist and twisted it with just enough power to spin my whole body round 360 degrees. The paparazzi, who'd been circling like hungry vultures, swooped down on their prey and devoured it with a salacious delight. Their flash photography created a strange strobe-light effect, giving the illusion of everything happening in slow motion, like a 1920s silent movie. Burt grabbed hold of my lapels, stuck out his right leg and, with what appeared to be very little effort, rolled my body over his right hip in a judo-style throw. I fell to the floor in a crumpled heap while Burt took up the classic kung-fu pose-of-a-warrior-style stance. The crowd of spectators burst into a spontaneous round of applause, which Burt coolly acknowledged. He adjusted his dickie bow, brushed some dirt from the arm of his tuxedo and continued walking into the cinema as if nothing had happened. I had to do my closing link to camera while being escorted down the red carpet by two St John Ambulance men.

When I eventually discharged myself from hospital, I returned home to find a message from Lizzi telling me she thought the whole thing was 'hilarious' and was looking forward to 'topping' it next week.

I can hardly wait.

15 NOV

PETERS MUST BE 'KWOUKERS' TO TAKE ON BURT

Once again I'm on the front page of every tabloid news-paper.

All the photographs show Burt in mid flight and me with a pained look on my face. Following my fight with Manky Mancini, I liked to think the public saw me as something of a tough guy. This image has now been completely dispelled. Without exception, every single paper highlighted the fact that Burt is actually seventy-three years old.

The shame of it; I don't think I'll ever leave the house again.

17 NOV

I'm still trying to come to terms with the fact that I'm genuinely famous now. Everyone seems to have an opinion on me. Journalists write about me, comedians make jokes about me and I even saw Alistair McGowan doing an impression of me (the voice was good, but he looked nothing like me).

Wherever I go people know who I am. They nudge each other and point and murmur and whisper and giggle. Today I nipped into Tesco for a pint of milk and two old women in the queue just stared at me.

'He's bought Tesco home brand,' whispered one.

'Cheapskate,' whispered her friend.

I'm also really struggling with the fact I might be a father. I thought being a father would make me feel different, more grown up, more responsible, but I don't. If anything I feel slightly detached from the whole situation, as if it's happening to someone else.

Maybe it is.

What if it is Manky's baby? Maybe that wouldn't be such a bad thing after all.

I called Mimi's agent, but when I said who I was, the secretary said I was the sixth person to say that today. I told her how desperate I was and begged and pleaded with her to tell me where Mimi and the baby were, but all she'd tell me was that they were 'on holiday' and she was unsure when they'd return.

18 NOV

Charley called me about my party.

'How many people are coming then?' she enquired.

'Oooh . . . erm . . . a couple.'

I didn't like to tell her it was *literally* a couple, as in two people. Charley and Archie Rimmer.

'Right, listen, Tamara Harvey-Wright was on *Coffee Morning* this morning presenting an item on the perfect party. Apparently she's a big fan of *Slebs*, I told her about your party and she said she'd organize it for you. She's going to call you at two o'clock this afternoon. You know who Tamara Harvey-Wright is, don't you?'

'Of course I do.'

Tamara Harvey-Wright is a legendary PR girl who organizes all the top parties in London. She only arranges A-list events and she's without doubt the best in the business. You're nobody until you've been to one of Tamara Harvey-Wright's parties.

I've never been to one.

Sure enough, at two o'clock the phone rang.

'Hello, Simon,' said the cut-glass voice at the other end of the line. 'Tamara Harvey-Wright here. I believe you need some friends, yah?'

I really didn't know what to say to that, which was just as well because she didn't give me time to.

'Now, because it's in December, dah-ling, how about a summer theme? Gals in bikinis, chaps in Hawaiian shirts? Yah? How does that sound?'

I thought it sounded a little tacky.

'Sounds great,' I said.

'We'll hire the Cosmo Bar, I know the owner, Piers Dubois, and he'll let me have it for free as long as we guarantee him a certain amount of press.'

I couldn't believe it. The Cosmo Bar in Central London is *the* place to be seen in and you always read in the gossip columns about famous people hanging out there. Personally I've never been able to get in, so holding my party there is a major coup.

'Cosmo holds about five hundred people, sweetie,' she continued, 'which means we can keep it purely A-list, yah?'

'Yah,' I said.

I didn't like to ask her if Archie Rimmer was A-list.

19 NOV

Tamara certainly doesn't waste any time. She called up and told me *OK!* and *Hello!* magazines are fighting over the exclusive rights to cover my party.

'It's definitely going to be six figures . . .' she said confidently.

Six figures? Once again, I saw the apartment, the Porsche, the villa, the yacht . . .

'So whatever I manage to get, that will cover my fee,' said Tamara, completely bursting my bubble.

'What do I get?'

'You get the publicity, sweetie. Yah?'

'Yah,' I said, somewhat despondently.

I cancelled the party in the upstairs room of the Red Lion pub. They weren't very happy about it because apparently the dominoes team were really looking forward to the occasion.

20 NOV

News travels fast and suddenly my birthday party is *the* hot ticket. Everybody wants to be on the guest list. My phone hasn't stopped ringing and I'm taking calls from people who claim to be friends of friends of people who I've never even heard of. I'd just put the phone down on a man who claimed to be Bobby Davro's next-door neighbour when it started to ring again.

'Hello?' I said wearily. By this point I was tiring of all the liggers and freeloaders.

'It's Pippa.'

The words sounded like a beautiful melody and it was a tune I could listen to for the rest of my life.

'Hi . . . wow . . . great . . . OK . . . wow.'

'How are you?' she said with the voice of an angel.

'Great . . . wow . . . great.'

I'd completely lost the ability to control my speech patterns and all I could do was stammer my way through various exclamations.

'How are you?' I said, snapping out of it. 'I've been watching all your bits on *Slebs*, they're really good.'

'Your bits are better,' she said with a slightly hard-edged tone (I don't think she meant to sound quite as bitter as she did).

There was a pause. Not an awkward pause but a pause all the same.

'Are you going to ask me then?' said Pippa.

I couldn't believe it. This was the moment I'd been waiting for.

'Yes, of course,' I said.

I took a deep breath and tried to control my nerves.

'Would you like to come out on a date with me? We could go for a drink, a meal . . . go to a club, whatever you want.'

There was another pause. This one could definitely be described as awkward.

'Yes . . . erm . . . OK.'

I couldn't help feeling she sounded a little disappointed.

We arranged to meet on Monday night at the Plush bar in Greek St. I'm so excited. Destiny has thrown us together once more and I feel it's only a matter of time before my love for her is requited.

21 NOV

Tonight was the third *Slebs* show. It's now the highest-rating entertainment show on British television. On the show, Claudia was in the studio interviewing Ryan Durwood, the winner of this year's Pop Legend competition. Ryan's Number One hit single is called 'Naked Love' and it was Lizzi's idea for both Claudia and Ryan to conduct the interview completely in the nude. The viewer at home never saw any rude bits, thanks to some strategically placed props. Whichever camera they cut to there was always a vase or a bowl of fruit or some vegetables in the way to spare their blushes. It was very funny and one of those TV moments, which people remember and talk about for a long long time.

Pippa was on VT interviewing John Travolta in the cockpit of his own Lear Jet. Pippa looked gorgeous in a tiny denim mini skirt. She was flirting outrageously and you could tell Travolta was bowled over by her (especially when she asked if she could have a go with his joystick). Watching her on the monitor I couldn't believe I was finally going to get the chance to take her out.

My item on the show wasn't that strong. I had to have a bare-knuckle fight with Keith Chegwin. After the show I voiced my concerns to Lizzi, saying I thought Keith was maybe a little passé.

'Exactly, dah-ling,' she said and went on to explain that it was post-modern irony and that 'people at home want nothing more than to see people like you and Cheggers knocking seven bells of shit out of each other.'

1.47 a.m.
What did she mean *'people like you and Cheggers'*? Surely I'm not like Cheggers. He's not A-list any more.

22 NOV

6 p.m.

Tonight is the night of my date with Pippa and it's just taken me three and a half hours to get ready.

I showered using Clarins Bain et Douche shower gel and shampooed and conditioned my hair with Aramis Nutriplexx System (for thinning hair). I towelled myself dry and allowed myself just a hint of Bouvoir's Jet Bronzer Self-Tanning Lotion, (so much better than that cheap Mr Bronzer stuff I used to wear). I applied L'Oréal Plenitude Deep Action Line Eraser Pure Retinol around my eyes and Clinique Oil Free Moisturising Formula to the rest of my face. I added a splash of Jean Paul Gaultier's aftershave behind my ears and used Tigi's Bed Head wax to give some definition to my hair.

I opened my wardrobe and took out the selection of clothes I now own courtesy of *Slebs*. I'm not really supposed to wear them until after I've worn them on the show, but I figured this was a special occasion, so I chose the black single-breasted Prada suit, the black Dolce & Gabbana shirt, the black Gucci tie, the black pearl Paul Smith cuff links, the black Patrick Cox shoes and some black Calvin Klein boxer shorts. Admittedly my black nylon socks are from Marks & Spencer, but there isn't a label on them, so that's OK.

6.45 p.m.

I've just looked in the mirror and I look cool and famous.

6.48 p.m.

If I am so cool and famous, why do I still feel so nerdy and nervous?

7.30 p.m.
I have to meet Pippa in the Plush bar in half an hour.

12.32 a.m.
I've just returned from the date and I am head over heels in love.

Pippa is the perfect woman and so different to anyone I've ever been out with before. I can't believe I've just spent the last hour in her company. I say *last hour* because she was actually two and a half hours late (I had to call her on her mobile and remind her she was supposed to be meeting me). By the time she arrived we only had time for one drink because she said she had to be up early in the morning. Even though she made me feel slightly over-dressed in my suit and tie, she looked absolutely stunning in a ragged old motorcycle jacket, white T-shirt and a pair of orange tracksuit bottoms. She's really skilled at making it look like she hasn't made any effort at all.

We didn't actually say much to each other during the course of the hour, but that didn't seem to be important. Pippa said it was more important to stand in the VIP section and ensure we could 'be seen'. Most new couples have to go through the motions and struggle through hours of inane smalltalk trying to get to know each other, but for Pippa and I it wasn't like that. Our relationship seems to have already transcended that point and the long silences, which some couples would find embarrassing, didn't matter to us. When she did speak for any length of time it was all about her hatred for Manky Mancini, which personally I could have listened to all night. She asked me if I thought it was true that Ricardo had slept with Mimi during the panto, but I said I didn't know. She didn't ask if I'd slept with Mimi and I appreciate the fact that she respects my privacy on that issue.

When we eventually moved off the subject of Manky, there was another long silence before she told me she'd been invited to lots of celebrity parties over the next couple of weeks.

I said that was nice for her.

After another minute of not saying anything she asked me if I'd like to accompany her to some of them.

Of course I jumped at the chance and said I'd love to.

After another long pause, she asked me if I knew of any parties to invite her to. Because she was late, I'd been drinking on my own since eight o'clock and I was slightly inebriated by this point, so I completely forgot about my own party. The only thing I could think of was my cousin Val's wedding in Birmingham in January. I invited Pippa to that and she accepted somewhat reluctantly.

That was pretty much all that was said.

We were about to leave the bar when Pippa spotted the paparazzi waiting outside. She insisted we leave separately, but told me to walk out exactly one minute after her, just to fuel speculation that we *had* been in each other's company. That, she explained, was actually better than being photographed together and would ensure the story 'had legs'. I wasn't entirely sure which story she was talking about, but because I'm totally in awe of her, I did exactly as she said.

As we parted, we arranged to meet up tomorrow night for the opening of a new musical in the West End. She gave me a peck on the cheek, and as she did so we both experienced a small electric shock. I told her it was a sign we were meant to be together. Pippa said it was static caused by nylon in the carpet.

23 NOV

Blockbuster! is a new musical at the Dominion Theatre about the rags-to-riches-to-rags tale of a young girl who starts off working in a video store and ends up starring in a Hollywood movie. It all goes horribly wrong and she ends up in the video store again, renting out the movie she once starred in. It sounds like it's going to be a great musical, but unfortunately the whole show is based around the music of the 1970s glam-rock band The Sweet and to be honest their music wasn't that good the first time around. Despite the musical being rubbish, the party afterwards was rather good, and even though there were some quite major stars there, Pippa and I were undoubtedly the most famous. Pippa looked gorgeous in a short, bright-pink dress (she said bright colours are starting to make a comeback).

I wore black.

Once again Pippa and I didn't have much to say to each other, but that really isn't important. Just being in her presence is enough for me. I've never been out with a beautiful woman before and she seems to radiate a natural confidence (which I know some people mistake for arrogance).

At a London party everybody checks you out to see if you're a 'somebody'. In the past I've always felt invisible, a nobody who everybody ignored, but now, with Pippa and the controversy surrounding *Slebs*, I feel highly visible, as if I'm sporting one of those luminous-green donkey jackets that motorway workers wear. Everybody notices us. One thing that does surprise me is that Pippa seems to attract lots of nasty comments from women.

Maybe they're just jealous of her for being with me?

At one point Richard Whiteley asked me for my autograph. He said it was for his nephew, but when I asked him what his nephew's name was he said it was Richard, which I found very amusing. Pippa didn't laugh, though; I think she was upset Richard didn't ask for hers.

Once again, Pippa insisted we leave separately to make the paparazzi 'desperate for a photo of us together'.

25 NOV

The *Sun*, the *Star* and the *Mirror* have all run stories speculating on whether or not Pippa and I are an item. They all claimed we've been seen together at several celebrity parties (which to me made it sound a bit tacky).

Later, when I met Pippa at the celebrity opening of a new Burger King in Leicester Square, she looked radiant in a low-cut, fluorescent-yellow dress. She said she was pleased about the publicity, but when I asked her whether we actually are an item, she changed the subject and said we shouldn't sit at the same table because she didn't want to blow the chances of an 'exclusive first photo deal' by having 'some pap catch us on a long lens'.

26 NOV

There's a brand-new club called Envelope and Pippa and I went to the opening of it.

We stood in the VIP bar (apart), had our photographs taken (individually) and then left (separately).

I want to invite Pippa to be guest of honour at my birthday party, but we never speak to each other long enough for me to ask her.

27 NOV

Pippa. Me. Film premiere. Red carpet. Celebrities. Champagne. Canapés. Paparazzi. Blah. Blah. Blah.

28 NOV

I've just finished the live broadcast of tonight's *Slebs* show and personally I think they're stretching the whole '*Simon fights people he doesn't like*' idea a little thin. Tonight I had to wrestle in a tag-team match with Neil and Christine Hamilton.

The idea was for me to ask the Hamiltons pertinent questions as we grappled on the canvas, but it soon became clear it wasn't going to happen. For the majority of the interview I was in too much pain to talk, as it quickly transpired that Neil was very handy with a half nelson and Christine had developed her own WWF speciality move called the 'Kiss of Death' (which, when I think of it, starts to make me feel quite queasy).

Why do Lizzi and the production team keep getting me to interview all these C-listers? Claudia and Pippa are always interviewing the big-hitters and major Hollywood players. Why can't I? I really feel I'm not being used to my full potential. Don't they realize I can do more?

I refuse to be packaged as just another vacuous celebrity.

29 NOV

I met Pippa in 'The Met Bar'. We only stayed for an hour, as Pippa was a little bit upset that there were no paparazzi there.

'What's the point of coming to the Met Bar if there are no paps to let everybody know you were here.'

She said this without a hint of irony, and for a fleeting moment I thought I saw a side of Pippa I didn't like. Surely the point of going out is to talk, laugh, giggle, flirt, eat, drink, have fun, entertain, be entertained and generally socialize and get to know each other better. Pippa seems to think the sole purpose of going out is to raise her profile and further her career. I was going to say this, but in the end I just agreed with her, mainly because she was wearing skin-tight jeans and a see-through blouse with no bra underneath.

Because there were no paparazzi, we left the bar together and walked out into the night air. Park Lane was cold, wet and deserted, but I felt a special warmth between the two of us. I gently took hold of Pippa's hand and knew the time was right.

'Would you like to be the special guest of honour at my birthday party?' I asked softly.

She looked at me with those big beautiful sparkling blue eyes. Suddenly she wasn't Pippa The Ambitious Dancer or Pippa The TV Star, she was just Pippa, a girl being asked out on a date. Momentarily, she was completely lost for words. She seemed to be overcome with emotion. Somewhere on Park Lane I could hear a violin softly playing. The pale moonlight bounced off the wet pavement and created a soft shimmering glow around the two of us. She smiled sweetly, but in a flash the smile was gone.

'About bloody time,' she snapped, snatching her hand away from mine. 'I thought you were never going to ask. Is Robbie Williams going to be there?'

The violin stopped and it started to rain again. Pippa hailed a cab and told me she'd see me at the party on Friday.

1 DEC

Something very strange happened today.

I was opening my mail and I had a telephone bill (£78.36), an electricity bill (£38.46) and a request from a man called Roger for a signed photograph and a pair of 'used underpants'.

That wasn't the strange thing.

I also had three pieces of junk mail, one giving me the opportunity to join a wine club, one offering me a low-interest credit card with a £10,000 upper limit and the other trying to sell me life insurance that *'pays even if you're only critically ill'* (I particularly like the way they say *'only'* critically ill). I worked out I could combine all three. I could use the credit card to buy two thousand bottles of wine, drink myself into a coma and then use the life-insurance money to pay it all off.

Once again, though, that wasn't the strange thing.

I had one other letter. I opened it and it was a cheque made out to me for £250,000.

That was the strange thing.

At first I thought it was another piece of junk mail. One of those crafty ones that says '£250,000 could be yours! All you have to do is call this number!' and then in small print: '(calls cost £250,000 per minute.)'

But it wasn't.

It was a Coutts cheque made out to me for £250,000.

It was signed by Mr L. Wynthorpe (senior) of Wynthorpe, Wynthorpe, Goldboom and Kaye (solicitors).

And that was it. No accompanying letter. Nothing.

Myriad thoughts shot through my mind. Maybe it was from a newspaper trying to bribe me to sell my story about Mimi and the baby? Maybe Pippa had done a deal for our first 'exclusive' photograph together? Maybe it was a birthday gift from my father? (I doubt it somehow.) Maybe Tamara Harvey-Wright had sold the rights to my party and decided to give me a cut after all? Maybe Max had landed me my own prime-time show without telling me and this was the initial payment? Maybe it was from a fan? Maybe it was payment from Roger for my unwashed pants?

I called Wynthorpe, Wynthorpe, Goldboom and Kaye (solicitors) to make sure there hadn't been some kind of mistake. The rather friendly secretary told me that Mr Wynthorpe (senior), who was handling this particular case, was on a winter break until 12 December and she was afraid she couldn't discuss where the money was from without his authority. What she could confirm was that the money was definitely mine.

£250,000 – the apartment, the Porsche, the villa, the yacht . . .

2 DEC

Tamara called me and said my party is going to be the 'party of the decade'. The guest list reads like a *Who's Who* of international showbusiness. Some of the people who have already confirmed include Posh and Becks, Robbie Williams, Jude Law, Kate Winslet, Liam Gallagher, Stella McCartney, David Bowie, Ewan McGregor, Kate Moss and Naomi Campbell. I always thought a birthday party was something you invited your family and closest friends to, but that clearly isn't the case. When I told Tamara I was worried I didn't know any of these people, she said, '*But they know you, dah-ling.*'

Also on the list were six lords, three ladies, two dukes and Christopher Biggins. The only person I said no to was Sir Elton John, which I think quite impressed Tamara.

She went on to tell me she'd done an exclusive deal with *Hello!* magazine for the photographic rights. When I asked her how much it was for, she quickly reminded me that we'd agreed she could keep the money as her fee (the mystery cheque was not from her then. I crossed that one off the list). Tamara then told me she had some very exciting news. She'd been speaking to Lizzi Rees-Morgan, who had agreed that this Friday night's *Slebs* show could be broadcast live from my birthday party. On hearing this, my first reaction was one of excitement. Surely this means I've made it. If having one's own birthday party broadcast live to the nation isn't confirmation of one's A-list status then I don't know what is. Tamara asked me if there was anybody I wanted to invite, but she asked me in such a way that suggested she hoped there wasn't.

I told her I'd like to invite Pippa (who was now going to be there for the show anyway), Charley, Max, Scary Babs and Archie Rimmer.

'What about your parents and family?' said Tamara, which I thought was quite considerate of her, but then she ruined it by adding, 'It might make a nice photo opportunity.'

I hesitated.

I was going to explain how my brother is an accountant in Sheffield and we don't really have much in common. I was going to explain how I hadn't spoken to my father for three years because of a petty argument which neither of us can remember. I was going to explain how my mother had died when I was young and how this had left me with a life-long sense of abandonment.

But I didn't.

'I don't think it's their sort of party,' I said.

4 DEC

I want this day to last for ever. I'm thirty years old tomorrow and I don't want to be. I want to be twenty-nine ad infinitum.

I was going to call Pippa and confide all my worries and fears, but on reflection I didn't think she'd understand (or be interested), so I called the one person who I knew would be: Charley. I started off by telling her about the mysterious £250,000 and her advice was to bank it, but not spend it

267

until I'd spoken to the solicitor and found out exactly who it was from and what it was for.

'How are you getting on with Pippa?' she asked. 'I've been reading all about you in the papers.'

'Fine,' I said. 'She's a really nice girl.'

'I bet you have a barrel of laughs.'

There was a pause, which quickly developed into a silence.

'I'm looking forward to your party,' she said, changing the subject. 'I've got a surprise for you.'

'I hate surprises.'

I was lying, of course. I love surprises. What I hate is having to wait for them. 'What is it?'

'You'll see at your party,' she said and wouldn't give me any more clues.

'What do you think about them broadcasting *Slebs* from my party?' I asked.

'I think it's the funniest thing I've ever heard. Don't they realize you're only Simon Peters?'

I told Charley I was quite worried about turning thirty. She said that last week on *Coffee Morning* they'd had a psychologist who said people should 'clear out the cupboards of their minds' by writing down a list of the pros and cons of the things they're most worried about.

I promised Charley I'd try it and here it is.

PROS OF TURNING THIRTY	CONS OF TURNING THIRTY
I have made it to thirty years of age	My mother won't be there to see it (neither will my father)
I am the father of a beautiful baby girl	I'm not sure the baby girl is that beautiful (I'm not entirely sure I'm the father)

I have a wonderful girlfriend in Pippa	I'm not sure Pippa is my girlfriend (I'm not entirely sure she's all that wonderful)
I'm eligible for cheaper car insurance	I'm nearer to sixty than I am to the day I was born (that, my friends, is a scary thought)
I'm rich	I don't know where the £250,000 came from
I'm famous	Being famous isn't as good as I thought it would be
My party is going to be broadcast to eighteen million people and there will be several hundred A-list celebrities in attendance	There is a niggling doubt gnawing away at the back of my mind that prevents me from completely embracing and enjoying the idea of my party. I can't help thinking it's not actually *my* party. The A-list celebrities aren't coming because of me; they're coming because it's going to be broadcast live to eighteen million people and eighteen million people won't be watching because of me, they'll be watching to see the A-list celebrities. I hate to be negative about these things, but part of me wishes I was still holding the party in the upstairs room at the Red Lion pub with Archie Rimmer and the dominoes team.

I called Tamara to make sure that everything was all right with the last-minute arrangements, but when I told her it was Simon Peters she said '*Simon who?*' When I explained who I was, she apologized and said it was because she'd already started working on Elton John's New Year's Eve party (I noticed she didn't invite me). She assured me everything was under control and told me not to worry.

'I'll see you tomorrow,' she said.

'Yes. I'll see you tomorrow, Tamara.'

I burst into a fit of giggles. I'd wanted to say that joke since I first spoke to her.

11.46 p.m.
I'm thirty years old tomorrow and I still make jokes like an eight-year-old schoolboy.

5 DEC

THIRTY!

Being a major TV star one would think I'd receive sackloads of birthday cards and presents, but no. In reality the only people to send me cards are the people who'd have sent them even if I wasn't on the telly, with the exception of Roger the Dirty-Underpants Fan . . . I do hope he's not becoming obsessive. Maybe everybody intends to give me their cards this evening.

I have to be at the Cosmo Bar for midday, ready to rehearse my segment for this evening's show. Lizzi and the scriptwriters have come up with what they think is a funny idea. For the duration of the programme, I'm not going to be allowed into my own party. I have to stand outside with a load of C-list celebrities who can't get in either. These include Su Pollard, Tony Blackburn and Keith Harris and Orville. Claudia and Pippa will be inside the party with all the A-listers and the running joke is that every time Claudia throws to me I have to try to find a different way past the large bouncers who keep refusing to let me in. Personally I think it's a bit of a weak idea and not particularly funny. Why not have me co-hosting the whole show with Claudia? It is my birthday after all.

3.02 a.m.
I have just returned from my party and I can't quite believe what happened . . .

The live show went without a hitch, and the only real problem came after we stopped broadcasting and the bouncers genuinely wouldn't let me in.

'If your name's not down, you're not coming in,' said the bouncer, without even a hint of irony.

'But it's my party,' I screamed, looking around me for someone to confirm it was true. Tony Blackburn, who was standing behind me, opened his mouth to speak. Go on, Tony, I thought, Tell him whose party it is.

'It's my party,' said Tony to the bouncer with a completely straight face.

There was a pause. I looked at Tony, astonished he was trying to get away with such an old trick.

'No, it's my party,' shouted someone else.

I span around to see it was Su Pollard.

Suddenly I was in the middle of the classic 'I'm Spartacus!' scene, with people all around me trying to claim the party as their own.

'It's my party,' chimed Keith Harris.

'No, it's my party,' said Orville the duck.

I hate that duck and always have. I took the opportunity to slap him on the beak and was quite surprised when it was Keith who said, 'Ow.'

Members of the public started to join in the mêlée and very soon there were about twenty people shouting, 'It's my party!' The paparazzi, who were outside covering the event, fired off endless reels of film and seemed to take a sinister pleasure in my obvious embarrassment.

After what seemed an age, the head bouncer called up Tamara on his two-way radio. She eventually came to the door and confirmed I was who I said I was. The bouncer unhooked the thick red rope from the polished brass pole and let me through. As I entered, Su Pollard seized the opportunity and quickly grabbed my arm and walked in with me. As soon as we were inside she kissed me on the lips, said, '*Thanks for that, chuck*,' and disappeared into the crowd, never to be seen again.

I walked down the stairs into the main area and was immediately aware of the incredible atmosphere that had been created. As Tamara had promised, the party had a Hawaiian theme. A steel band played in the corner, there were fire-eaters, limbo dancers and hula girls handing out garlands of flowers. Everyone in attendance seemed to have entered into the spirit of it. The women wore bikinis and grass skirts and all the men wore brightly coloured Hawaiian shirts. I overheard somebody saying that Hawaiian shirts are going to be the next big thing.

'Hawaiian shirts are the new black,' said one person.

'Black is so passé,' said another.

I felt slightly conspicuous and self-conscious in the black suit, black shirt and black tie Lizzi had made me wear for the show.

I was amazed by the number of genuine A-list celebrities who had turned up. Tamara had done a great job with the guest list, and everywhere I looked there was a familiar face. As I made my way to the VIP area (or the VVIP area as Tamara called it), I passed movie stars, rock stars, pop stars, soap stars, models, presenters and Christopher Biggins. Not one person said hello or wished me happy birthday.

I saw Claudia standing just inside the roped-off area. She kissed me on the cheek.

'Great show,' she said. 'I think it's the best one yet.'

Lizzi was standing next to her sipping mineral water, which I thought was unusual for her. She nodded in agreement at what Claudia was saying, but at the same time gave me a very strange look. I asked Claudia if she'd seen Pippa and she said she'd last seen her speaking to Mick Hucknall.

'Which is strange,' said Claudia, 'because I don't think he can help her career in any way.'

Meowww. Saucer of milk for table two.

At that moment Teri Anderson from The Foxy Girls came into the VVIP area. She totally ignored me and started chatting to Claudia. I thought I'd try to strike up a conversation with Lizzi, but she turned her back on me and headed off in the direction of the toilets.

I turned around and suddenly came face to face with Barry Chuckle.

We stood there for a moment, just staring at each other.

It was Barry who broke the silence.

'You won't believe this,' he said, grabbing my hand and shaking it. 'People are always coming up to me and telling me I look like Simon Peters. Hey, maybe you could join the act.'

He started to chuckle (he really did chuckle). This was the first time I'd seen him close up and he was older than I'd imagined. How could people say we were alike? I studied his features and, whilst I admit there were some similarities, I came to the conclusion I was definitely better looking than him.

I wonder if he was thinking the same thing?

'I'll catch you later,' said Barry and it wasn't until he'd gone that I started to wonder how Barry Chuckle got into the VVIP area. Come to think of it, how had he got into the party? He definitely wasn't on the list. I started to worry that with him and Su Pollard roaming around, people might not see it as an A-list event. My fears were quickly laid to rest when the famous Australian supermodel Anna Maya-Montague approached me. She was wearing a short grass miniskirt but no bikini top. The only thing covering her large, surgically enhanced breasts were three strategically placed garlands of flowers and two small strips of toupee tape. She looked gorgeous.

'Do you want coke?' she said in that matter-of-fact-straight-to-the-point-totally-up-front Australian way of hers.

By this point the Hawaiian music was really loud, and whilst I heard what she said, it took a moment for it to sink in, because I was still looking at her breasts.

'Pardon,' I said.

She leant forward and pressed her collagen-implanted lips to my ear.

'Do you want coke?'

'Well erm . . . I don't really . . . erm.'

'You look like you need some coke . . . wait here.'

She melted into the crowd. I couldn't believe it, a Grade-A supermodel was offering me Class-A drugs at an A-list party. This was the sort of thing I'd dreamt about for years. My head was full of images of Anna and I using her platinum Amex card to chop Charlie in the toilets. We would then use rolled-up fifty-pound notes to sniff it up off the white porcelain cistern and then make mad passionate love right there in the cubicle without worrying about who could hear us. I waited for about five minutes and finally she returned.

'This will pep you up a bit,' she said, handing me a glass of Coca-Cola.

I looked at the glass. Then at Anna. Then back at the glass.

'Cheers,' I said and started sipping the Coke through the straw. 'Rock 'n' Roll, man.'

I think my irony was lost on her.

The American movie star Hank Wells came over and, without even acknowledging my existence, started to speak to Anna. After a couple of minutes I felt slightly uncomfortable and I was about to move on when, from behind me, somebody covered my eyes with their hands. I quickly span around and was genuinely delighted to see Charley. She wore a Hawaiian shirt, which was tied in a knot exposing her midriff, and a long grass skirt, which offered an occasional glimpse of her legs. She had three green flowers in her long flowing hair, which served to accentuate her emerald-green eyes. She looked absolutely stunning and I was quite surprised to find myself thinking she was the most beautiful girl there.

'Happy birthday,' she shouted, planting a delicate kiss on my cheek.

'You're the first person to say that all night,' I shouted back, trying not to sound too bitter about it.

'Aren't you enjoying yourself then?'

'Kind of,' I said. 'Su Pollard kissed me on the lips, Barry Chuckle thinks I should join the act and Anna Maya-Montague gave me some Coke.'

Charley shot me a surprised look.

'It's diet, though, and personally I prefer regular.'

She laughed.

'All these people are here for you,' she shouted excitedly, struggling to make herself heard over the sound of the music.

Even though I knew it wasn't true and Charley knew I knew it wasn't true, she still managed to make me feel good about it all. Charley has a way of always doing that.

'How's your love life?' she asked.

'Oh, you know . . .'

I let the sentence trail away to nothing.

'That's a surprise,' she said, 'because Pippa seems such a sweet girl.'

'Another saucer of milk over here, please.'

At that moment the DJ started playing the theme tune from *Hawaii Five-O* and everyone on the dance floor started doing the rowing-a-canoe style dance routine.

'Do you want your surprise now?' asked Charley.

I was wondering when she was going to get around to that.

'Yes, please.'

She grabbed my hand and led me through the crowd of people who had gathered by the bar. We made our way up the stairs and passed Bono talking to David Bowie. I couldn't stop staring at them. *Bono* talking to *David Bowie* at *my* party. To make this moment last a little longer I pulled Charley's hand to slow her down, but she seemed to be on something of a mission. At the top of the stairs we turned left and Charley took me through a door marked private. We walked along a dark narrow corridor and, as we did so, the noise of the party became a distant rumble.

'That was David Bowie talking to Bono,' I said, but Charley just ignored me. 'Where are you taking me?'

I was slightly concerned that maybe we shouldn't have been there.

'Shhhhh.'

We went through a fire door, up one more flight of stairs and then along another long corridor.

'Hopefully this is going to be the best birthday present ever,' she said, crossing her fingers.

'I hope you're not planning on having your wicked way with me.'

'Not yet,' she said with a big grin on her face.

We walked along the corridor and stopped outside what looked like an office.

'This is it,' she said.

'You've bought me an office. Just what I've always wanted.'

Charley didn't laugh, in fact she looked quite serious. She took a deep breath and gave me a look as if to say, *I hope you like this.*

She slowly opened the door and once it was fully ajar I could see there were two men sitting at a desk, one of them with his back to me. I instantly recognized the man facing me. I'd seen his face in lots of magazine articles. It was Piers Dubois, the flamboyant and outrageously camp owner of the Cosmo Bar and several other high-class clubs and restaurants in London. He stood up and smiled at me. I couldn't help noticing that he was wearing lip-gloss and pink nail varnish. I smiled back, still not entirely sure what was going on. Piers looked back at the other man, who was still sitting down. I glanced at Charley, but she too was staring at the man with his back to us. I looked at him and thought I recognized him, but from the back it was difficult to tell. As he slowly turned around to face me I realized I did know him.

I knew him very well.

It was my father.

'We'll leave you two to it,' said Piers as he minced towards the door.

'Thanks for doing this for us, Piers,' said Charley.

'No problem,' he said as the two of them left the room. 'I feel like Cilla on *Surprise Surprise.*'

Once they were gone the silence hung in the air and my

277

father and I stood there staring at each other. I always knew I'd see my father again, but I never thought it would be in a bright-pink office on the second floor of a nightclub in Soho.

I was in a state of shock.

At that moment I wasn't sure what my emotions were or what they were meant to be, and once they did kick in, I wasn't entirely sure I'd be able to control them.

'Hello, son, it's been a long time.'

My dad always was the master of understatement.

He seemed older than I remembered, gentler, frailer.

'Hello, Dad.'

I didn't know whether to hit him or hug him. I felt like Robert Mitchum in *Night of the Hunter* with LOVE tattooed on one fist and HATE tattooed on the other.

'How . . . how come you're here?'

'Piers said we could use the office,' said my father with feigned innocence. 'Nice fellow for a poofter.'

It was only one line, but it was enough. I surprised myself by how quickly I felt the anger. Years of pent-up frustration quickly bubbled to the surface and into the cauldron with it came annoyance, fury and irritation.

'I don't mean how come you're here in the office,' I snapped, desperately trying to channel my emotions. 'I mean how come you're here in London . . . here at the party.'

'Charley called me and said it would be the best birthday present ever if I was here.'

Just as quickly the anger subsided.

I suddenly realized that for my father to travel down from Rotherham on his own was a big deal. I know for a fact that my Dad has only been to London three times in his life. Even as a comedian he only ever played in the north. '*What does thee want to go down there for.*

Everything thee can get down there, thee can git up 'ere for 'alf the price.'

I went to hug my dad as he held out his hand for me to shake. We both realized our mistake and simultaneously tried to rectify it by copying what the other had done. I held out my hand while Dad went to hug me. Then I went to hug him while he held out his hand. This went on for about ten seconds until it started to look like a Marx Brothers comedy routine. In the end we settled on shaking hands with the right hand while embracing awkwardly and patting each other on the back with the left.

'Is it true I'm a grandad?' he said. 'I'd love it if I were.'

I noticed his eyes were all misty, but there was no way he was going to let himself cry (it's not the Yorkshire thing to cry in front of your son).

'I'm going to have to let you know on that one,' I said, desperately trying to hide my own tears (it's not the Yorkshire thing to cry in front of your father).

We sat down on either side of the desk and started a somewhat stilted conversation. I asked him about my brother, David, and he said he was fine. I asked him about his beloved garden and he said it was fine. I asked him about Rotherham and he said that was fine.

'How's the weather going to be tomorrow?'

'Fine.'

He looked at me and realized I was joking. He started to giggle. It was an infectious giggle I'd only ever heard when he was performing on stage.

We started to talk about nothing in particular. We spoke about the weather, music, parties, nightclubs, David Bowie and Bono (who he'd never heard of), newspapers, smoking, holidays, haircuts, painting and decorating, gangster movies of the 1930s, and Rotherham United Football Club. At one point he even asked me if I could get Su Pollard's autograph for him and I promised I'd try. During the conversation I noticed that my Yorkshire accent, which I'd tried so hard to lose when I first came to London, had suddenly reappeared.

I wanted to talk to him about my mother, but I knew this wasn't the time or the place. If tonight was all about building bridges, we'd somehow managed to get halfway across the river.

After about an hour, Piers and Charley knocked on the door and asked if everything was OK. We told them it was and I asked my father if he'd like to come downstairs and join the party, but he said it wasn't really his thing. He said that, as he was heading back to Rotherham early in the morning, he thought it best if he went back to the hotel he was staying in, which was just off Tottenham Court Road. Piers very kindly offered one of the famous pink Cosmo limos to take him there, but my father declined, saying he could do with the fresh air. Shame, I'd have loved to have seen my dad in a pink limousine.

I walked with him to the door of the club. We said goodbye and promised to keep in touch in a slightly bizarre conversation that sounded more like two people who'd just met on holiday rather than a father and son who hadn't spoken for three years. He asked me if I wanted to go and visit him on Boxing Day and I told him I would.

'See you soon, son,' he said.

'See you soon, Dad.'

Once again there was a slight hesitation before we shook hands and patted each other on the back. He went to leave, but then stopped and turned back to face me.

'I've seen you on the telly, lad,' he said. 'I think you're quite funny.'

And with that he disappeared into the London night. I stood there in silence, stunned by what I'd heard. My father has always been a man of very few words, but when he says them he certainly makes them count. A 'quite funny' from him was the highest compliment he could pay. To him, Eric Morecambe was only ever 'quite funny'. As he walked away I had a feeling of sheer elation and tears rolled down my cheeks. I took a deep breath, swallowed hard and went back into the club. As I walked down the stairs, Bono and David Bowie were still standing there talking. This time I wasn't quite as impressed.

Charley was right, that was the best birthday present ever.

6 DEC

My party was a hit. Every single tabloid ran a story on the front page. *The Sun* said it was a *'celeb-fest'*, the *Star* said it was *'a major A-list event'* and the *Mirror* called it *'the party of the millennium'*. Every paper carried a picture of me leaving with Pippa. She'd pushed Charley out the way and used Su Pollard's trick of grabbing my arm as I was about to leave . . . she'd let it go again as soon as we were away from the cameras.

I know I should be pleased with all of the publicity, but now it's finally happening to me, it just leaves me feeling empty, shallow and detached. When they mention Simon Peters, it's as if they're talking about someone else, and in many ways they are. Maybe it's The Confident Me, The Show-Off Me, The Desperately-Seeking-Attention Me.

The Other Me.

The Real Me was the one who cried when his father told him he was 'quite funny'.

8 DEC

Tonight I'm supposed to be meeting up with Pippa at Harpo's in Wardour Street. To be honest, I'm getting a little bored of going out every night. Sometimes I just want to stay in and watch television. I'm also getting bored of Pippa. We never actually speak to each other; all we do is sit in the VIP section pretending we don't want to be noticed. Whenever I get the chance to speak to her, she seems slightly distant and is always looking over my shoulder. She claims she's watching out for paparazzi, but I think she's just looking to see if there's someone more famous than me to talk to. There never is, though. I'm always the most famous person there, but it still doesn't seem to make me interesting.

9 DEC

'It's over,' I said.

'What's over?' she said.

'Our relationship.'

'What relationship?'

I think that said it all.

'I'll phone my publicist,' said Pippa. 'She'll let all the tabloids know. I don't think the 3 a.m. Girls are going to be very happy about this.'

For the first time in my life I really didn't care what the 3 a.m. Girls thought.

10 DEC

I've reached the top of the celebrity ladder, but there's nothing up here. I think I preferred it in the middle. At least in the middle you've still got something to aim for and it's not such a long way to fall.

I thought fame would help me lead a better life and make me a more attractive person. I thought it would provide the answer, but I'm not entirely sure what the question was in the first place.

Why have I spent so much time and energy in the pursuit of fame? Where did this desperation to be recognized by complete strangers come from? Why can't I be satisfied with the cloak of anonymity that the majority of the public seem happy to wear? I keep telling myself I should be happy that I'm leading the showbiz lifestyle so many people aspire to: the celebrity friends, the paparazzi, the publicity, the premieres, the parties, the glitz and the glamour. It all seems so exciting when you see the photos in magazines, but the reality has such a hollow ring to it. I thought I would feel different when I was 'famous', I thought all my problems would disappear, but if anything the opposite is true and it seems to intensify the paranoia. I don't like reporters hanging around outside my house and taking my photograph every time I take the rubbish out. I don't like the fact that every person in the country has an opinion on whether they think I'm the father of Mimi's baby or not. I never wanted to be judged; that's not the sort of fame I wanted. I just wanted to be a celebrity. I wanted people to know my name, I wanted to be a somebody. It was my driving force, my burning ambition, it was at the very core of my being. Now I realize that for all these years I was searching for the wrong Holy Grail. What I really wanted was my dad's approval and on the night of the party I finally got it.

13 DEC

David Mulryan was waiting for me outside my flat. I immediately looked for the camera but he appeared to be alone. I ignored him and hurried quickly towards Ringo.

'Mr Peters,' he said with more than just a hint of sarcasm in his voice. 'I just thought it would be a courtesy to let you know *The Sword of Truth* is going to be broadcast live to the nation in three days' time. Mimi Lawson's agreed to an interview and she's going to reveal who the father is on the programme.'

This came as a shock, but I didn't want to let Mulryan see I was interested.

'I'm the father,' I said flatly.

'We'll see.'

'I've already admitted it on live television. It's old news. I don't think anybody's interested.'

'*Au contraire*,' he said grandly. 'I think the whole country's interested. How do you feel about having millions of people talking about you?'

'I don't care!' I screamed with pure vitriol.

As soon as I'd said it I realized I'd fallen into his trap. From the corner of my eye I saw the tell-tale sign of the camera's red light and I could just make out the shape and form of a cameraman hiding behind a car on the opposite side of the road.

Something inside me snapped.

Releasing a stream of obscenities I leapt across the bonnet of my car (like David Soul used to at the beginning of *Starsky & Hutch*) and sprinted across the road to where the cameraman was hiding. I pushed him backwards and put my hand over his lens in a classic no-publicity-style pose. I looked at his face and was quite surprised to see it wasn't the cameraman Mulryan usually had with him. He didn't even look like a cameraman, but I was too angry to register the fact. I grabbed him by the lapels and screamed something about making sure he was getting my best side.

'I'm sorry,' he said, his eyes starting to fill with tears. 'My name's Roger. I'm your Number One fan.'

'Roger? Not Roger the Underpants Fan?'

I suddenly felt very stupid. I looked back across the road to Mulryan. Standing next to him was his usual cameraman, and on his shoulder was a camera pointing straight at me as I held Roger by the lapels. I looked at Roger, then at the camera, and then back at Roger again.

'Sorry about that, Roger,' I said, helping him to his feet and dusting him down. 'I'll get you some tickets to a recording of *Slebs* by way of an apology.'

'I'd rather have some dirty pants,' he said.

I told him I'd see what I could do.

I sheepishly crossed the road, opened my car door and climbed into the driver's seat. As I fired up the engine, Mulryan poked his head through the window and flashed me a sly smile.

'Don't forget to watch on the sixteenth,' he said.

14 DEC

The ITV Network is heavily promoting Mulryan's *The Sword of Truth*. One of the trailers used some of the footage from *Slebs*. Set to a piece of classical music it showed Manky and me fighting in slow motion.

The voice-over said 'Who's the daddy? Find out Monday at eight o'clock. Live on ITV1.'

Another trailer was made in the style of a cheesy game show. Against the backdrop of gold lamé curtains, they showed a picture of me, a picture of Manky and a silhouette of someone with a question mark over his head. They called the game show *Who's the Father?* and in true *Blind Date* style (it sounded like they'd actually got '*our Graham*' to do it) the voice-over said, 'Who's the father of Mimi

Lawson's baby? Will it be number one, Simon Peters the professional "sleb" who's willing to fight to prove he's the daddy? Will it be number two, Ricardo Mancini, game-show host and long-term Lothario, who is hoping that the whole thing isn't a "swizz"? Or will it be mystery man number three . . .'

At that point they made it look as if there was interference on the television, only for the picture to return seconds later with Graham informing us we would find out who the father was on Monday night at eight o'clock . . .

'. . . Live on ITV1.'

15 DEC

WYNTHORPE, WYNTHORPE, GOLDBOOM AND KAYE (SOLICITORS)

112–114 Gt Portland St, London W1 8TA

12 Dec 2002

Dear Mr Peters,

The accompanying letter should have been forwarded to you on 30 November. Due to a clerical error it was not. Please accept my apologies in this matter.

Yours sincerely,
Mr Lionel Wynthorpe (senior partner)

WYNTHORPE, WYNTHORPE, GOLDBOOM AND KAYE (SOLICITORS)

112–114 Gt Portland St, London W1 8TA

30 November 2002

Dear Mr Peters,

We are acting on behalf of the estate of the late Mr Vince Envy. This is to inform you that you are sole beneficiary under the terms of his will. As according to his last will and testament, you are bequeathed a legacy of £250,000. Having already applied for a grant of probate to the estate, please find enclosed a cheque for said amount. Also find enclosed a handwritten note from Mr Envy, which he requested be passed on to you.

We would appreciate it if you would acknowledge receipt of this letter and cheque.

Yours sincerely,

Mr Lionel Wynthorpe (senior)

Attached to this letter by a paper clip was a scrappy piece of lined notepaper. I unfolded it and in Vince's inimitable messy handwriting it said,

For the son I never had,

It seems I had more money than sense. You'll know what to do with this money when the time is right.

Good luck, pal,

Vince

PS God bless the people of Albania, they know talent when they see it. Maybe you should try your luck out there!

I called the solicitors to confirm that I'd received the cheque. I spoke to Lionel Wynthorpe (senior) and he explained the money was paid to Vince in the last couple of weeks of his life as royalties from the sales of his hit record 'Cream Sweater, Blue Jeans'. Apparently it was the biggest-selling record ever in Albania, having sold over two million copies. It had been at Number One for seven months and had just started to slip down the charts when it was announced in June that Vince had died. The record went back to Number One and has stayed there ever since. Mr Wynthorpe (senior) told me that, as sole beneficiary to Vince's estate, I could expect a similar cheque once every six months for as long as the record continued to be played on Albanian radio. Mr Wynthorpe went on to point out that as 'Cream Sweater, Blue Jeans' is one of only five records actually allowed to be played on Albanian radio, I'd be receiving the cheques for quite some time.

I put the phone down and started to cry. They were tears of joy mixed with tears of guilt. I have to admit the tears of guilt didn't last long, though. I spent the rest of the day humming the tune to 'Cream Sweater, Blue Jeans' and looking at a map of Albania in my atlas.

'You'll know what to do with the money when the time is right.'

I think the time is right to buy a brand-new Porsche (all in the memory of Vince, of course).

16 DEC

I always thought I'd find out if I was a father in the traditional way. A doctor wearing a green mask, gown and rubber gloves would come out of the delivery room, shake my hand, pass me a cigar and say, 'Congratulations, Simon, you're a father.' What I didn't expect was to have to tune in to ITV1 and find out at the same time as twelve million other people.

The Sword of Truth started and I felt numb. I wasn't sure how I would react when Mimi finally revealed the father's name. Would I feel elated if I was the father? Would I feel disappointed if I wasn't? Would I feel elated if I wasn't the father? Would I feel disappointed if I was?

As I watched the opening credits I realized I hate David Mulryan, maybe not as much as I hate Ricardo Mancini, but the capacity is certainly there. The title sequence was every bit as arrogant and pretentious as the man himself. There was a loud, driving, classical rock soundtrack with lots of black and white shots of Mulryan running and jumping, inter-cut with big close-ups of him trying to look earnest. The sequence ended and the shot dissolved through to Mulryan standing in the middle of a run-down council estate, which I immediately recognized as the place where Mimi lived.

I started to feel guilty.

'An inner-city slum,' announced Mulryan pompously as he walked passed a derelict building. When he talked, he did so really slowly and he had an annoying habit of over-emphasizing the word *this*. 'There are council estates like *this* all over the country. But *this* one, in Hackney, is different. *This* one houses one of the most talked-about mothers in the country. *This* is where Mimi Lawson lives.'

They showed a montage of highlights from Mimi's career. All the familiar images were there: *Tomorrow's Stars Today, Here's Mimi!, The Morecambe and Wise Show,* Mimi curtseying and laughing with the Queen.

When it cut back to Mulryan he was walking up the steps of one of the graffiti-covered stairwells.

'It's the mystery that's gripped the nation for the past nine months. Everybody has been talking about it from royalty to refugees, from politicians to pop stars. Tonight, live on ITV1, in an exclusive interview with the lady herself, we're going to find out the answer to *this* question: Who is the father of Mimi Lawson's baby?'

Another montage. This time using news footage and tabloid headlines, they told the story of Mimi's pregnancy and the controversy surrounding it. There were vox pops of the public saying who they thought the father was, clips of comedians telling jokes about it and then once again footage of Manky and me fighting on the set of *Swizz Quiz*.

This time when it cut back to Mulryan, he was sitting in what was obviously Mimi's flat. It looked scruffy, dirty and desperately in need of redecoration. Mulryan introduced Mimi and, as they showed a close-up of her, I thought she looked burned out and abandoned, like the cars that littered her estate. Motherhood and the strain of the past few months had obviously taken its toll.

Mulryan eased her gently into the conversation by saying the public would probably be surprised that she lived on a council estate in Hackney. Mimi explained that she'd fallen on hard times during the Eighties and even now, with all the publicity surrounding the birth of the baby, she was still struggling to pay off all her debts.

'The public think people in showbusiness earn more money than they actually do,' said Mimi and I couldn't help but agree with her.

The way it was being shot, I was reminded of the Martin Bashir/Princess Diana interview. Mulryan was probing yet understanding, Mimi was coy yet articulate. He asked her about her career as a child star and about her tempestuous relationship with her mother. He touched lightly on her three failed marriages and her battle with the bottle, but all this, of course, was just a warm-up for the killer question.

After about fifteen minutes of amiable chit-chat,

Mulryan steered the conversation onto the subject of Mimi's baby.

'How is Jessica?' he asked smarmily.

'She's fine, thank you,' replied Mimi coolly.

'Now we understand that for private reasons you don't want us to film the baby, but are you prepared to reveal who the father is?'

The camera shot tightened in on Mimi until her face filled the screen.

'Yes, David, I am.'

I held my breath.

'You'll tell us tonight on live television,' said Mulryan, desperately trying to eke out the tension.

'Yes, David, I will.'

A bead of sweat trickled down the back of my neck.

'Mimi Lawson. Who is the father of your baby?'

There was a pause. My heart stopped beating.

'. . . is a question the whole country wants to know the answer to.' Mulryan turned to look at the camera. 'We'll have the answer to that question right after this break. Don't go away.'

I couldn't believe Mulryan had done the old Chris Tarrant trick of prolonging the suspense over the commercial break. I went to the fridge to get myself a beer. As I popped the ring-pull, I realized it was my fifth of the evening. When the show returned, Mulryan addressed the camera and reminded the viewing millions that we were just moments away from finding out who the father was.

'But before we find out for sure,' he said condescendingly, 'let's have a look at some of the prime suspects.'

They rolled the VT and there was a shot of Manky Mancini walking down the street. Mulryan appeared from behind a hedge and fired a barrage of questions at him. Mancini was really squirming and every time he answered a question they cut to a tabloid headline about his dubious love life, several of them hinting at the fact that he was a latent homosexual. I was just starting to enjoy Manky's obvious discomfort when they suddenly cut to a wide shot of the exterior of my flat. It then cut to a mid shot of me closing the door and walking to my car. Next came a big close-up of Mulryan asking me how I would feel if I was the father of Mimi Lawson's baby – I know for a fact that he never asked me that question and that the shot had obviously been filmed at a completely different location. It then cut back to me screaming, '*I don't care!*', which I'd actually said in response to a completely different question.

'It was at this point', said Mulryan's voiceover, 'that Peters savagely attacked my cameraman.'

It cut to the shot of me holding Roger the Dirty Underpants Fan by the lapels and screaming at him that he wasn't getting my best side. By clever editing Mulryan had managed to make me look utterly self-obsessed. This was a total travesty and a complete misrepresentation of the truth. I was about to call Max about the possibility of suing when the VT finished and they cut back to Mulryan and Mimi sitting in her flat.

'Those are the two prime suspects,' said Mulryan. 'Simon Peters and Ricardo Mancini. To be honest, I'm not sure I'd want either of them as a father.'

He laughed at his own joke.

'Now, Mimi,' he continued. 'I have some questions for you. Do you swear to tell the whole truth?'

'I do,' said Mimi, assiduously.

The lights in Mimi's flat dimmed, a spotlight shone on her face and dramatic music started to play as an underscore. They were certainly giving this the full theatrical effect.

'Here we go then. Question number one, while you were

in pantomime in Grimsby, did you have an affair with Ricardo Mancini?'

'Not what I'd call an affair, no.'

'Did you have a fling?'

'Yes, I'd call it a fling.'

'Is Ricardo Mancini the father of your baby?'

There was a pause.

'No,' said Mimi flatly. 'Ricardo Mancini is not the father of my baby.'

'*How can you be sure?*' I shouted at the television.

'How can you be sure?' asked Mulryan calmly.

'Because when I went to bed with him he couldn't get an erection.'

I burst out laughing, and I knew twelve million other people would be doing exactly the same. Twelve million people with the exception of one, of course. I tried to imagine Manky sitting at home with his head in his hands, knowing full well that that line would haunt him for the rest of his life.

'Simon Peters,' said Mulryan.

I stopped laughing.

'What about him?' asked Mimi, ice cool under the pressure.

'Did you have an affair with him?'

'Not what I'd call an affair, no.'

'A fling?'

'Yes, let's call it a fling.'

'Did you at any time sleep with Simon Peters?'

'I did,' said Mimi.

'You're admitting that you slept with him?'

'I am.'

I reached for another beer.

'I'm forced to ask the question then,' said Mulryan. 'Is Simon Peters the father?'

Mimi didn't answer and instead leant forward and took a sip of water.

'I ask you again,' said Mulryan. 'Is Simon Peters the father of your baby?'

Another long pause. The music seemed to intensify and once again the camera tightened in for a close-up.

'No,' said Mimi, totally void of emotion. 'Simon Peters is not the father of my baby.'

In answer to my earlier question, I felt a jolt of elation and a stab of disappointment at exactly the same time.

'*How can you be sure?*' I screamed.

'How can you be sure?' asked Mulryan calmly.

'Because we slept together in the sleeping sense of the word, but that was all. It was after the company meal. We went back to my hotel, but Simon was so drunk he just fell asleep.'

'*What about the mooing?*' I shouted. '*Ask her about the mooing.*'

'During my investigations,' said Mulryan, 'some people claim to have heard certain . . . "noises" coming from your hotel room on the night in question.'

'Yes, that was Simon,' she said. 'He kept mooing in his sleep.'

This time it was my turn to hide my head in my hands. I could actually hear my next-door neighbours laughing at this, and I knew people were going to moo at me in the street for years to come.

'So, Mimi, if it's not Ricardo Mancini and it's not Simon Peters, the question remains: who is the father of your baby?'

Mimi took another sip of water and exhaled slowly. She closed her eyes for a moment, and when she opened them, looked straight down the lens as if she wanted to personally set the record straight with each and every single viewer.

'Vince Envy,' she said.

I couldn't believe it.

'Vince Envy, the former rock 'n' roll star who tragically died in June of this year?'

'We were lovers for years,' said Mimi.

She seemed genuinely upset when she thought of him and her eyes started to mist over. I'd never seen her looking so vulnerable.

'It was what you might call an on-off relationship. More off than on. We first met in the West End production of *Flares* in the early Eighties. He was a handsome leading man and I was a love-struck teenager. We became lovers and it stayed that way for years.'

'Was he married at the time?'

'He was separated. It became a standing joke between us, whenever either of us got divorced we'd automatically go running back to the other one.'

'But he never asked you to marry him?'

'No, but I think he was going to. I think that's why he arranged for me to do the panto in Grimsby. It was one last roll of the dice for our relationship, one last chance for us to get together.'

'Did it work?'

'Vince was drinking heavily by that point and all we seemed to do was argue.'

'Hence the flirting with Peters and Mancini?'

'That was just to make Vince jealous, but to be honest he was always too pissed to notice . . . I'm sorry, am I allowed to say pissed?'

Mulryan held up his hands, as if to say it wasn't allowed but it was too late now.

'Why would Peters and Mancini think you were stalking them?'

'I wasn't stalking them,' said Mimi indignantly. 'After

the panto, Vince seemed to just disappear. I was desperately trying to get in touch with him to let him know he was going to be a father. I thought Simon and Ricardo might know where he was, but even though they claimed to be his friends, they just didn't seem to be interested.'

'So did you manage to let Vince know that he was going to be a father?'

The tears were starting to well up in Mimi's eyes. She took a deep breath and exhaled slowly.

'No,' she said. 'After the panto I never saw him again. He . . . he died before I could tell him. The one thing Vince always wanted was a child and now with the birth of Jessica – that was the name of one of his hits, by the way – I feel I've given him that gift, even if he isn't around to see her.'

'Would you say she takes after her father?'

'Yes, she reminds me so much of Vince,' said Mimi. 'She's definitely Daddy's Little Girl.'

Mimi began to weep silently, and it was at this point I realized I was crying too. Great big fat tears rolled down my cheeks and I began to sob uncontrollably.

It was then I knew the Porsche was going to have to wait.

17 DEC

I walked past the deserted buildings and dilapidated cars, and as I made my way up the graffiti-covered stairwell the stench of urine hung heavily in the air. I arrived outside the door. The blue paint had started to peel and one of the panes of glass had been smashed and replaced by a piece of cardboard. From inside my pocket I took an envelope; inside the envelope was a Christmas card and inside the Christmas card was a cheque for £250,000 made out to Jessica Lawson. On the envelope I wrote 'To the

Daughter I Never Had'. I pushed it through Mimi's letter-box and left feeling a better man.

18 DEC

In *The Sun*'s 'Bizarre' column it was announced that Vince's 1964 hit 'Cream Sweater, Blue Jeans' is going to be used in the next Levi's advert and that Polydor, who own the rights to the song, are going to rush release it in time for Christmas ('Jessica' is going to the B-side). Victoria Newton, *The Sun*'s showbusiness editor, even tipped it as the Christmas Number One.

19 DEC

Every tabloid newspaper has started hailing Vince as a genius, and today Polydor announced they're going to re-release his entire back catalogue, including one previously unreleased album called *The Vegas Years*. The *Daily Mirror* reported Andrew Lloyd Webber is planning a musical about Vince's life (the script is to be written by Ben Elton). *A Life of Envy* will open at the Palladium next autumn.

I called Lionel Wynthorpe (senior) and asked him to set up a trust fund in Jessica's name and to make sure all of Vince's royalties be paid into it.

20 DEC

The scales have been removed from my eyes and I see the world in a new light.

This is *The New Me*.

I called Charley up and told her I was a changing man. I told her how I viewed things differently now that I'd made up with my father and how good it made me feel when I set up the trust fund for Jessica. I told her I was tired of being so self-serving and how I didn't want to be famous any more.

'What do you want to be then?'

'I want to be a philanthropist, a humanitarian, an altruist, a benefactor, a doer of good deeds.'

'Oh my God,' said Charley. 'You haven't seen the light, have you?'

'No . . . I just want to be a *nice* person.'

'You are a *nice* person.'

'Really?'

'Yes,' said Charley.

She paused.

'Even when you were a bitter and twisted self-obsessed egomaniac with more ambition than talent and a chip on your shoulder the size of Yorkshire, you were always a really nice, sweet, caring, thoughtful person.'

Even though she was joking about the bitter and twisted, self-obsessed egomaniac bit, I couldn't help thinking she was being genuine about the sweet, caring and thoughtful part.

'I've always thought that,' she said, suddenly sounding very serious. 'You must have been blind not to notice.'

This was entering uncharted waters.

I took a deep breath and nodded, but because we were on the phone she couldn't see me nodding and instead there was an embarrassing silence. Then Charley asked me if I wanted to go round to her flat on Christmas Day for a candlelit Christmas dinner.

'If I didn't know you better, I'd think you were asking me for a date.'

'Maybe I am,' said Charley.

I took a deep breath.

'Are you sure?'

'I've been sure for about twelve months,' she said.

I was aware of a strange tingling sensation in the pit of my stomach. Nerves? Butterflies? Love?

'I'll see you at seven o'clock on Christmas Day,' I said.

Maybe this really is the new me.

21 DEC

Slebs has finished its run, so I was quite surprised to see Lizzi Rees-Morgan driving past my flat in her convertible BMW. I waved, but I don't think she saw me because she didn't wave back. She had a very serious expression on her face; it was the same look she had at my party when she wouldn't speak to me.

Lizzi lives in north London. What was she doing driving down my road?

22 DEC

Lizzi left a message on my answer machine. She sounded really upset about something but she was crying so much I couldn't understand what she was saying.

3.06 a.m.
I'm getting a terrible sense of déjà-vu.

23 DEC

I received what I thought was a Christmas card. I opened it up, but inside was just a piece of paper. It was from Lizzi. In what looked like a childish scrawl she'd written, *'I'm late, call me.'*

24 DEC

'How would you like to take part in a *Celebrity Big Brother Christmas Special*?'

It was Max.

He told me one of the celebrities had dropped out and the producers wanted to know if I'd be interested. He explained I would have to spend two weeks in the house and, as with the real *Big Brother*, every waking (and sleeping) moment would be monitored, recorded and televised, and then the public would vote on who they wanted to be evicted.

'When does it start?' I asked.

'Tomorrow.'

'Christmas Day?'

'They thought it would make it a bit different,' said Max. 'You're not allowed to take any writing material with you so that diary of yours is a no-no. By the way, I might have a publisher who's interested in that.'

'Who are the other celebs?'

If you're going to spend two weeks cooped up in a confined space, you need to know you're going to get on with the people in there.

'I only know three of them,' said Max. 'Mimi Lawson, Ricardo Mancini and one of the Chuckle Brothers . . . Barry I think.'

'Mimi Lawson?' I said, suddenly full of paternal concern. 'What about the baby?'

'Apparently Mimi's mother, who she hadn't spoken to since she was fifteen, got in touch with her after *The Sword of Truth* programme. They made up their differences and she's going to look after the baby.'

I felt pleased for Mimi. After everything she's been through she's finally got her mother back.

I was having doubts about *Big Brother* though.

'I'm going to have to think about it.'

'What is there to think about?' said Max. 'Simon, my boy, this show is a guaranteed hit. The fact that it starts on Christmas Day means everyone will tune in. They're expecting thirty million people to be watching. *Thirty million!* This will make you more famous than you've ever imagined.'

There was a pause

I thought about *The New Me*. I thought about Charley and the candlelit Christmas dinner and the fact that I was supposed to be seeing my father on Boxing Day. Did I really want to go into the *Big Brother* house and have my every word dissected, scrutinized and analysed? I thought about the awful reality of having to spend two weeks in a house with Ricardo Mancini, Mimi Lawson and a Chuckle Brother (especially if it was Barry). Then I thought about Lizzi's note and Max telling me this show would make me more famous than I'd ever imagined.

'I'll do it,' I said.

4.16 a.m.

How did Max know about my diary?

THE END

ACKNOWLEDGEMENTS

Thank you to Simon Taylor and all at Transworld for their confidence and to Guy, Rachel and Alex at Futerman Rose for their continued support. Thanks to my Mum, Dad, family and friends who didn't laugh too loudly when I told them I was writing a novel but then laughed really loudly when they read it. Last, but by no means least, thank you to Emily, who read every single draft and was there to always check for split infinitives.

www.paulhendy.com